FLESH CIRCUS

LILITH SAINTCROW

www.orbitbooks.net

New York   London

Copyright © 2009 by Lilith Saintcrow
Excerpt from *Heaven's Spite* copyright © 2009 by Lilith Saintcrow
All rights reserved. Except as permitted under the U.S. Copyright Act of 1976, no part of this publication may be reproduced, distributed, or transmitted in any form or by any means, or stored in a database or retrieval system, without the prior written permission of the publisher.

Orbit
Hachette Book Group
237 Park Avenue, New York, NY 10017
Visit our website at www.orbitbooks.net

Orbit is an imprint of Hachette Book Group. The Orbit name and logo are trademarks of Little, Brown Book Group Limited.

Printed in the United States of America

First mass market Orbit edition, December 2009

10 9 8 7 6 5 4 3 2

ATTENTION CORPORATIONS AND ORGANIZATIONS:
Most HACHETTE BOOK GROUP books are available at quantity discounts with bulk purchase for educational, business, or sales promotional use. For information, please call or write:

Special Markets Department, Hachette Book Group
237 Park Avenue, New York, NY 10017
Telephone: 1-800-222-6747 Fax: 1-800-477-5925

I screamed and leapt, the whip coming free and flicking forward, silver flechettes jingling as it wrapped around one of the zombie's legs and almost tore itself out of my hand.

The leather popped hard, once, like a good open-hand shot to the face or a piece of wet laundry shaken in just the right way, and the zombie went down in a splattering heap.

Then I was on the thing, its foul sponginess running away as I broke its neck with a louder crack than the other ones. *This guy must be pretty fresh, too.* I balled up my right fist, my knees popping foul, slipping skin and sinking through muscle turned to ropy porridge.

I *punched,* pulling it at the last second so my fist didn't go through the head and straight on into the dying lawn. Newspapers ruffled in a sudden burst of cold air and the smell of natron. The wet splorching sound was louder than it had any right to be, and brain oatmeal splattered. The body twitched feebly.

I just wished it wasn't so messy. You'd think I'd be used to it by now, though.

Praise for Lilith Saintcrow:

"Lyrical language and movie-worthy fight scenes are staples in Saintcrow's novels, and this one is no exception."

—midwestbookreview.com on *Night Shift*

BOOKS BY LILITH SAINTCROW

JILL KISMET NOVELS

Night Shift

Hunter's Prayer

Redemption Alley

Flesh Circus

DANTE VALENTINE NOVELS

Working for the Devil

Dead Man Rising

The Devil's Right Hand

Saint City Sinners

To Hell and Back

Dark Watcher

Storm Watcher

Fire Watcher

Cloud Watcher

The Society

Hunter, Healer

Mindhealer

Steelflower

To L.I.

Acknowledgments

Thanks for this book go first and foremost to Mel Sanders, who listened to me talk about it for hours and hours. And next to Maddy, Nicky, and Gates—who listened to me talk about it for hours and hours. Next-to-last, but certainly not least, to Devi and Miriam, who also put up with me when I talked about it . . . for hours and hours.

And as usual, the biggest thanks to you, the Reader. Step right up, sit on down. And let me tell you a story.

I promise it won't take long.

Bonitas non est pessimis esse meliorem.
—Seneca

1

Just outside the Santa Luz city limits, the caravan halted. I rolled my shoulders back under heavy leather, my fingers resting on a gun butt. They tapped, once, four times, bitten nails drumming.

Out here in the desert, the two-lane highway was a ribbon reaching to nowhere. The stars glimmered, hard cold points of light. A new moon, already tired, was a nail-paring in the sky, weak compared to the shine of cityglow from the valley. I'd parked on the shoulder, and dust was still settling with little whispering sounds.

They were pulled aside, on a gravel access road, as custom dictated. Or fear demanded.

Their headlights were separate stars, the limousine pointed directly at my city, a long raggletaggle spreading out behind it. Minivans, trucks, trailers, and one old Chevy flatbed still wheezing from the '60s with bright spatters of glittering tie-dye paint all over its cab. One black limousine, crouched low to the dusty ground. The animals were sprawling or pacing in semi trailers.

I could smell them all, dung and sweat and glitter and fried food with the bright sweet corruption of hellbreed laid over the top.

Another pair of headlights pierced the distance. I waited, leaning against a wine-red 1968 Pontiac Bonneville. She wasn't as sweet as my Impala, or as forgiving on tight corners, but she was a good car.

Cirque de Charnu was painted on everything except the glossy limo, in baroque lettering highlighted with gold. Under the fierce desert sun it would look washed-out and tawdry. At night it glittered, taunted. Seduced.

They're good at that. I sometimes wonder if they hold classes for it in Hell. It wouldn't surprise me. Nothing much would surprise me about that place, or about hell-breed.

Saul lit a Charvil, a brief flare of orange light. He studied each and every car, and the taut silence around him was almost as tense as the way he tilted his chin up, slightly, sniffing the air. Testing the wind.

"I don't like this," he murmured, and turned his sleek, new-shorn head slightly to watch the headlights arrowing toward us. A few silver charms were knotted into his hair with red thread. He had a small copper bowl of them in the bathroom, all the ones he'd worn before his mother died, tied back in as his hair got longer.

I contented myself with a shrug. The scar on my right wrist pulsed, the bloom of corruption on the caravan plucking at it. I'd stuffed the leather wristcuff in my pocket, wanting my full measure of helltainted strength tonight.

Just in case.

Baked, sage-touched wind off the cooling desert ruffled my hair, made the silver charms tied into long dark curls tinkle sweetly. I had no reason to draw silence over me like a cloak right now. We'd arrived at the meeting spot first, slightly after dusk. They'd shown up as soon as true dark folded over the desert, a long chain of bright, hungry headlights. The caravan still popped and pinged with cooling metal, its engines shut off one by one. Nobody moved, though I could see a few faint flickers when someone lit a cigarette, and a restive stamping sounded from one of the semis. Their lights were a glare, but not directed at me. Instead, the flood of white speared the desert toward my city, etching sharp, hurtful shadows behind every pebble and scrubby bush.

The other headlights, coming up from the city's well, came closer. My pulse tried to ratchet up, was strictly controlled.

Anticipation. Fear. Which one was I feeling at the prospect of seeing him?

Faint dips in the road made the sword of light from the approaching car waver. Still it came, smooth and silent like a shark. Mostly, you can see a long way in the flat high desert. But he was speeding, smoothly taking the dips and curves. It took less time than you'd think for the other car's engine—another limo, sleek and freshly waxed—to become audible, purring away.

"I don't like it either," I murmured. A hunter spends so much time holding back the tide of Hell, it feels just-damn-*wrong* to be inviting hellbreed in. *Come into my parlor*—only it was the fly saying it this time, while the spider just lolled and grinned.

And I would much rather put off seeing Perry again. No visits to the Monde to pay for a share of a hellbreed's power, thundering through the scar on my wrist. And I'd used the mark more or less freely for months now.

I was in the right, of course, and he'd welshed on the deal first, but . . . it made me more nervous than I liked to admit. Especially since it seemed stronger now than it ever had while I was visiting the Monde every month. Strong enough that I had trouble controlling it every once in a while.

Strong enough that it worried me.

His limousine coasted over the near rises. The wind dropped off, the desert finishing its long slow exhale that starts just after dusk. I marked the position of every vehicle in the caravan again.

There were a lot of them.

I heard it was always a shock to see how big the Cirque was when set up. How many souls they pulled in for their nightly games. How during daylight it always seemed exponentially smaller but still the shadows held secrets and dangers. And *eyes*.

It wasn't comforting information. And some of the pictures and old woodcuts Hutch had dug up for me before he went on vacation were thought-provoking and stomach-churning at once.

The black limo coasted to a stop. Sat in its lane, purring away, the gloss of its paint job powder-bloomed with fine crackling threads of bruised etheric energy.

The engine roused again, and for a mad moment I thought it was going to peel some rubber and speed off into the dark. Of course, if it did, I would be able to refuse entry. The Cirque would go on its way, and I'd breathe a huge sigh of relief.

But no, the shark-gleaming car just executed a perfect

three-point turnaround, brought to a controlled stop on the other side of the road.

"Show-off," Saul muttered, and I was hard-pressed not to grin.

The urge died on my face as the door opened and Perry rose from the back of the limo, immaculate as always. Only this time he didn't wear his usual pale linen suit. It was almost a shock to see him in a tuxedo, his pale hair slicked back and the blandness of his face turned by a trick of light into a sword-sharp handsomeness before settling into its accustomed contours. His eyes lit gasflame-blue, and he didn't glance at the dingy collection of cars huddling on the access road.

No, first he looked at me for a long, tense-ticking ninety seconds, while the limo idled and he rested his bent arm on the door. There was no bodyguard to open it for him, no gorilla-built Trader or slim beautiful hellbreed to stand attentively beside him.

Another oddity, seeing him without a posse.

Why, Perry, what a nice penguin suit you're wearing. A nasty snigger rose over a deep well of something too hot and acid to be fear, killed just as surely and swiftly as the smile. The contact of cooler night air on my skin turned unbearably sharp, little prickling needles of sensory acuity.

The scar turned hard, drawing across the nerves of my right arm like a violin bow.

I kept thinking the memory of him pressing his lips there would fade. Silly me.

He finally stepped away from the limo. The door swung closed, and I tensed, muscle by muscle. Perry strode loosely across the road, gliding as if on his own personal dancefloor, and the caravan took a deep breath. Another door swung open, I heard feet hitting the dusty ground. Two pairs, both with the sound of hellbreed or Trader—too light on the toes, or too heavy, a distribution of weight no human musculature would be capable of—and if my ears were right, from the limo.

Hellbreed like limousines. I've heard politicians do too. Oh, and rock stars. Thought-provoking, isn't it?

I peeled myself away from the Bonneville's hood. Saul stayed where he was, but I felt his attention. It was like sunlight against my back as I strode forward, steel-shod bootheels cracking down with authority.

If it was a dance, it was one that brought us all together just where the road met the shoulder. I ended up with one foot on the tarmac and the other on dirt. Perry, to my left, stopped a respectable six feet away on the road, and as he came to a halt I saw he was wearing mirror-polished wingtips. The crease in his pants was sharp enough to cut.

To my left, the Ringmaster halted. Thin membranous curls of dust rose from his footprints, settling reluctantly with little flinching sounds.

The Ringmaster. A tall thin hellbreed with a thatch of crow-dark hair over a sweet, innocent face with bladed cheekbones. They're all beautiful, the damned. It's the blush of a tubercular apple, that beauty, and it rots in the gaze if you keep looking steadily enough. Little things that don't add up—bones a millimeter too high, a skin-sheen just a degree or two off, a chin angled in a simulacrum of humanity but with *something else* under the skin—grab the attention, then the attractiveness reasserts itself. It's the mask they wear to fool their prey, but a hunter back from Hell can see under it.

We can see the *twisting*.

This one wore a thin-lipped smile that was far, far too wide. I looked for his cane and didn't see it. His black suit was a shabby, fraying copy of Perry's, a worn top hat dangling from loose, expressive strangler's fingers. When his lips parted, a long ridge of sharp bone with faint shadows that could be tooth demarcations showed. The ridge came down to points where the canines would be, then swept back into the cavern of his mouth.

In very dim light, human eyes might mistake him for one of their own. A hunter never would. Diamond insect feet walked up my back, leaving gooseflesh in their wake. A muscle in the Ringmaster's elegant cheek twitched, but it was Perry who spoke first.

"Kiss. A delight, as usual."

Don't call me that, Perry. I eyed the second one from the Cirque, a small, soft boyish Trader with huge blue eyes and a fine down on his round apple cheeks. My stomach turned over, hard. "Let's just get this over with." I sounded bored even to myself. "I have work to do tonight." *Got a childkilling Trader to catch, and you assholes are wasting my time.*

"As do we all." The Ringmaster's voice was a surprise—as hearty and jolly as he was thin and waspish. And under that, a buzz like chrome flies in chlorinated bottles.

The rumble of a different language. Helletöng.

The speech of the damned.

"Always business." Perry shrugged, a loose easy movement, and I passed my gaze down the small, doe-innocent Trader. He was thin and birdlike, in a white T-shirt and jeans, and he made me uneasy. Most of the time the bad is right out there where you can see it. If it's not, you have to keep watching until it shows itself. "Welcome to Santa Luz, Henri."

The Trader leaned into the Ringmaster's side, and the 'breed put one stick-thin arm over him. A flick of the loose fingers against the T-shirt's sleeve, probably meant to be soothing, and the parody of parental posture almost made acid crawl up the back of my throat.

"Thank you, Hyperion. This is Ikaros," the Ringmaster said. He focused on me. "Do you have the collar?"

I reached into a left-hand pocket, my trench coat rustling slightly. Cool metal resounded under my fingertips, and I had another serious run of thoughts about stepping back, turning on my heel, and heading for the Pontiac.

But you can't do that when the Cirque comes to town. The compact they live under is unbreakable, a treaty between dark and light. They serve a purpose, and any hunter on their worldwide circuit knows as much.

It just goes against every instinct a decent hunter possesses to let the fuckers keep breathing.

Perry rumbled something in Helletöng, the sound of freight trains painfully rubbing against each other at midnight, in some deserted hopeless trainyard.

I paused. My right hand ached for a gun. "English, Perry." *None of your goddamn rumblespeak here.*

"So rude of me. I was merely remarking on your beauty tonight, my dear."

Oh, for fuck's sake. I shouldn't have dignified it with a response. "The next time one of you hellspawn rumbles in töng, I'm going back to work, the Cirque can go on down the line, and you, Perry, can go suck a few eggs."

"Charming." The Ringmaster's smile had dropped like a bad habit. "Is she always this way?"

"Oh, yes. Always a winsome delight, our Kiss." Perry's slight smile hadn't changed, and the faint blue shine from his irises didn't waver either. He looked far too amused, and the scar was quiescent against my skin.

Usually he played with it, waves of pain or sick pleasure pouring up my arm. Fiddling with my internal thermostat, trying to make me respond. Tonight, he didn't.

And that was thought-provoking as well. Only I wasn't sure what thoughts it was supposed to provoke, which was probably the point.

My fingers curled around the metal and brought it out.

The collar was a serious piece of business, a spiked circle of silver, supple and deadly-looking. Each spike was as long as my thumb from middle knuckle to fingertip, and wicked sharp. Blue light flowed under the surface of the metal, not quite breaking free in response to the contamination of two hellbreed and a Trader so close. My silver apprentice-ring, snug against my left third finger, *did* crack a single spark, and it was gratifying to see the little Trader shiver slightly.

I shook the collar a little, the hinges moving freely. It trembled like a live thing, hypnotic blue swirling. "Rules." I had their attention. My right hand wanted to twitch for a knife so bad I almost did it, keeping myself loose with an effort. The charms in my hair rattled against each other, blessed silver reacting. "Actually, just one rule. Don't fuck with my town. You're here on sufferance."

"Next she'll start in about blood atonement," Perry offered helpfully.

I held the Ringmaster's gaze. My smart eye—the left one, the blue one—was dry, but I didn't blink. He did—first one eye, then the other, slight lizardlike movements.

The Trader slid away from under his hand. Still, their auras swirled together, and I could almost-see the thick spiraled rope of a blood bond between them. Ikaros took two steps toward me and paused, looking up with those big blue eyes.

The flat shine of the dust lying over his irises was the same as every other Trader's. It was a reminder that this kid, however old he really was, had bargained with Hell. Traded away something essential in return for something else.

His lashes quivered. That was his first mistake.

The next was his hands, twisting together as if he was nervous. If the Ringmaster's hands were flaccid and delicate, the Trader's were broad farmboy's paws, at odds with the rest of his delicate beauty.

I wondered what he'd Traded for to end up here.

"We'll be good." His voice was a sweet piping, without the candy-sick corruption of a hellbreed's. He gave me a tremulous smile. There was a shadow of something ancient over his face, a wrongness in the expression.

He was no child.

"Save it." I jingled the collar again and watched him flinch just a little. The hellbreed had gone still. "And get down on your knees."

"That isn't necessary." The Ringmaster's tone was a warning.

So was mine. "I'm the hunter here, hellspawn. *I* decide what's necessary. Get. Down on. Your knees."

The Trader sank down gracefully, but not before his fingers clenched for the barest second. Big, broad hands, and if they closed around my neck it might be a job and a half to pry them away.

He might have looked like the sort of tchotchke doll old ladies like to put on their shelves, but he was *Trader.* If he looked innocent and harmless, it was only the lure used to get someone close enough for those strong fingers. And that tremulous smile would be the last thing a victim ever saw.

I clipped the collar on, tested it. He smelled like sawdust and healthy young male, but the tang of sugared corruption riding it only made the sweetness of false youth less appetizing. Like a hooker turning her face, and the light picking out damage under a screen of makeup. The stubble on his neck rasped and my knuckles brushed a different texture—the band of scar tissue resting just above his collarbone. It was all but invisible in the dimness, and I wondered what he'd look like in daylight.

I don't want to find out. I've had enough of this already, and we're only ten minutes in.

I stepped back. The collar glinted. My apprentice-ring thrummed with force, and I twitched my hand, experimentally.

The Trader let out a small sound, tipping forward as he was pulled off-center. His knees ground into the dust. Every bit of silver I wore—apprentice-ring, silver chain holding the blessed carved ruby at my throat, the charms

in my hair—made a faint chiming sound. My stomach
turned. It was just like having a dog on a leash.

I nodded. Let my hand drop. "You can get up now."

"Not just yet." Perry stepped forward, and little bits
of cooling breeze lifted my hair. I didn't move, but every
nerve in my body pulled itself tight as a drumhead and
my pulse gave a nasty leap. They could hear it, of course,
and if they took it for a show of weakness things might
get nasty.

Ikaros hunched, thin shoulders coming up.

My left hand touched a gun butt, cool metal under my
fingertips. "That's close enough, Perry."

"Oh, not nearly." He shifted his weight, and the breeze
freshened again. His aura deepened, like a bruise, and
the scar woke to prickling, stinging life.

A whisper of sound, and I had the gun level, barrel
glinting. "That's close *enough*." *Give me a reason. Dear
God, just give me a reason.*

He shrugged and remained where he was. The Ringmaster was smiling faintly, his thin lips closed over the
tooth-ridges.

I backed up two steps. Did not holster the gun. Faint
starlight silvered its metal. "The chain, Perry. Hurry
up."

He smiled, a good-tempered grin with razor blades
underneath. It was the type of smile that said he was
contemplating a good piece of art or ass, something he
could pick up with very little trouble. His eyes all but
danced. A quick flicking motion with his fingers, the
scar plucking, and a loop of darkness coiled in his hands,
dipping down with a wrongly musical clashing. His left

hand snapped forward, the darkness solidified, and the Trader jerked again, a small cry wrung out of him.

Ikaros's eyes rolled up into his head and he collapsed. Spidery lines of darkness crawled up every inch of pale exposed flesh, spiked writing marching in even rows as if a tattoo had come to life and started colonizing his skin.

Perry's hands dropped. The Trader lay in the dust, gasping.

"Done, and done." The Ringmaster sighed, a short sound under the moan of freshening breeze. "He is your hostage." Now his cane had appeared, a slim black length with a round faceted crystal the size of a pool ball set atop it. He tapped the ground twice, paused, tapped a third time with the coppershod bottom. The crystal—it looked like an almighty big glass doorknob except for the sick greenish light in its depths—made a sound like billiard balls clicking together, underlining his words. "Should we break the Law he will suffer, and through him, I will suffer; through me, all shall suffer. He is our pledge to the hunter and to the Power in this city."

The Trader struggled up to his hands and knees. The collar sparked, once, a single point of blue light etching sharp shadows behind the pebbles and dirt underneath him. He coughed, dryly. Retched.

"So it is." Perry grinned. The greenish light from the Ringmaster's cane etched shadows on his face, exposing a breath of what lived under the mask of banal humanity. "May your efforts be fruitful, brother."

"No less than your own." The Ringmaster glanced at me. "Are you satisfied, hunter? May we pass?"

"Go on in." The words were bitter ash in my mouth. "Just behave yourselves."

Ikaros struggled to his feet. He moved slowly, as if it hurt. I finally lowered the gun, watching Perry. Who was grinning like he'd just discovered gold in his underpants. His face wavered between sharply handsome and bland as usual, and the tip of his tongue flickered out briefly to touch the corner of his thin lips. Even in the darkness the color—a wet cherry-red, seen in an instant and then gone—was wrong. I had to clamp down on myself to stop the sweat rising along the curve of my lower back.

The Ringmaster took the Trader's elbow and steered him away, back toward the convoy. Their engines roused one by one, and they pulled out, a creaking train of etheric bruising, tires shushing as they bounced up onto the hardtop from the access road and gained speed, heading for the well of light that was my city below.

Last of all went the limo. The Trader slumped against a back passenger-side window, and the inside of the vehicle crawled with green phosphorescence, shining out past the tinting. Its engine made a sound like chattering teeth and laughter, and its taillights flashed once as it hopped up onto the road and passed the city limits.

As they wound down the highway, they started to glitter. Each car, even the ancient Chevy, dewed with hard candy of false sparkling. They wasted no time in starting the seduction.

Jesus.

Perry stood, watching. I swallowed. Took another two steps back. The scar was still hard and hot against my wrist, like almost-burning metal clapped against cool skin.

I waited for him to do something. A conversational gambit, or a physical one, to make me react.

"Good night, sweetheart." He finally moved, turning on his heel and striding for the limousine.

It was amazing. It was probably the first time in years he hadn't fucked with me.

It rattled me more than it should. But then again, when the Cirque de Charnu comes to town, a hunter is right to feel a little rattled.

2

$\mathcal{M}$ine is definitely not a day job. The day is for sleeping. A long golden time of sunny safety hits about noon and peters out at about five in the winter, somewhere around eight in the summer. I like to be home, curled up in bed with Saul's arms around me.

I do *not* like wrestling with a Trader in a filthy storm sewer reeking of the death of small animals. I don't like being thrown and hitting concrete so hard bones break, and I hate it when they try to drown me.

So many people have tried to drown me. And I live in the *desert,* for Chrissake.

This close to the river there's always seepage in the bottom of the tunnels, and the Trader—a long thin grasshopper who had once been a man, filed teeth champing and yellow-green saliva spewing as he screamed— shoved me down further, sludge squirting up and fouling my coat even more.

I clocked him on the side of the head with a knifehilt-braced fist, got a mouthful of usable air, and almost wished I hadn't breathed. The smell was *that* bad.

Candlelight splashed the crusted, weeping walls. The Trader had set up an altar down here, bits of rotting flesh and blood-stiffened fur festooning the low concrete shelf. Cats and dogs had gone missing in this area for a while, but the Trader hadn't bumped above the radar until small children started disappearing.

I had more than a sneaking suspicion where some of those children could be found. Or *parts* of them, anyway.

The Trader yelped, losing his grip on me in the slime and scudge. The knife spun around my fingers, silver loaded along the flat of the blade hissing blue sparks like the charms in my hair, and I slashed with every ounce of strength my bent-back left arm could come up with.

The blade bit deep across one bulbous compound eye. I've long since stopped wondering why a lot of Traders go in for the pairing of hellish beauty and bizarre body modifications. It's almost as if they want to be Weres, but without the responsibility and decency Weres hold themselves to.

Green stuff splattered, too thick to be slime but too thin to be pudding. The Trader howled. I exploded up from the bottom of shin-deep water, the carved ruby at my throat crackling with a single bloody spark, and shot him twice. The recoil kicked almost too hard for even my helltainted strength—I'd finally gotten around to getting a custom set of guns, like most hunters do after a while, and I'd wondered since why it had taken me so long. Nine-millimeters are nice, but there's nothing like something bigger to pop a hole in a Trader.

Some male hunters go for guns on the maxim that "bigger is better." Female hunters generally go for accuracy of fire. I decided to go for both, since I've got the strength and have no complex about the size of my dick.

My pager went off in its padded pocket. I hoped it hadn't gotten wet, ignored the buzzing, shot the Trader a third time, and flung my left hand forward. The knife flew, blue light streaking like oil along its blade, and hit with a solid *tchuk!* in his ribs. Even that didn't take the pep out of him.

Kill kids in my town, will you? I blew out a short huff of rancid foulness, clearing my nose and mouth at the same time, wet warmth dribbling down from my forehead, more wet sliminess sliding down from my nostrils. My chin was slick with the stuff. Right hand blurred to holster the gun, other hand already full of knife, my feet moved independently of me and I hurled myself at him.

We collided with ribsnapping force. I feinted with my left hand and he took the bait, grabbing at my arm since the knife was heading for his face again. Stupid fucker.

It was my right hand he should have worried about. No gun meant I was moving in for the kill, since knifework is my forte. I'm on the tall side for a woman, but comparatively small and fast compared to 'breed and Traders.

Even without the hellbreed scar jacking me up past human and closer to the things I kill.

My right hand flicked, sudden drag of resistance against the blade, and we were almost cheek to cheek for a moment. I exhaled, inhaled, almost wished I hadn't because the smell of a ripped gut exploded out, a foul carrion stench.

Who knew what he'd been eating down here in the drains?

I did. I had an idea, at least.

The scar pulsed wetly against my wrist, feeding hell-ish strength through my arm. I twisted my wrist, hard, breaking the suction of muscle against the blade. My knee came up, I shoved, and he went down in a tangle of too-thin arms and legs, twisting and jerking as death claimed him and the corruption of Hell raced through his tissues. It devours everything in its path, the bargain they make claiming the flesh and quite possibly the soul, and the body dances like a half-smashed spider.

Some hunters swear they can see the soul streaking out of the body. Even with my blue eye I can't see it. Sometimes I've sensed a person leaving, but I don't talk about it. It seems so . . . personal. And once you've gone down and seen the shifting forest of suicides border-ing Hell, a lot of New Age white-light fluff palls pretty quickly.

The Trader collapsed, his compound eyes falling in, runnels of foulness greasing his cheeks. The stench took on a whole new depth. I watched until I was sure he was dead, noticing for the first time that my ribs were twitch-ing as they healed, the bone painfully fusing itself back together. I was bleeding, and my right leg felt a little unsteady. Liquid sloshed around my shins. I took in sip-ping breaths, my lungs starved for oxygen but the reek, dear God, it was amazing.

The candles kept burning. Lumpy, misshapen tapers, their thin flames struggling in the noxious air, stuck to any surfaces above the water's edge. I waded toward the altar, my blue eye smarting and filling with hot water as it untangled the web of etheric bruising hanging over every surface. Little crawling strands, pools of sickness a normal person would feel like a chill draft on the nape or an uncomfortable feeling it seems best to ignore.

The drift of small bones on the altar, some tangled with fur, others with bits of cloth that might have once been clothes, made small clicking sounds as I approached. Random bits of meat quivered, and if I hadn't already been on the verge of retching from the stench I'd probably have lost my breakfast right there. As it was, it had been a while since I'd eaten, and my stomach was near empty.

My fingers tingled. It took a short while before the thin blue whispering flames of banefire would stay lit along my fingers, a sorcery of cleansing almost drowned by the tenebrous air.

I'm sorry. My lips twitched. I almost said it. *It's my job to protect you. I'm sorry.*

Four kids we knew about. Three we suspected, another two I was reasonably sure of. Nine little vulnerable lives, sucked dry by a monster who had bargained with Hell.

Who knew what those kids would have grown up to do? Save lives, find a cure for cancer, bring some joy to the world. But not now. Now there was only this vengeance in a filthy, stinking sewer.

I cast the banefire, my fingers flicking forward and long thin jets of blue flame splitting the dimness. The candles hissed, banefire chuckled, and I stumbled back, blinking the blood out of my watering eyes. The bane would burn clean and leave a blessing in its wake, a thin layer inimical to hellbreed and other contagion.

I'm so, so sorry.

It was getting harder and harder to keep the words to myself.

The banefire had taken hold and was whispering to itself, a sound like children crying. I tried not to think about it as I went through the sodden pockets of whatever was left of the corpse on the floor. Luck was with me, and I found a wallet. It went in my pocket, and I half-dragged, half-floated the squishing, still sluggishly contorting body over to the burning altar. When I dumped him on it, a shower of snapping sparks went up, and I suddenly felt queasy at the thought that he was lying on top of his victims. Nothing to be done about that—I had to burn them all, or the hellbreed he'd Traded with might be able to reach out and get himself or herself a nice fresh-rotten zombie corpse or two.

Now that I had his ID I had a fighting chance of finding whatever 'breed he'd Traded with and serving justice on him, her, or it. I headed back, sliding and slipping, for the tunnels that would take me to the surface. It hadn't been a long or particularly grueling hunt, physically. No, this one had just hurt inside.

God, I hate the kid cases. The cops agree with me. There's no case that will drain you drier or turn you cynical faster.

It took me a good twenty minutes to retrace the route I'd tracked him along. When I finally found my entry point—a set of metal rungs leading up to an open manhole, welcome sunlight pouring down and picking out bits of rust on each step—I looked up, and a familiar shadow moved at the top.

"Hello, kitten," Saul called down. I started climbing, testing each rung—that's the price of greater strength and endurance, a muscle-heavy ass. And I hadn't precisely climbed through, just dropped into the manhole after my quarry, hoping I didn't hit anything on the way down.

I wish that wasn't so much business as usual.

"Hey," I called. "How's everything up in the daylight, catkin?"

"Quiet as a mouse." He laughed, and it sounded so good I almost hurried up. Exhaustion dragged against my shoulders. "Smells like you had a good time."

"The fun just never ends." Crumbling concrete held a spider-map of veins right in front of my nose. I kept climbing. "He's bagged."

"Good deal." Tension under the light bantering tone—he hadn't wanted to stay topside, but I'd needed him up there watching the manhole in case the Trader doubled back.

Or at least, that's what I'd told him. He didn't make any fuss over it, but his tone warned me that he was an unhappy Were, and we were probably going to have a talk about it soon.

There were other things to talk about, too. Big fun.

I reached the top, skipping a rung or two that didn't look sanguine about holding me, and Saul put a hand out. I grabbed and hung on, and he pulled me easily out of the darkness. He magnanimously didn't mention how bad I must have smelled. "You okay?"

My boots found solid ground. It was a dead-end street

down near Barazada Park, the spire of Santa Esperanza
lifting into the heat haze. Blessed sunlight poured hot
and heavy over me, just like syrup. In the distance the
barrio weltered.

"Fine." I paused for a moment. "Not really."

He reeled me in. Closed his arms around my shoulders and we stood for a moment, me staring at his chest
where the small vial of blessed water hung on a silver
chain. No blue swirled in the vial's depths.

He pulled me even closer, slid an arm around my
waist, and I could finally lay my head down on his chest.
We stood like that, his heartbeat a comforting thunder
in my ear, for a long time. The rumble of his purr—a
cat Were's response to a mate's distress—went straight
through me, turning my bones into jelly. It didn't stop the
way I was quivering, though, body amped up into red-
line and adrenaline dumping through the bloodstream.

When the shakes finally went down I let out a long
breath, and immediately felt bad about smearing gunk
on him. He didn't seem to mind much—he never did—
but I felt bad all the same.

"Want to tell me about it?" He didn't try to keep me
when I eased away from him. He just let go a fraction of
a second later than he *had* to.

I sighed, shook my head. "It's over. That's all." A flood
of sunlight poured over the dusty pavement, the drop-off
at the end ending in a gully that meandered behind busi-
nesses and the chain-link fence of a car dealership.

"Good enough." His hands dropped down to his
sides, and he studied me for a long moment before turning away. The manhole was flung to the side—I hadn't
been particularly careful at that point, I just wanted to

get *at* the motherfucker. It was bulky, but he got his fingers under it and hauled it around, and I fished my pager out of its padded pocket, the silver in my hair chiming in a hot draft. "Who's calling?"

The number was familiar. "Galina. Probably got another load of silver in." *Christ, I hope it's not more trouble.*

"Least it's not Monty." The manhole cover made a hollow, heavy metallic sound as he flipped it, gauging the force perfectly so it seated itself in its hole like it had never intended to come loose.

"You're such an optimist." The smile tugging at my lips felt unnatural, especially with the stink simmering off my clothes and the sick rage turning in small circles under my heart. The scar twinged, the bloom of corruption on my aura drawing itself smaller and tighter, a live coal.

He smiled back, crouching easily next to the manhole cover. The light was kind to him, bringing out the red-black burnish in his cropped, charm-sprinkled hair, and the perfect texture of his skin. He tanned well, and a fine crinkle of laugh lines fanned out from his eyes when he grinned. They smoothed away as he sobered, looking up at me.

We regarded each other. He of all people never had any trouble meeting my mismatched gaze. And each time he looked at me like this, dark eyes wide open and depthless velvet, I got the same little electric zing of contact. Like he was seeing past every wall I'd ever built to protect myself, seeing *me*.

It never got old. Or less scary. Being looked at like

that will give you a whole new definition of naked. It's just one of the things about dating a Were that'll do it.

We stood there, oven heat reflecting off the concrete, each yellowed weed laid flat under the assault of sunlight. Finally my shoulders dropped, and I slipped the pager back in its pocket. "I'm sorry." The words came out easily enough. "I just . . ."

"No need, Jillybean." He rose fluidly, soft boots whispering as he took two steps away from the manhole. I was dripping on the concrete, but drying rapidly.

"I don't mean to—"

"I said there was no need." He glanced at the street over my shoulder. The Pontiac crouched, parked cockeyed to block anyone from coming down here, a looping trail of rubber smeared on the road behind it. I'd been going at least seventy before I stood on the brakes. "You really wanted this guy."

I really want them all, sweetheart. The words died on my lips. *And each time I kill one, the itch is scratched. But it always comes back.* "Kids." Just one word made it out.

"Yeah." He scratched at his ear, his mouth pulling down in a grimace. Weres don't understand a lot of things about regular humans, but their baffled incomprehension when faced with kid cases is in a league all its own. "You must be hungry. We can stop for a burrito on the way to Galina's."

In other words, *you haven't eaten in a while, shame on you. Come on, Jill. Buck up.*

I took a deep breath, squared my shoulders. "Sounds like a good idea. That shack on Sullivan Street is probably still open."

The pager went off again. I fished it out again, my hair stiffening as it dried. Ugh.

This time it was Avery. It never rains but it pours. "Shit. On second thought, maybe we'd better just go. Avery probably needs an exorcism, and I can call Galina from his office afterward." I stuffed the pager away and turned on one steelshod heel, headed for the Pontiac.

"Dinner after that?"

"Sure. Unless the world's going to end." Adrenaline receded, leaving only unsteadiness in its wake. I made sure my stride was long and authoritative, shook out my fingers, wrinkled my nose again at the simmering reek drifting up from my clothes.

He fell into step beside me. "You know, that sort of thing is depressingly routine. How about calzones, at home? I've got that dough left over."

It *was* routine. People have no idea how close the world skates to the edge of apocalypse every week. If they did know, would it make them stop killing each other?

I used to think maybe there was a vanishing chance it would. But I'm getting to be a cynic. "Calzones sound good." I was already wondering what Avery needed, and the pager finished its buzzing as I walked. "Let's get a move on."

3

The apartment was on Silverado, in a slumping, tired-looking concrete building—the old kind with incinerators in the basement and metal chickenwire in front of the elevator doors. The wallpaper had once been expensive, but was now faded, torn, and a haven for creeping mold. If the elevator worked the place could probably have gotten on a historical register.

As it was, the whole building smelled of fried food, beer, and desperation. We took the stairs, found the right hall, and the door was cracked open.

I don't usually show up for exorcisms covered in gunk and stinking to high heaven. The victim doesn't give a rat's ass by the time I'm called in, but my fellow exorcists probably do.

This time, however, Avery didn't even seem to notice. His brown eyes sparked with feverish intensity, his mournful-handsome face animated and sharp despite the bruising spreading up his left cheek. A gurgling noise scraped across my nerves, and we came to a halt at the foot of the bed.

I studied the body thrashing against restraints for a few moments. Don't ever, ever rush an exorcism in the beginning stages, no matter how pressed for time you think you are. That was the first thing Mikhail said when he began training me to rip Possessors out of people.

"Guy's name is Emilio Ricardo. Thirty. Dishwasher. Not the usual victim." Avery spoke softly, but his entire body quivered with leashed energy. I folded my arms. The carved ruby on its short silver chain at my throat sparked once, a bloody flash in the dimness. Silver moved uneasily in my hair. Saul stood near the door, leaning against the wall with his eyes half-closed.

The apartment was small, with none of the usual signs of possession. No hint that the victim was a shut-in, nothing covering the windows, no scribbles of demented writing in whatever substance was on hand on the walls or mirrors. No smell of rotting food. No foul slick of etheric bruising over every surface.

And Possessors aren't that fond of poverty. They like to get their flabby little mental fingers in the middle and upper class. It's almost enough to make you feel charitable, finding at least *one* thing that doesn't prey on the poor.

There was a metal bed the victim was tied to, a chair and a table in the greasy kitchen, and an old heavy television balanced on a TV cart. The floor was linoleum, and the whole place was the size of a crackerbox.

No, definitely not the usual victim. But they are creatures of opportunity too, the Possessors.

The victim was male, another almost-oddity. Women

get possessed more often, between the higher incidence
of psychic talent and the constant cultural training to be
a victim. But a man wasn't unheard of. It's about sixty-
forty.

Still. . . . Male, dark-haired, babbling while he strained
against the restraints, leather creaking. "How did you
get him tied down?"

"Cold-cocked him. He'll have a headache for a while."
Avery didn't sound sorry in the slightest. He rubbed at
his jaw, gingerly. "Assuming he ever wakes up."

I kept my arms folded. Ave had done a good job strap-
ping the man down. He looked thin but wiry-strong,
fighting against the restraints, his skin rippling. The
candy-sick scent of corruption was missing.

That was what bothered me. "He doesn't smell
right."

"Smells like BO and fish." Ave's nose wrinkled. "But
it just seems off. That's why I called you. Didn't feel
right, and you're always bitching about trusting those
instincts."

"Because when you don't, you end up getting your ass
handed to you." I paused. "And then you get all embar-
rassed when I do show up to bail you out."

"Humility's a virtue, Kismet."

"So's discretion. I suck at both. Didn't you notice?"

The banter wasn't easing our nerves, but he gave me
a tight, game smile. The bruise was coloring up quite
nicely. "I was too bowled over by your witty repartee.
Not to mention your leather pants. What do you think?"

"I think he's possessed, but I don't know by what yet.
Grab a mirror."

He backed up two steps and bent to dig in his little

black exorcist's bag on the greasy linoleum floor, metal
and glass clinking. I approached the end of the bed and
considered the thin man, who was still ranting and rav-
ing in glottal stops and harsh sibilants. It didn't sound
Chaldean. It had a lilt to it unlike Helletöng, and it was
vaguely familiar.

"Here." Avery had a small round hand mirror, the
type exorcists buy by the case. I took it and hopped over
the end of the bed, which squeaked and shuddered as my
feet landed on either side of the victim's hips. I crouched
easily and kept the mirror out of sight, tucked against
my leg.

My trench coat settled over the victim's legs, and I
could see his eyes were blind—filmed with gray. A fine
tracery of overloaded veins crawled away from the corners of his eyes, right where laugh lines should be. They
were gray as well, pulsing as if thin threads of mercury
were running under his skin.

Now *that* was interesting.

Let's see what we're dealing with here, shall we? I
leaned down, examining him closely, my gaze avoiding
his blindness. My aura quivered, sea-urchin spikes almost visible, my blue eye turning hot and dry.

The victim kept twisting against the restraints.
I shifted my weight, the cot groaning. Waited. The
blind eyes wandered, back and forth in random arcs.
He didn't respond to my nearness, which could have
meant anything.

Seconds ticked by. Avery was breathing high and
hard, tension spreading out from him in waves. Saul was
a quietness by the door, watching. I settled, my heart-

beat picking up just a little. I forgot what I smelled like, crouching there, my attention narrowing to stillness.

The mirror jabbed forward just as his gray-filmed eyes wandered across the precise, unavoidable point in space that would force him to look at himself. The reflection caught and held, my blue eye straining to pierce layers of etheric interference—like fine-tuning a radio dial to catch the familiar bars of an old song—and I caught a glimpse of it before the mirror's surface disintegrated with a sharp horrified sound and the bed itself heaved and bucked three different ways at once.

The mirror went flying, jerked from my grip; restraints creaked and the bed jolted. I moved quick as a striking snake, my hellbreed-strong right hand flashing to close around the victim's throat as leather groaned, restraining a force it was never meant to bear. The chanting rose, the victim's mouth loose and sloppy, and I knew what I had hold of.

Oh, goddammit.

I bore down hard, a nonphysical movement accompanied by a hardening of physical muscles. The sea-urchin shape of my aura trembled on the surface of the visible, spikes starring out hard against the air, light popping on the points. My aura, like any exorcist's, has grown hard and thick over the course of hundreds of exorcisms, each of them unique—the only commonality is the undeniable will needed to press something inimical out of its unwilling host.

But this case needed something a little different. Silver rattled in my hair, and I heard my own voice.

"Begone, in nomine Patrii, Filii, et Spiritus Sancti!

I command you, I abjure you, I demand you release this—"

That was as far as I got before what was in the man exploded, my fingers slipping free, and threw me ass-over-teakettle. The cot shredded itself, screeching as it tore. The restraints held, just barely—once-living tissue more resilient than brittle metal, for once. Avery yelled, diving, and Saul gave a short sharp bark of surprise.

I landed hard, skidding on my hip, hit the wall. Drywall crumbled, puffing out chalk dust. I was on my feet again without knowing quite how, moving faster than I had any right to, adrenaline pouring copper through my blood. Two skipping steps across the room, a leap, and I realized just as soon as I was committed to the motion that I was going to miss.

Crap.

Avery was still yelling as I twisted in midair. The victim rose from the ruins of the bed, leather restraints squealing as his body strained against them, a sound like the wind rushing from the mouth of a subway tunnel thundering through the apartment and blowing out the windows in a tinkle of glass.

He was shouting, still in that lyrical tongue, and the curse flew past me as I twisted even further, my coat snapping taut like a flag in a stiff breeze. I touched down, pulling etheric energy recklessly through the scar, a pucker of hurtful acid wetness inside my right wrist humming with power. My foot flashed out, weight shifting back, and I caught him full in the face right before full extension, the precise point where a kick has the most juice. The jolt went all the way up my leg.

He went flying, Avery yelled something else shapeless, and I coiled myself, getting my feet under me. Now I was prepared.

The wall disintegrated as the victim hit it, and I had no time to think about the damage that might be done to the host body. I centered myself, drew myself up to my full height, and the charms in my hair rattled and buzzed.

"Papa Legba!" I had to shout to hear myself through the volume of noise the victim was producing, gabbling and screaming. *"Papa Legba! Papa Legba close the door! Papa Legba close the door! PAPA LEGBA CLOSE THE DOOR!"*

Silence fell, sharp as a knife. My blue eye—the left one, the smart one—watered. The ether swirled, the sensitized fabric of the room resounding like a plucked thread. Everything halted, droplets of crystallized water hanging in the air—Avery, chucking a bottle of holy water at the victim, whose mouth was open in a trapped, contorted scream.

Well, at least Ave was thinking. Holy water's far from the worst ally in a situation like this.

The room filled with a colorless cigar-smoke fume. I tasted rum, thrown back hard against the palate, and spat, spraying the air. A silver nail ran through me from crown to soles, and I remembered Mikhail's pale face after my first introduction to this type of magic.

Be careful it does not eat you alive, milaya, he'd said. *These sorts of things do.*

The victim toppled, a long slow fall to the greasy linoleum floor. Before he hit I was on him, my aura sparking in sudden swirling darkness despite the flood of sunlight rushing through the windows. The shape of the things inhabiting him rose like smoke—three small humanoid forms, weaving in and out of each other. There was a high chilling childish laugh, and a gabble of weirdly accented Spanish.

"Usted va a pesar de que, bruja." For a moment I saw them—little boy and little girl, both with crystalline eyes and bowl-cut black hair, the girl in a shift and the boy in a brown loincloth. The shape between them was androgynous, melting first into the girl's body, she mutated into the boy, and the third shape whisked them both back out of sight, receding down a long tunnel. The sound of a door closing, sharp and firm, echoed through shocked air.

I sagged. The victim was unconscious, his face slack and empty. "Ogoun," I whispered. "Legba, Ogoun, thank you. *Muchas gracias.* Thank you very much."

"What. The. Hell?" Avery didn't finish the thought. He didn't have to.

"It's bad news." I glanced at Saul, who hadn't moved from the door. He leaned forward, though, tense and expectant, his dark eyes not leaving me. He was pale under his coloring, and I found out I was still smelling like rotting goop.

I couldn't *wait* to get home and take a shower.

"I got that much." Avery crouched gingerly. I let go of the victim, who slumped to the floor, breathing heavily. "That smelled like cigars. And . . . rum?"

"Put him in a holding tank downtown. Get me a file on him, too. I need two headshots." I straightened. Every muscle in my body cried out in pain, then subsided into a dull howling. "Keep the door bolted. Watch him. If you have to, buzz me again."

"Great. Okay." Ave visibly restrained himself from asking me why, and I checked. I get so used to dealing with one thing after another that sometimes letting someone else in on the situation doesn't occur to me. But Ave would do his job better if he knew what he was dealing with.

"You've never seen a *loa* before? An *orisha?*"

"Holy crap." His eyes got really wide, and he eased back a few steps, as if it was catching. "That was a—"

"Not a normal one, no." I cast a critical eye over the apartment. "Get going. He won't stay knocked out forever, but you should be able to get him downtown. If he wakes up in the back of the car and gives you trouble, smack him in the face with holy water and keep repeating a Hail Mary or something."

"I'm *Protestant.*"

For Christ's sake, like that matters. "Then recite the Nicene. Or the goddamn Wheelwrights lineup, whatever works." I straightened. "Go on. I'm going to look around."

"What for?"

"For signs of what he's mixed up in. You don't just trip and fall and get a spirit in you, you know." Even Possessors had to spend weeks of effort to worm their way into a human host.

"Ha ha. I suppose you're not going to help me carry him?"

"Saul will." I glanced over at my Were again. He nodded slightly, and his jaw was set. I couldn't think why, until something warm and stinging dropped into my eyes. "Shit." I touched my forehead, discovered a shallow slice. "I'm bleeding." I actually sounded surprised.

Avery rolled his eyes. "Hanging around you is a never-ending adventure."

It's that way for me too. "Shut up and get this guy locked up before he does anything else."

Bare fridge, bare cupboards—only a can of refried beans and a paper bag of Maseca, as well as a bottle of vinegar, for some reason. Threadbare clothes, two uniform shirts with the victim's name embroidered on them. A pair of busted sneakers in the closet. It was like a monk's cell.

I poked at the remnants of the cot. Was standing, staring at the twisted curlicues of metal and sharp sheared-off ends, when Saul reappeared, closing the door with a slight click. "Anything?"

"Nothing. If he's a follower, he's got it well hidden."

"That wasn't a Possessor."

"Nope, it wasn't. It was an *orisha*. Or a *loa*. Six of one, half a dozen of the other. Whatever branch of magic this guy's into—"

"He didn't smell like magic." Saul paced forward, stopped at my shoulder, and looked down at the mess of the broken bed. "Why didn't it cut the leather?"

"Leather was once living. And it has a greater elasticity when it comes to that kind of load. No, he didn't smell like magic. And the Twins don't usually take people without—"

"The Twins?"

"Yeah. You've heard of voodoo, right?" I glanced up. He looked blank. I tried again. "Santeria? Candomblé?"

"Santeria? A little. Popular down in the barrio." A

shadow of a grin eased the tension in his face. He hadn't even had time to smear warpaint along his beautiful cheekbones, we'd been running so hard and fast. "I suppose now isn't the time to admit I'm behind on my reading."

This is why Weres run backup—they don't have the breadth of knowledge a hunter does. They're busy with their own spirits, their own particular sorceries. They rarely mess around with human magics.

Or human predators.

"Well, forget what you've seen in the movies. Voodoo is different. People don't just make bargains with hellbreed—there's a bunch of other inhuman intelligences out there. They make contact for all sorts of reasons. We have things spirits want, they have things we want, and everybody trades."

"Got that. So, voodoo in particular? Santeria? Candomblé?" His pronunciation wasn't off by much.

"Basically they interact with the same *species* of intelligence, but not the same *groups*. There's some crossover, but they're like different families. Spirits halfway between us and God, they say." I had to choose what to tell him, boiling a complex subject down to a few sentences. "They're not from Hell, and generally a practitioner is safe from being contaminated by a Possessor." I frowned down at the shattered bed. "Though they're not immune to physical harm from a hellbreed. Hell generally doesn't mix with voodoo." Now I was thinking out loud, good to do with him in the room.

"That's not what's bothering you, though." His fingers touched my hip. He crowded a little closer, his heat wrapping around me. It felt nice.

I let out a long breath. "What's bothering me is that the *loa* don't step in where they're not invited. At least, not without a good reason. And that was the Twins. At least, I'm reasonably sure it was one of their aspects."

"Bad news?"

Well, not particularly good news. I shrugged. "We'll see. If he was mixed up in something, we'll find out. I'll pick up the file from Avery and—"

"Dinner first?" It wasn't like him to interrupt me.

I was tired, my head hurt, and I smelled like death warmed over. "Dinner first," I agreed, scrubbing at the quick-drying blood on my face with my free hand. "This doesn't look right. It makes my weird-o-meter tingle like mad."

"That's saying something. Come on. Let's close this up and go home."

"In a second." I gave him a squeeze, freed myself, and checked the small bathroom. A bar of coal-tar soap in the ringed bathtub; toothbrush, box of baking soda, and a straight razor in a ceramic mug next to the sink.

The razor was a nice one, antique. Had to be 1920s, if my guess was good. A black scale with mother-of-pearl inlay, and a well-preserved steel, sharp as a suicide's whisper. I flicked it open, saw the shadow of blue swirling under the surface of the metal. I blinked, and it was gone.

Now that's interesting. I closed it carefully, dug in my pocket for a Ziploc baggie, and found one. Slid the straight razor in and sealed it. *I wonder . . .*

"What have you got there?" Saul said from the door.

"Clue." I slipped the razor in my pocket, turned. My

coat brushed the sink, and the mug clattered down into its rusted bowl, spilling the toothbrush as well. "Shit."

"Which one? Clue or shit?" It was a pale attempt at humor, but one I appreciated.

"The former, catkin. Come on, I'm hungry." *And I need to work some of these nerves off. Maybe you'll help me with that.*

"Mh." He let me out of the tiny, tiny bathroom. Hot air soughed through the broken windows. "Sure made a mess."

"Can't have an exorcism without breaking a few beds. If he's clean we'll figure something out."

"And if he's not?"

I didn't have to work to sound tired. "Then a smashed-up apartment is the least of his worries."

4

$\mathcal{D}$ust swirled like oil, covering my city in waves. Autumn was moving across the mountains, the nights getting chillier and the days only slightly less hot. Soon the thunderstorms would start rolling in. But for now the far hills were tawny, and the clouds only stayed, threateningly, in the distance.

I hit the ground hard. Drew my knees up and shot my bare feet out, using the momentum to fuel a leap, propelling myself up. Whirled, my hand shooting out; he avoided it with a liquid jump to the side. My hand turned into a blade, chopped down.

He caught my wrist, brown fingers locking, and twisted, pulling back as he dropped into a crouch, swinging his center of gravity down and back. My arm almost yanked out of its socket, his foot smacked into my midriff as he hit the mats on his back, and I flew. Twisted in midair, doubling on myself like a gymnast, and landed a bare half-second before he was on me, a fast hard flurry of strikes and parries. Each one pushed aside, combat like a dance, no more than the barest touch needed to redirect, to score a hit, pulled at the last fraction of a second.

A hunter relies on firepower and sorcery to even the playing field. Still, we never fight Weres, even rogues. They're just too quick, too powerful, too graceful. They have no corruption, like in a hellbreed, that a human can latch onto and track.

I've wondered about that. I wonder about a lot of things, the more I work this job.

I'm harder to hit now, and a hell of a lot harder to hurt. And it was times like this that the bargain seemed a better thing than just a stopgap measure until I could figure out how to send Perry screaming back to Hell.

Hard.

Saul drove me across the length of the sparring room, dying sunlight falling liquid through the windows, sweat on both of us and the sounds of deadly serious mock-combat echoing. I stamped my back foot down hard, dipped, and spun as he advanced on me, taking his legs out from under him. He hit hard. I leapt and had my fist drawn back, my other hand tangled in his silver-scarred shorn hair.

"Give up?" I asked, sweetly.

A fine sheen of sweat highlighted each plane of his face. He blinked, a cat's quick flicker of eyelids. "You haven't won yet."

I grinned, lips pulling back from teeth. "Wanna keep going? Best two out of three, or should we take this somewhere else?"

"Don't know if you're ready." An answering grin, but his teeth kept well hidden.

Oh, I'm ready. I was ready for more than just sparring.

He heaved up, I pushed him back down. A few more seconds of wrestling ended with me still on top for once, the scar burning against my wrist and hot strength spilling through my bones. "It's looking like you're the one not ready, catkin."

"Just biding my time." He surged again, I pushed him down and realized my mistake a split second too late as his knees came up, my balance off by a critical fraction. A confused welter of movement, his forehead hit me in the mouth, and we rolled. Judo took over, and I began fighting in earnest. Reflex turned me into a dangerous snake writhing in his arms, but Saul knew how to handle this.

He always did. Or at least, he always *had.*

Stinging salt, my body suddenly just a welter of reaction. Saul held me down, silver chiming as his head dipped. Smell of leather, of cherry Charvil smoke, the good scent of a healthy male and the dry sleekness of catfur. We became one body with twisting limbs, rolling and seeking advantage, the floor a hard sea we only touched the surface of.

His mouth found mine, and it was no longer tossing on an ocean. It was a softness blooming, nailing me in place. My body loosened, tingles flooding me. It was a far cleaner feeling than the scar's sick heat. I kissed him with my heart flooding out through the play of tongue and lips. He was purring, a rumble spreading out in waves. Each concentric circle of that purr stroked along my skin.

I broke away to take a breath. He nuzzled down my

jawline, his mouth settling lower, just over my pulse. I quieted, the instinct of struggle sliding away.

"Saul," I whispered.

"Hm?" He nipped, playfully, and I arched.

"I think we should take this somewhere else." *Like a bed. Like* our *bed*.

"Here's nice." He nuzzled again. I squirmed in a new way.

"Saul—"

"Shhh."

I stilled. He inhaled deeply. Let out the breath in a chuff, a warm spot on my vulnerable throat. My pulse strained toward him. I held still as long as I possibly could. Finally wriggled a little bit, and he didn't immediately move. "What's wrong?" My wrists, braceleted by his fingers, both throbbed. He was holding me a little too tightly.

"Nothing," he whispered back. "I just want to hold you."

Goddammit. I want something else entirely. But I breathed in, the urge retreating low in my pelvis, a dull ache spiking for a moment as bloodflow reversed itself. *I'm going to be cranky if this keeps up.* "Okay." I swallowed, my throat moving against his lips. Another slight touch; it became very difficult to throttle my hormones back.

Mikhail had always been on me to control my pulse. I was much better at it than I ever had been, but one whiff of my cat-boy and the hormones started jacking me up again.

As problems went, it was a nice one.

Deep breathing. My eyes closed. The dark behind my

lids was safe for once. Pushing the feeling down and away, reasserting control.

It used to be damn near every sparring session ended with us rolling around in an entirely different way to take the edge off. Since Saul had come back from the Rez with his hair cropped, it hadn't happened. He wanted to be close, and wanted to be held.

I was okay with that. But the no-sex thing was beginning to take its toll.

God, Jill, how selfish can you be? His mom's dead. For a Were, that's like the end of the world. I kept my breathing slow and even. He didn't let go. We stayed that way, knotted together. Frozen.

"I love you," he finally said against my skin. "Jill?"

"I know that." And I did. "I love you too, catkin. Just rest for a minute. It's okay." I told the persistent tension in the bottom of my belly to go away. *I refuse to be dragged around by my clitoris, for God's sake. Come on, Jill. Rule the body, the body doesn't rule you.*

"I . . ." Maddeningly, he stopped. We lay like that for another thirty seconds or so, hardwood floor holding me up but not in the most comfortable way.

He levered himself up all in a rush, easing over to the side and ending up cross-legged, sitting and watching me. Something flared in his dark eyes. I watched his face, alert for any sign.

"I'm sorry." The little bottle of holy water on its silver chain around his neck shifted as he moved again, twitching, and stilled. "I thought . . ."

"Don't worry about it." I pushed myself up on my elbows. My T-shirt was rucked up, muscle moving under my abdominal skin, scars crisscrossing me. I'd put on a little more weight, but not a lot, and most of it more muscle. "Really."

"Jill . . ." A helpless shrug. You wouldn't think he was so much bigger than me, he looked so small and lost right now.

"Hey." I scrambled, got my knees under me, threw my arms around him. "Hey, don't. Please don't. Don't *worry* about it."

"I just . . . I want to . . ." I'd never known him to be incoherent before. Quiet, yes. Unable to find the words?

No. That was my job, wasn't it? To be the one who couldn't express a single goddamn important thing. I searched for the right thing to say. "I know, baby. Don't worry so much. It's only temporary."

His face fell. "You think so?" It wasn't like him to sound so questioning. Or so tentative.

"Of *course.*" I said it far more firmly than I felt. Maybe it wasn't temporary. Maybe he was just having second thoughts about marrying a hellbreed-tainted hunter. Weres don't divorce—they just pick their mates and settle down—but Weres didn't date hunters all that often either, and almost never got hitched to them.

So if this distance between us wasn't temporary, would he go back to his tribe? As far as they were concerned the fireside ceremony with his mother officiating made me his mate. But . . . I was an anomaly, and a big one. If he went back to his tribe, I couldn't see anyone protesting.

Least of all me. I'd commence and finish quiet internal bleeding before I said a peep. He deserved that much from me. If he really wanted to go back, I couldn't blame him one bit.

God knows you're not the easiest person in the world to live with, Jill. Buck up. Comfort him.

I held him, stroking his hair, touching the silver charms knotted in with red thread. Rubbed his nape just the way he liked it, scraping with my bitten-down nails. He eased a little and purred again, in fits and starts. "It's okay," I repeated. "Really and truly. It's all okay."

I don't know what else I would have said if the doorbell hadn't sounded loud enough to cut my ears in half. The thing goes off so seldom, I always forget between times that I have it deliberately loud. I like to hear everything scuttling in the warehouse's walls, down to the smallest insect.

Not that I ever have many insects around, what with sorcery burning all through the paneling and studs, but you get the idea.

I straightened. There wasn't a quiver or a peep from my hackles. My intuition was quiet, for once. "Huh."

Which didn't mean there wasn't something bad at the door. It could be just a very *quiet* something bad. Then again, why would anything that valued its life and had mayhem on its mind ring my doorbell instead of just busting in to lay some hurt on me?

"Jill—" Saul made a small movement, like he wanted to catch my wrist.

"Hang on, catkin." I bounced to my feet and stalked for the door. A convenient table on the way gave me a gun; I checked the magazine as I slipped cat-footed down the hall and toward the front door.

Nothing. Not even a tingle. A series of raps—*human,* I decided, since they didn't have the odd too-light or too-heavy edge that meant something else. I slid up to the door.

Breathing. Slightly asthmatic. A human pulse, just a little elevated. I jerked the door open, the locks parting like water.

A skinny Hispanic teenager smelling of Corona and refried beans stood on my front step. He wore 51 colors, a red bandanna knotted around one thin bicep. Beneath the edge of a hairnet keeping his dark, limp hair back, he had a face that belonged on an Aztec codex.

Or at least, his proud, bird-beak nose did. Sallow, pitted skin and a pair of dead, empty eyes showed why he'd never be handsome. I recognized him a split second after I realized what he was standing there for.

He had the look.

Oh, no. Not now. "What the hell do you want?"

Gilberto Rosario Gonzalez-Ayala blinked once. *"Hola, bruja."*

"Hello, *Señor* Gonzalez-Ayala. I repeat, what the bloody blue blazes do you want?"

"Took me a while to find your house." A ghost of good humor slid through the bottom of his dark, shark-flat eyes.

You're not packing a .22, are you? I eyed him, taking in the flannel shirt, the torn jeans—and there it was under the stark flatness of his expression.

I knew that look. It was hunger.

Crap. I knew I hadn't seen the last of this kid. "There's a reason for that," I said finally. Behind him, the street was empty. The warehouse is on the wrong side of the tracks, of course. I spent the first half of my life trying to get away from the wrong side, and now it's where I spend most of my time. I barely have any idea what it's like over on the decent side of town, unless I'm working a case with its tentacles up among the rich and powerful.

I think that's referred to as *irony*.

He kept quiet, watching me. The sun was going down, dusk dyeing the west in bright pink and orange scarves. It was almost time to get ready for the night. Which would mean racking in more ammo and dropping by Galina's, since she had another load of blessed silver for me. Before that, I had to do some quiet digging, starting with the file on Avery's victim from the last night—

"You know why I'm here, *bruja*." His eyes were fixed on my face. "I owe you a beer. And we got business."

Yes, I do know why you're here. You still have to say it. "What kind of business? I'm not involved with petty gang warfare." *No matter how useful you guys were last time I had big trouble in town.* My heart squeezed down on itself, thinking of a grave and a coffin, and a good cop laid to rest.

My fault. If I had known . . .

But you never do. I brought myself back to the present with a conscious effort.

The boy on my front step shrugged. "I ain't here for Ramon. We got other business."

"Like what, Gilberto?" *Go away while you still can.*

"*Bruja* business. With what you do."

I held his gaze for a long fifteen seconds, feeling Saul appear behind me, a silent presence. My nostrils flared. It was there, too, the flat odorless reek of desperation with the burnt-sugar edge of wanting.

He didn't quite break, but he did pale the slightest bit and step back, as if my mismatched eyes had somehow changed. I knew they hadn't—there was none of the dry burning that would tell me my blue eye was doing funny things. But even the bravest tend to get a little weirded out when I stare at the bridge of the nose. The gaze grows piercing when you do that, especially if you just soft-focus, and you begin to look like you're staring through someone's head, riffling through their most intimate memories.

It's a tough look to pull off while covered in dry sweat, fucked-up in a T-shirt and leather pants, and frustrated enough to chew nails. I still managed.

"I know what you do." Gilberto dropped his hands. They dangled loosely, reminding me of the strangler-fingered Trader. "I want to do it, too."

I didn't have to put any more bitterness into my laugh. It was already bitter enough. "Go home, *poquito*. Leave the night alone and don't darken my door again." I swept said door to and closed it in his face.

No sound from the other side. None that you could hear with human ears, that is. I could still hear his heart-beat, pounding a little harder and faster now. Accelerated breathing, too.

I'll bet that didn't go the way you thought it would. I half-turned, and Saul stood close behind me, his hair mussed and high color blooming in his cheeks, one dark eyebrow elegantly lifted.

I shrugged. "Hopefully he'll go away. I'm going to hit the shower."

"What if he rings the bell again?"

"Ignore him." I swung past him, already planning out the rest of the night. "Want a snack before we head out again?"

His broad shoulders dropped. "I'll make you eggs." He even managed to make that sound tentative. His hand twitched again, like he wanted to touch me, but he refrained.

Why?

You've got other problems, Jill. Just let him be. Be supportive, for once. "Good deal. Thanks, sweetie." I paced away, a little faster than I should have, trying not to feel like I was retreating.

Now *that* was a losing battle.

5

Avery's desk always looked about to disappear under a mound of paper and ranks of liquor bottles. He'd stuck slim candles into bottle mouths, some burned down and others pristine, though I never saw a burning one. If he ever lit them up, it was probably when he was alone.

Cops aren't supposed to drink on duty, but exorcists get a little bit of leeway. However, Ave didn't immediately reach for the mini-fridge under his desk to get me a beer, and that was odd.

The tiled passageway behind me resounded with faint echoes from the downtown jail above. Here, at the very bottom, the long corridor terminated in Ave's office and three rooms, each barred with cold iron. Each with a circle carved into the concrete floor to hold victims hosting a Possessor—or those who had been cleaned out but had to be protected from the demon coming *back* to crawl right in and set up housekeeping.

He handed over the file. "This is seriously weird."

When isn't it? I rolled my shoulders back in their sockets, my coat creaking a little. "What's weird? Where's our boy?"

"He's the winner in Room One. Didn't flinch at the circle or anything. Didn't even know he was awake until I peeked in the porthole about an hour ago, when I finally got the file all together. There's some headshots in there too. He has a record."

I flipped it open and took a look. A couple of drug arrests, one breaking and entering dismissed with time served, and nothing for the last three years. Emilio Ricardo, thirty-six, brown and brown, employed halfway across town at a Mexican restaurant. Avery had even, bless his thoroughgoing little heart, pulled his recent renewal of a food-handler's card. "Huh."

"Yeah. The address on his food permit isn't the place on Silverado where I found him." Avery scratched at his forehead under a flop of brown hair. "It just tingled too funny. I got called in by a patrol car—they'd gone in for a domestic disturbance in the same apartment building and ended up hearing this guy screaming. Couldn't break the door down, and one of them—Jughead Vanner, you know, blond kid, looks like an advertisement for Clairol—radioed me in. He said it made him feel hinky."

That's odd. "Poor Jughead. You know he came across a Trader a couple months ago?"

Ave's sleepy smile bloomed. "He told me. Not in so many words, but . . . he wanted nothing to do with anything weird. I had to jiggle the door to get it open, and the vic tried to cold-cock me when I stepped in. I returned the favor, we tussled, I knocked him out."

"Where was he when you came in? Right next to the door?"

"Guess so. Why?"

"No reason." The straight razor was still in my pocket. For some reason, it bothered me. "So he's been quiet?"

"As a mouse." Avery's eyebrows were struggling not to rise. "Something wrong, Jill?"

"Not yet." *But this is strange.* "I'll peek in on him, then I've got a couple other things to do. Can you hold him for a bit?"

He made an expansive motion, rolling his eyes. "All things should be so easy. It's been quiet on the exorcism front."

I didn't tell him that with the Cirque in town, exorcisms would probably bottom out for a while. He didn't need that kind of uneasiness weighing him down. "Yeah. I haven't pulled something out of someone for at least two weeks, before this."

"No rest for the wicked." He indicated the first door. "Wanna take a look? Eva and I are going out for beers after I get off-shift. In about twenty minutes."

"You've been spending a lot of time with her. Speaking of Eva, how's Benito? And Wallace? Is Benny's leg okay?"

"Oh, yeah, it itches like hell under that cast but he's all right. Says he feels more stupid than anything else." Avery pointedly didn't mention Eva again, and—was he *blushing?*

I stared at him, my jaw threatening to drop. Ave's got a sleepy smile and big brown eyes, both of which draw women like honey. They don't stay—girls don't like it when their man spends his nights somewhere else, even if it's with possessed people. And Avery never makes much of an effort to keep them, either.

But he and Eva had been hanging out an awful lot lately. She's smart, tough, and a capable exorcist, even if she'd never make a hunter. Both Benito and Wallace have a little-sister thing going for her, and she handles it as gracefully as any woman in a predominantly male field does.

That is, with a smart mouth and twice the moxie of any mere man.

I swallowed the smile struggling to rise to my face. "Mmmh. Serves him right, taking on an exorcism-plus like that without calling me." I put the file under my arm and stepped up to the first door, my back itching a little because it was to the hallway. Only one entrance and one exit to any exorcist's lair.

Getting trapped is a risk we'll take. Letting a Possessor or a victim escape without being cleaned out isn't.

"Eh, well. None of us want to call you without reason." He shrugged when I glanced at him. "I know, I know. Better to call you without need than to need you and not call you. Believe me, I'm down with that."

I eased the bolt on the porthole free, slid the small reinforced square aside. Even this aperture was barred with cold iron, blue light running under its pitted, rusting surface. Reinforcing the protections on a space like this was an every-day, every-other-day job at most. Some exorcists do it twice a day, even.

Considering the alternative, I don't blame them.

Emilio Ricardo crouched in the center of the circle scored in the concrete floor. He rocked back and forth, subvocalizing, and now that the peephole was open I could hear it, a tuneless buzzing plucking at the air. He was hugging himself, and the rags of his shirt fluttered. The restraints lay in a corner, a jumble of leather straps.

Interesting. "Did you untie him?"

"Yeah. Figured he was going to be in there awhile. I'll trank him through the door if we need to take him out for a walk." Avery shivered. "I got a bad feeling about this, Kiss."

Don't call me that. "Me too." I shut my dumb right eye and peered through, concentrating.

There was only a slight, fading quiver of the unnatural around Ricardo. He was just keening, probably in psychological shock. Either that, or . . .

"Huh." I looked closer, my smart eye dry and buzzing.

"I hate it when you say that," Avery muttered.

Lingering cheesecloth veils hung around him, pulsing every time he took a breath. It looked like he was fighting free of the contamination—though contamination isn't the right word when it comes to voodoo or any of her cousins. He was definitely struggling with the mental and emotional damage done by having something inhuman use your body as a hotel room—or getting that something violently evicted.

It didn't look like the regular event of a *loa* or *orisha* "riding a horse." The bargains that priests and priestesses make with those spirits are well-defined on both sides, and initiation into the secrets of any voodoo-esque branch carries a protection against unwanted possession as well as methods of doing it safely.

That is, if any possession can be called "safe."

They are jealous of their followers, those spirits. I learned as much doing a residency, working the voodoo beat in New Orleans. Now *that* had been an education. Just goes to show there's always something more you can learn, even as a hunter.

I slid the porthole closed, locked it. "Has he eaten anything?"

Avery shook his sleek dark head. "Nothing yet. I slide the food in, he doesn't touch it."

I don't like this. I restrained the urge to flip through the file again. "Okay. I'm going to ask some questions. Hopefully I—" My pager buzzed, I broke off and dug for it. "Jesus. Never rains but it pours."

"You say that a lot. I'll just keep feeding him, then."

"Be careful. I'm not exactly sure what's going on here, and until I am I don't want him going anywhere. Okay?" I checked the pager. Galina, again. Which meant I had to get over there—it wasn't like her to buzz right after I'd visited her unless something was going on. Usually she'll just wait for me to drop by every couple of weeks, figuring I have other irons in the fire.

"Okay. Say hi to Saul for me, will you?"

"I will." I pocketed my pager, took another long look at the closed door holding a mystery behind it, shook my head, and turned on my heel. "Say hi to Eva for us."

He *was* blushing. He should've known I wouldn't leave without twitting him. "Go fuck yourself, Kismet."

I laughed and was on my way, pushing up the stairs lightly with each foot. Outside the jail, the Pontiac was parked in a fire lane, Saul leaning against the front left quarter-panel and smoking. The streetlamp shine of just-past-dark was kind, and I stopped on the steps for a moment, just taking a good look at him.

Tall, dark man, silver in his short black hair, jeans and combat boots and a black T-shirt. Broad-shouldered and lean-hipped, and almost too delicious to be real. Weres are generally striking if not beautiful. They just look more *finished* than regular humans.

He was studying the street, presenting me with a three-quarter profile hard-edged as a statue. There were dark circles under his eyes, I noticed, and his mouth was drawn tight. And his shoulders were hunched in a way I'd never seen before.

He looked tired. *Well, his mom just died. Leave it alone, Jill. Be supportive.*

My pager buzzed again, and I fished it out.

Galina, again. A chill touched my nape. "Fuckity."

That got Saul's attention. He ditched his cigarette, a long, thin stream of smoke following its arc into the gutter. "What's up?"

"Galina's buzzing. Twice. I should get over there. Avery says hi, by the way. I think he and Eva are dating." I waited for him to give me a quick smile, waited for his eyebrow to quirk.

Instead, his mouth turned even thinner. "Huh."

He really did look tired. My fingers tightened on the manila folder, making it creak and crackle slightly. "I can drop you off at home."

That earned me a look sharp enough to break a window. "You don't want me along?"

What? "Of course I do. You just look a little under the weather, that's all." *You look tired, and I don't blame you.*

He didn't scowl, but it was close. "I'm *fine*." He slid along the side of the car, opened his door, and dropped in as my pager sounded again.

Goddammit. I stalked around the front, popped the driver's door, and got in, tossing the file in the backseat. I'd go over it after we found out what was going down at Galina's. "Saul—"

"I'm fine." He lit another Charvil. "If that's Galina we'd better hurry."

"You're actually telling me to drive fast?"

He grabbed for the seat belt as I twisted the key. The Pontiac purred into life. "Christ, when do you *not* drive fast, kitten?"

When indeed. I dropped the Pontiac into gear. My pager buzzed again, and I floored it while Saul was still trying to get his seat belt on.

6

Galina's shop windows shone with featureless yellow light behind paper-thin blinds. The telephone poles marching alongside the road in this part of town were festooned with paper. As I cut the engine, looking at the one right next to the car, I saw a huge painted poster stapled over the weathered drift of concert announcements and nudie-bar placards.

Come To The Circus! Art Deco flowers festooned the edges, and in the middle was a grinning clown's face, deep lines in its paint, leering at the street. A suggestion of fangs touched the greased lower lip, and the clown's eyebrows came up to high peaks. A dusting of corruption lay over the paper, visible only to my blue eye.

There was no address. Of course, the people who wanted to would find it. That's the way it works.

My mouth went dry. "Jeez."

Saul barely gave it a glance. "Trashy." He opened his door, flicking his Charvil into the gutter.

A shadow moved in the plate-glass front of the shop

across the street. I eyed it for a few moments, took my time opening my door. Blue fuzzy dice hanging from the rearview mirror rocked slowly to a halt—Galina's gift, a replacement for the red ones that had gone up in flames with my Impala.

The thought *still* pissed me off. I'd nursed that car back into shape from a rusted hulk in a wrecking yard. All that work and effort gone in a few heartbeats, dying in the barrio.

Saul hadn't asked any questions when I picked him up from the train station in the Pontiac. I was glad about that.

The shadow in Galina's window moved again. I slid out of the car, slammed my door, and eased a gun free of the holster. Saul had paused at the rear of the car, his head up, hot wind touching his hip-length leather jacket and making the fringe move a little. His dark eyes flicked to the gun in my hand, and he straightened infinitesimally before stepping out into the road.

He followed two steps behind and to my left, carefully out of the way but close enough if I should need him. The skin between my shoulder blades twitched a little when I crossed the centerline—it hadn't been so long ago that I'd been right in the middle of the street and got chewed up by an assault rifle. They'd used copper-jacketed lead, the dumb bunnies, instead of silver to hurt a helltainted hunter.

Everyone skipping and scrambling to kill me, when if they'd just left me alone they could have quietly had their bioweapon and their higher-up from Hell stepping through to make my entire city—hell, probably the entire *country*—a wasteland before I could stop them.

There wouldn't have been a damn thing I could do about it. I'd only been poking around the suicide of Monty's old partner, not looking for a serious dose of lead poisoning or a firebombed car.

I wasn't far enough away from that case yet for my body to forget. A prickle of chill touched the curve of my lower back.

The body remembers, and the body knows. You can override that knowing with enough training, but it's still never pleasant.

The blinds twitched and one moved aside slightly. The shape in the window was Galina, her marcel-waved hair an immaculate cap as always. Her green eyes sparked as the sheet of etheric energy folding over her shop changed slightly, like light refracting through a waterfall. Even my dumb eye could sense the reverberations, watering and tingling. The scar prickled.

"She looks worried," Saul murmured.

"No shit," I muttered back. Inside her shop, Galina's will is law—she is, after all, a Sanctuary. But anything could happen on the way up to her doorstep.

And who knew what was waiting for us around here? It wasn't like her to call more than once. They all know the drill, everyone who dials me—I'll get around to you sooner or later, unless I'm being shot, strangled, knifed, electrocuted, thrown off a building, or doing anything else fun and interesting.

I opened the door cautiously. The bell jingled. I stepped carefully through the curtain of Sanc warding.

"Thank God." She was in her robes, the pigeon-throat gray shifting and the mark of the Order—a silver medallion, the quartered circle inside a serpent's hoop, snake eating its own tail—at her throat. I gave the shop a quick glance—nothing visible. I relaxed fractionally, didn't reholster the gun. Something was off here. "You won't need that, Jill, I've got everything—"

"Is it her?" A rumble of Helletöng slid under the words, and the windows chattered, both with Galina's wordless shout and the lash of a hellbreed's voice.

Coming from *inside*.

Usually, my instinct would be to dive *away* from something like that. This time, though, I pitched forward, my shoulder smacking hard against the bottom of a display case running along the right side of the store. Glass shivered and whickered loose. Saul let out a short sharp yell, I finished rolling, gaining my feet in a single convulsive movement and ending up with both guns pointed straight at a very familiar-looking 'breed.

The Ringmaster held his cane like a staff, the crystal at its head spitting with venomous green as he stood next to the cash register. His eyes ran with wet orange hellfire. His hair was lifting on a slight screaming breeze from nowhere, standing up in wet black spikes. This time he was in a battered red velvet coat and actual *jodhpurs,* but it didn't make him look ridiculous.

No, he looked like he belonged on a carton of animal crackers. A really twisted, ugly carton sopping with blood and other nasty liquids.

"We came to this town in good faith, hunter." The faint lines on the ridge of bone masquerading as teeth were grimed with something dark. "We came to cleanse and to—"

"Stand down." My voice sliced through his. Behind me, Saul's warning growl rose, rattling the entire place no less than Galina's anger or the wave of hellbreed agitation. "This is a Sanctuary. Calm the fuck *down*."

"*Both* of you." The air hardened under Galina's words. "You. Stand over there, or I will send you back to Hell. I'm *not* joking."

"She isn't, you know." This was Perry, who stood with his back to the rest of us, bending down to peer inside a glass display case that held several crystal balls, mummified alligators, and a stacked display of Etteila tarot cards. Something rippled on his back, under the white linen suit jacket. "I suggest you calm yourself."

"What the hell's going on?" I didn't lower the gun, and Galina's walls ran with rivulets of etheric force, cascading in sheets. The lightshow was amazing, but it could just as easily turn on me as on the hellbreed. "Galina?"

"Stand *over there*." Her voice rang like a gong, and the Ringmaster grudgingly paced to the exact spot she pointed to on the hardwood floor, his thin body twitching with mutiny. His hair actually writhed, the spikes touching each other with little balloon-squealing sounds. The fraying nap of his red velvet coat crawled with corruption-dust, and his fingers twisted and twitched.

Galina gave me a meaningful look, and I slowly, slowly lowered my guns. The glass shards on the floor stirred, quivering. "Someone give me a vowel."

"We are in a very special place right now, Kismet." Perry still didn't turn to face any of us. "Let us absorb the full implications."

"Where have you been, hunter?" The Ringmaster jabbed his cane at me, the crystal popping off one diseased-green spark. "We came here in *good faith!*"

"I've been chasing a child-killer and doing exorcisms." Every nerve in my body cried out in protest when I holstered the guns. "More than enough fun and games to keep me busy. Whatever's happened to you, I'm not involved with it." I licked my dry lips. Saul straightened from his crouch behind me. It was good to feel him there, even while I was worrying about two hellbreed in front of me and the look on Galina's face. "Yet."

"There has been an attack." Perry finally turned, slowly, and it was almost a relief to see him still wearing his blond, bland face. He was also grinning, lips pulled back in a rictus and his eyes burning gasflame-blue. There was no indigo spreading and scarring the whites, though.

That was good news. How good remained to be seen. "Attack?" That was the bad news. "What kind of attack?"

"A Cirque performer, my dear." Perry stuffed his hands in his pockets and tilted his blond head. It ruined the lines of his suit, but I suppose he thought it made him look less dangerous. Or something. "A certain fortune-teller appears to have gone to collect her eternal reward. With some help, I might add."

For a few seconds the words refused to make sense. Then they slammed home, and I took a deep breath. My face felt very cold, and I suspected I'd gone even paler than my usual night-working fishbelly. "You're kidding." It was the only thing I could think of to say.

"You see?" Perry's grin didn't alter in the slightest. "I vouch for her shock, brother. My Kismet is altogether too intelligent for such a blatant act."

"Shut up, Hyperion." The Ringmaster's cane dipped.

He watched me, his orange gaze swirling with dust and crawling all down my body. "You will swear you had no part in this, hunter?"

"For Christ's sake." I resisted the urge to draw a knife, or better yet, limber my gun up and make the world a better place with a few well-placed headshots. "The hostage is your good behavior. Why the hell would I want to attack any of your people?" *Other than their being hell-breed, which is enough reason to seriously tempt me.*

"To erase the rest of—" The Ringmaster's eyes flicked toward Perry, who pursed his lips. A number of things occurred to me just then, and I actually had to stuff my tongue into my cheek and bite down to keep from making a snarky comment.

They were actually thinking I'd go after the entire Cirque, given enough reason. But the Ringmaster wouldn't be so upset unless he seriously thought I had a chance at actually pulling it off.

It was an unintentional compliment. Being feared by hellbreed isn't a nice thing, but it's damn useful, and pleasant when it can smooth your way a little bit.

My heart rate eased a little bit. Saul crowded closer behind me. The bell on the door jangled slightly, thrumming under the murderous tension. Galina relaxed, fractionally.

"All right." I tried not to sound relieved. "This is the first I've heard about an attack on the Cirque—which I consider just as bad news for me as it is for you. I give you my word I have nothing to do with it. But I'm about to." I took a deep breath. My pulse smoothed out a little bit more, and my eyes skipped between the two 'breed, each of them vibrating with barely controlled rage. Perry hid it better, but I've been around him too much, for too long, to trust his outward appearance. "I've got some business to transact with my Sanctuary, here. Then I'll be out at the Cirque to take a look at what's going on. I'll find out who's behind this and take appropriate action. In the meantime, you'll keep your noses clean." *Put the sting in the tail, Jill.* "Perry, you'll meet me at the Cirque."

"I do not—" The Ringmaster began.

"I think it's best, don't you?" Perry interjected smoothly, taking a single step closer. "So nobody is tempted to run amok while my dear Kiss is on the scene. It would be so embarrassing to have a hunter become justified in killing a few *more* of your performers." He didn't look at the other 'breed, though. Instead, he was staring at me like he was hungry and I was a bowl of lunch.

I wish I could say I didn't know that look. But men have been giving it to me all my life.

The other 'breed stared at me, the pumpkin hellfire smearing from his irises not abating one iota. I was suddenly glad we were inside Galina's shop. If he moved on me she'd drop him—or more precisely, the Sanctuary warding on the walls would. If all else failed, it would give me enough time to put a few silverjacket slugs in him. And maybe sink a knife right into one of those orange-glowing eyes.

"If I find that you are, indeed, involved in this . . . unfortunate . . . event—" The cane twirled smartly, the crystal hissing as it clove unresisting air.

That's the trouble with this job. It's full of threats, both veiled and naked. After a while it gets ho-hum. Except when you're dealing with Hell's scions. The slippery, twisting, twitchy bastards threaten all the time—and they'll get away with what they can.

"I sure hope that wasn't a threat," I remarked to the empty air over his black-spiked head. "Because for a member of the Cirque de Charnu to threaten a resident hunter is exceeding bad taste. Not to mention stupid. And dangerous. And—"

"That's it." Galina stepped forward just as the Ringmaster did, a synchronized movement that would have been funny if the hellbreed hadn't been hissing like a steam kettle. "Both Perry and I vouch for our hunter's innocence. Go back to your home and wait. You've said and done enough here."

Our hunter. A pucker of hot liquid prickling filled the scar. The bottom dropped out of my stomach. Perry grinned like he had just gotten a Christmas present full of snackable entrails. Galina, however, didn't notice anything.

Great.

Crackling tension rose another notch. The Ringmaster paced toward me, and I realized he would have to pass very close to get out the front door. I stepped aside, so did Saul, and I did my best to keep myself between him and the 'breed. The smooth incense quiet of Galina's shop trembled like the skin atop fresh milk. My hands literally itched for a weapon.

The Ringmaster halted for a bare second. Adrenaline spiked through my bloodstream. I caught a whiff of sawdust and glitter, spice and fried food, with the faint thunderous note of rotting underneath. The edges of his red frock coat twitched, as if tiny insect feet were stabbing the threadbare crimson velvet from underneath.

Amazingly, he didn't stop to threaten me again. He just passed by with a sound like fresh-tanned leather crumpling and banged out the door, leaving a scrim of evil little laughter in his wake. I let out the breath I hadn't been holding—I'd inhaled deeply, ready for the explosion.

"Now you, Perry." Thunder smoked and roiled under Galina's voice. "I've business to transact with Jill."

"What if I do, too?" He grinned and leaned forward, his toes digging into the floor. "Business with *my* hunter."

"Perry." Just the one word. Galina's eyes turned incandescent. The silver at her throat sparked, a clean springtime green swirling at the surface of the metal. "It would be *undignified* to be tossed out of here on your ass."

"True." He rocked back on his heels, grinned at both of us. "I bid you a civil adieu, then, ladies." A wink and a flash of pearly teeth between his bloodless lips, and he slid past me like a burning wind. Halfway out the door he vanished, leaving behind strangled little whispers before the door banged closed and I heard footsteps pattering away down the street, far too fast and light to be human.

My shoulders dropped. I let out another, far gustier sigh, and Galina swayed before she pulled herself upright. The glass on the floor quivered again. I watched as the broken pieces of the display case twitched slightly, arranged along spiraling rays of reaction.

Huh. That's interesting.

Saul's hands caught my shoulders. "You okay?" He sounded worried.

I realized the scar was twitching against the underside of my arm as if an enthusiastic seamstress was pleating the skin. At least Perry hadn't really tried to play with it. "Just ducky. Jesus, Mary, and Joseph. Someone's looking to kill Cirque performers?"

Galina said it, so I didn't have to. "Or they have a deeper plan, and they're going to try to pin anything that happens on you. I don't like this."

"Sorry about your display case." I stared, willing the pattern to come clear, and finally blinked it away when it refused. Hunters always become full-blown psychics before the end of their apprenticeships; damn useful when dealing with the nightside. But sometimes intuition won't tell you anything. It will just muddy the waters.

I looked up to find the Sanctuary studying me, a line between her dark eyebrows. "Don't worry about that." Galina was pale, and shaking just the slightest bit.

"Oh, Christ," I said. "Drop the other shoe. And get me some more ammo. I've got a bad feeling about this."

7

You could find just about anything a serious practitioner needed at Galina's, and if your credit was good you could get a whole lot more. A neutral supply of necessities for all concerned is the least of the services a Sanctuary provides to a city's nightside inhabitants.

She poured us tea up in her kitchen. The night pressed against the bay window over the sink, the green bank of herbs in a cast-iron shelving unit stirring slightly.

Sancs like growing things. They are gentle souls, really. It's a shame so few people pass their entrance exams.

Galina set the tray of silverjacket ammo down on the butcher-block table. "What do you know about the last time the Cirque was here?"

Saul blew across his tea to cool it. He was looking everywhere except at me.

I stared at her for a few seconds, the chill down my back growing more pronounced. "It was the hunter before Mikhail. I know he told them not to come back until

he wasn't the hunter here either. Bad blood between him
and the last Ringmaster. Or is that the same one?"

"It's the same one. He's been controlling the Cirque
for a few generations, which means he's nasty and smart."
Her fingers were steady on the teapot; she poured and
pushed the ammo tray toward me. It was really strange
to see her so pale. Not much disturbs Galina's serenity.
"With that goddamn cane of his. The last time . . ."

I waited while she set the teapot down, the walls
echoing slightly with her distress. Sancs don't go outside
much; it's the price they pay for being almost godlike
inside their nice thick defenses. Being inside a Sanctuary's space when they lose their cool is an uncomfortable experience at best.

Saul slurped loudly. The scar ran with prickles, like
icy water on burning skin. I began checking the ammo
automatically, sliding yet more extra cartridges into the
loops sewn inside my coat. I could probably do this in
my sleep, I've done it so many times.

And hell, while I was here for the second time today
I might as well load up.

"There was some trouble," Galina finally said, low-
ering herself down to sit on a stool opposite me. "The
hunter before Mikhail was Emerson Sloane; he had a
sort-of apprentice. Everything went sideways."

Sort-of apprentice? That doesn't happen. But there
are wannabes in this business, just the same as any other.
Fucking amateurs trying to get themselves killed, since
they're unfit for the job one way or another, or they'd be
trained.

Silence stretched between us. I finally broke it.
"Mikhail never told me about that."

"He wasn't an *actual* apprentice." The kitchen, with its mellow shining counters and wood-faced cabinets, wavered slightly and solidified around her. "He just kept following Sloane around until Sloane gave up and began training him."

That's how it usually starts. My own apprenticeship hadn't begun that way, but . . . Mikhail had been an exception all over.

And so, I suppose, was I. And if I was lucky, Gilberto would have vanished off my front step by the time I got home.

Galina sighed. "He got into trouble. There were some problems."

"What type of problems?"

Her brow furrowed. "I . . . didn't hear much. Sloane never opened up about it. I do know the kid ended up dead, after something terrible."

There's certainly no shortage of terrible things on the nightside. "And no word on what 'something terrible' entailed? Did it have to do with the Cirque, or—"

"I just don't know, Jill." She picked up her own cup, took a small sip. Her shoulders were sharp points under the robes. Some of the shaking had eased out of her. The walls had stopped quivering with etheric distress. "The Ringmaster seemed to think you had a hand in this attack, and he was . . . excited when he showed up. Perry was right behind him."

Goddammit. I'll just bet he was, with his little fingers in the pie as usual. I couldn't help myself—a sigh to match hers came out hard on the end of the sentence. The smell of incense, dust, and sleepy power in her shop mixed uneasily with the aroma of spaghetti sauce and the fading tang of 'breed—she'd probably been at dinner when they dropped by. "What can you tell me about this trouble?"

The line between her eyebrows got deeper. "Not much that I can recall. It had to do with the apprentice and a woman over near Greenlea, I think, back when that part of town wasn't very nice. Had to be, oh, around 1926 or so. Before the barrio moved, before the big outbreak, and before all that new money moved in and turned it into a shopping district. The kid . . ." She frowned. "There was something about him. I can't remember. I'll dig through my diaries, see if I can suss it out."

Hm. "It's not like you to have a bad memory."

She gave me an exquisitely sarcastic look. "When you've put in almost a century of tending a Sanctuary, Jill, then we'll talk. Mikhail and Sloane both liked things close to the vest, too. Most of the time I didn't have a clue what either of them were up to."

And I was no different when a case was heating up. It was my turn to shrug as I finished stowing the ammo. "Mischa was a private person, all right. I didn't hear much about the former hunter either. Except that Sloane wasn't of our lineage, he was part of Ben Cross's crowd."

"Yes. Sloane died after the outbreak in 1929." She stared into her tea mug like it held the secrets of the universe. "We were in freefall for years. That was a bad time for any hunter."

"Yeah." The second-biggest demonic outbreak of the past century, 1929 was a bad year for hunters all over the United States, and it got exponentially worse in Europe ten years later. So much of what was unleashed during

the two decades after '29 is still out running around—
it's like the Middle Ages all over again, only this time
we have more firepower to put things down.

Still, the firepower's no good without people trained
to use it. And quality apprentices are few and far
between.

I thought again of Gilberto and hoped he was gone by
the time I got home. Which might not be soon. This had
all the makings of a complex situation, which meant a
lot of blood and screaming. Not to mention gunfire and
ugliness.

"Oh." A sudden, abrupt movement. Galina finished
trolling through her memory and blinked. "Gregory.
That was the kid's name. Something Gregory. I'll look
through my diaries."

"I'd appreciate it." *Great. And I really have to get
over to Greenlea, now that you mention it. I've got business there too.* "Hey, has anyone been in to buy voodoo
stuff lately? Anyone making a big serious purchase?"

"No. I don't do much voodoo or Santeria here.
That's more Mama Zamba on the edge of the barrio, or
Melendez. I sometimes send people to either of them."
A curious look crossed her round, pretty face. "I
wonder . . ."

I hate going to either of them. Jesus. "Well, give ol'
Zamba a call as soon as I leave. Let her know I've got
a few questions. It's about time I went and scared her
again." I fished out a fifty-dollar bill. "Here's all I've got
on me for this load of ammo; I'll take care of the rest
when I get my municipal check. Okay?"

"You can put it on account, you know." But instead of

saying it with a grin, Galina looked troubled. "Jill, are
you sure you want to go out to the Cirque?"

"I'll go where I have to." *You should know that.* "It's
just a bunch of hellbreed playing games. Nothing I
haven't seen before."

"I really hope you don't mean that," she muttered, but
she let it go.

It wasn't like her not to get the last word in, so I left it
at that. Saul finished his tea, I got a few more odds and
ends, and we left her up in her kitchen, tracing the ring
of spilled tea from the bottom of her cup, drawing it on
the table like it might give her an answer.

Of course they would settle near the trainyards, far north
of my warehouse and on the fringes of the industrial section. A cold night wind came off the river, laden with
flat iron-chemical scent. It was usually a space of empty,
weed-strewn lots, a few squares of concrete left over
from trailers or something, and a festooning of hypo-
dermics and debris from when it used to be a shackville.
The homeless were rousted out during a huge urban renewal drive five years ago, but the drive petered out and
the fencing around the lots turned that bleached color
everything gets after a winter or two in the desert.

Now it was cleaned up, the fencing was taken down
in some parts, replaced in others, and it was starred with
lights.

Everyone who told me about the Cirque was right. It
does look bigger than its sorry little caravan would ever
lead you to dream of. It sprawled like a blowsy drunk on
a tattered divan, cheap paste jewels glittering.

Cirque de Charnu, the painted boards on the fence barked. The bigtop was up, canvas daubed with leering clown faces and swirls of watery glitter. Faint music rode the flat, whispering wind. The smell of fried food mixed uneasily with the blood-tang of the river, and I caught the undertone of sweat and animal manure too. Shouts and laughter, and a Ferris wheel I would have sworn wasn't part of the caravan spun like a confection of whipped cream and glass. Its winking lights were sterile eyes, and it shuddered as the wind changed. One pair of lights winked out, and I heard the faint ghost of a scream before it righted itself and went whirling merrily on.

We sat in the car overlooking the spectacle; there was a footpath down the embankment leading to the temporary parking lot, already full of vehicles. Little dust devils danced between the neat rows. The fringes of contamination and corruption were thin flabby fingers poking at each tire and dashboard.

Saul was smoking again, cherry tobacco smoke drifting out his window. The tiny bottle of holy water on a chain around his neck swirled with faint blue. "Smells like a trap," he finally said.

"It is." *A trap for the weak or unwary. Or just for those who don't care anymore.* "You sure you want to come with me?"

A shadow crossed his face. He tapped the ash from the cigarette with a quick, angry motion.

I glanced quickly away, over the carnival. The Ferris wheel halted, its cars swinging and trembling slightly, like leaves in a soft breeze. Its gaunt gantry looked hungry, and a couple lights flickered on the verge of going out.

"I haven't changed my mind yet." He took another drag. His face settled against itself.

I'm not so sure about that. But I didn't say it. "You realize we can't interfere down there. Once we step through the gate—"

"I know the rules. You repeated 'em twice. I'm not stupid, Jill."

"You're right, you're not stupid. But maybe I am." I eyed the layout again. The alleys between the tents looked regular and even, but they also ran like ink on wet paper in the corner of my vision. I had the idea that if I looked away they would move, and snap back together in a different configuration once my gaze returned.

The music halted as the wind veered, then started again. Calliope music, faint and cheery, with screaming underneath. It sounded like a cartoon. The Ferris wheel shuddered again, and another light blinked out. It restarted, creaking, and the music swallowed any sound that might have made its way out.

I blew out between my teeth. Measured off a space on the steering wheel between two index fingers, tapped them both rapidly, a tattoo of dissatisfaction. *Time's wasting, Jill. Get moving.*

When I reached for the door-handle he did too. The Pontiac sat in shadows, her paint job glistening dully. It was a cleaner gleam than the cars in the lot below, or the bright winking lures beyond.

The music struggled up to us as we made our way down the hill, my bootheels occasionally ringing against a stone, Saul silent and graceful. Between the rows of cars, windshields already filmed with dust, gravel shifting under our feet. There was no need to be quiet.

There wasn't much of a crowd milling around the ticket booth. The scattered people were mostly normal, and they looked dazed. I kept my mouth shut, watching for a few moments as a round brunette in her mid-thirties tilted her head, listening. The calliope music sharpened, predatory glee running under its surface, and she finally stepped up to the booth and handed over a fistful of something. It looked like wet pennies, and the Trader manning the booth—female, heart-shaped face and short black Bettie Page bangs, big dark eyes, and a pair of needle-sharp fangs dimpling her candy-red lower lip—made a complex gesture, then stamped the woman's hand and waved her past.

Saul let out a short sigh. We strode through the confused, each of them averting their eyes like we were some sort of plague. A couple Traders milled with the normals, uncertainly. Most of them flinched and drew into the shadows when they saw me.

The Trader in the booth studied us. She opened her mouth, and I saw all her teeth were sharp and pointed, not just the fangs.

I beat her to the punch. "I'm here on business, Trader. Where's the Ringmaster?"

She shrugged slim, bare flour-white shoulders, her rhinestone-studded Lycra top moving supple over high, perky breasts. Visibly reconsidered when I didn't respond. "Around and about. Probably in the bigtop. Want your hand stamped?"

I snorted. "Of course not. Come on, Saul." I took two steps to the side, heading for the turnstile.

Her sloe eyes narrowed. "Just what are you—" The
words died as I stared at her. The corruption blooming
over her was strong, and I'd bet diamonds she had weapons under the sightline of the flimsy booth. She tried
again. "You can come in. But I'm not so sure *he* can."
She actually pointed at Saul with one lacquered-yellow
fingernail. It was amazing—I wondered how she wiped
herself with claws that long.

Oh, yeah? Quit pointing at my Were, bitch. "He's
with me. Go back to seducing suicides," I snapped. We
strode past, through the clicking turnstile. Each separate
bar of the stile ended in a cheap chrome ram's head, lips
drawn back and blunt teeth blackened with grime. The
Trader didn't say anything else, but the swirl of corruption lying over the entire complex of canvas and wood
tightened.

The spider knows the fly's home.

I didn't like that thought. I also didn't like how the
air was suddenly close and warm, almost balmy with
a slight edge of humidity. It even smelled wrong—no
clean tang of dry desert, no metallic ring from the river
or any of the hundred other little components that make
up a subconscious map of my city. You spend enough
time breathing a place and it'll get into your bones—and
when it isn't what it should be, that's when the uneasiness starts right below the hackles.

It was also—surprise, surprise—more crowded inside than out. There wasn't a crush, but it was work
threading my way through. The flat shine of the dusted
on Trader irises, dazed incomprehension on the shuffling normals, rubbing shoulders and shuffling feet. I
saw men in pajamas, a woman in filmy lingerie with her

hair in pink curlers, a fiftyish man in work clothes carrying a dripping-wet hammer and wandering walleyed and fishmouthed like he was six again.

The midway bloomed around us. Pasteboard and flashing lights, buzzing strings of electric bulbs.

"Throw the ball, win a prize!" This was an actual 'breed, female in a red cotton peasant dress. A sleepy-eyed teenager stopped in front of her; she licked her pale lips and smiled at him. Her white, white hands touched his shoulders in a butterfly's caress, but she saw me watching and pushed him aside. He stumbled and rejoined the flow of the crowd.

"Catch a fish!" A Trader in suspenders, a white wife-beater, and a newsboy hat, his ears coming to high hairy points, motioned at a crystal bowl. The fish inside glittered too sharply to be anything but metallic, globules of clear oil bubbling from their mouths. "Win a dream! Lovely dream, freshly colored! Catch a fish!"

A woman hesitated before putting her hand in the bowl. I silently urged her not to, and turned away before she could make her decision. There was a wet, deep crunch. The fish-catcher's savage cry of triumph rose behind me, and I let out a sharp breath, my stomach turning over.

This was what the Cirque did. It separated the weak and suicidal from the just vaguely disaffected. I caught sight of a young woman, mascara dribbling down her cheeks on a flood of tears, mouthing words that seemed to fit the dim seaweed sound of the calliope. Something like "Camptown Races," married to a more savage beat.

Doo-dah, dooo dah. . . . She shivered, and walked

slowly toward an open tent exhaling a flood of beeps and boops like a video arcade. God alone knew what waited for her in there.

Funny, the music should be louder. I shivered, kept pacing. They parted in front of me like heavy molasses, drawing slowly away.

The normals didn't look at me, lost in whatever the calliope was whispering. But the Traders flinched aside, and the 'breed sometimes bared their teeth, or fangs. One, dolled up like a fortune-teller and outside a tent swathed with fluttering nylon scarves, a chipped crystal ball on the round satin-draped table in front of her, actually snarled.

I stopped and stared at her for a good twenty seconds, unblinking, before she dropped her yellow gaze. Her eyes matched her tongue, a jaundiced, scaled thing that flickered past thin lips and dabbed the point of her chin before reeling back into her mouth.

"There's a lot of them," Saul murmured. He kept close, the comforting heat of him touching my back. The silver in my hair was shifting, and the carved ruby at my throat spat a single, bloody spark just as he spoke.

"There always are." *And when the sun rises, maybe a third of them will make it home safe. Those who decide they do want to live after all—or those smart enough to run like hell and make no agreements. Even implicit ones.*

And here I thought I was such a cynic. Probably a lot less than a third would get home.

Lean four-legged shapes slunk in the shadows. Their colorless eyes flashed, and they followed us through the midway. The Ferris wheel rocked at one end, another light winked out, and I heard a shapeless scream, like a man waking from a nightmare in a cold bath of sweat. The calliope music surged, swallowing it. Paper ruffled at our feet—wrappers still hot from popcorn or sticky with cotton candy, gnawed sticks still holding traces of corn-dog mustard or clinging caramel. A man's gold Patek Philippe glittered, flung carelessly on the packed, scuffed dirt. Thick electric cables creaked back and forth under the slow warm breeze.

The entrance to the bigtop was huge, easily as big as a triple garage door. Oiled canvas rubbed against the ropes; tattered pennants fluttered and snapped on seven high-peaked poles. Crowd-noise swelled, and for the first time I heard the rumble of Helletöng bruising the air.

A gangling scarecrow of a male hellbreed lolled in a chair next to a post holding one end of the tattered red velvet rope barring the way. His top hat was pulled down over his eyes, and his spiderlike fingers—six on each hand, and a thumb too, bones and tendons flickering under the mottled skin—twitched as I halted.

I eyed him. Threadbare, skintight burlap pants straining every time a skinny leg moved. Biceps so thin I could probably have spanned them with thumb and forefinger. For all that, it was a hellbreed, and usually they aren't so flagrantly unhuman.

Usually they're beautiful, and they like to show it. Except Perry. This one could be a surprise too.

I stepped forward, my heels clicking on gravel, and eyed him. The hat lifted a little, and mad silvery eyes gleamed under a hank of silky dirt-dark hair. The fingers twitched again.

I held the 'breed's gaze for maybe fifteen long seconds, the calliope music drifting up around me in skeins of etheric foulness. The hounds, slinking in the shadows, drew nearer. Saul didn't make a restless movement, but I could guess maybe he wanted to.

"Cut the act." Silver jangled, underscoring my words. "Get me the Ringmaster."

The 'breed tipped his head back further. A pointed chin, hollow cheeks—he was a walking skeleton with mottled skin stretched drum-tight over bones, and I suddenly knew what he was. The knowledge made my hands ache for a weapon again; I controlled the urge.

"Are you sure you want to see him? He's not in a good mood." The 'breed smirked, pointed yellow teeth flashing for just a moment. Strings of thick saliva bubbled behind his lips. I was almost sorry I'd eaten.

"Snap inspection, plague-bearer. And the mood you should be worrying about right now is *mine*. I'm giving you less than two seconds to haul that skinny ass of yours up, and less than ten to bring me the Ringmaster. Or I start shooting 'breed and Traders. Your choice."

It was a nice bluff. Technically, a hunter can snap-inspect any part of the Cirque at any time, and serve summary judgment on any 'breed or Trader caught breaking the rules—for example, pressuring a victim into making a bargain, or in my city, playing with anyone under eighteen. That's pretty much why the Cirque obeys the strictures—first there's the hostage, and then there's *us,* swallowing bile and watching, waiting for them to step out of line.

Of course, people vanish all the time. It's a goddamn epidemic, and whenever the Cirque finally leaves town there's a lull in exorcisms, disappearances, and other nastiness. They eat all they can hold in each town, I guess. And with the pickings so easy once the calliope starts singing, they would be foolish to take any unwilling meat.

Hellbreed aren't fools.

He jolted to his feet, elbows and knees moving in ways human joints weren't designed to, and I almost twitched toward a gun. But he just capered over the red velvet rope and into the bigtop, leaving his chair rocking back and forth, a bloom of powdery yellow dust left behind, eating little holes in the painted wood.

"Plague-bearer?" Saul murmured.

"You don't want to touch that stuff." My nerves were scraped raw, my back crawling with the thought of so many of Hell's citizens in one place, a cancer in the middle of my vulnerable city.

My apprentice-ring cooled, turning to ice on my finger. It twitched, sharply, twice. It was the first time since I'd met the Cirque outside town that it had made any sort of motion at all.

I tilted my head, listening. The calliope music surged, screaming puffs through chrome-throated pipes. I shut it away, despite the plucking underneath the music—*come in, come in, lay your troubles down, play a game, become one of us, one of us, just give in, stop struggling.*

My attention turned, coasting through the flood of sensory information. Dust, hot frying fat, screams, chewing noises, stamping feet, a horse's screaming whinny.

And a long, drawn-out rattling gasp.

I came back to myself with a jolt, spun on my heel, and leapt into a run. Saul's footsteps were soundless behind me.

The bigtop blurred past on one side, yards and yards of canvas. It drew away like a wave threatening to crest, and I plunged into a network of tents and alleys, half-lit. Here was one of the older parts of the carnival—the air was thick with a reek of spilled sex, and the tent flaps were always half-open. Moans and ghastly shrieks ribboned past, the calliope suddenly crooning. Traders with gem-bright eyes, hellbreed with seashell hips and candied mouths, lounging in the entrances to their tents, seducing and beckoning—

I veered off to the left, my apprentice-ring pulling like a fish on a thin line. The tents gave way to trailers, and I passed the limousine sitting still and polished under a rigged-up canvas canopy. The headlights flickered once, green, as I flashed past.

A huge silver Airstream rocked as I left the ground in a flying kick, etheric force booming through the scar and filling my veins with sick heat. My boot hit the door, which crumpled and exploded in. A terrible, sour-sewer smell puffed past me, and I heard Saul's surprised half-yell.

The trailer was small, and every surface inside was crawling. Little bits of darkness moved, fluttering chitinous legs and wings twitched as the roaches spilled over every surface. A pinprick of laser-red light glowed on the back of every goddamn insect, and they startled into flight as I let out a half-swallowed, childlike cry of revulsion.

Hey, they were bugs, and they surprised me.

The tide of insect life streamed past me, little hairy legs touching and brushing. Saul's coughing growl warned me.

I couldn't worry about the inside of the trailer just at the moment. There was something behind me, and Saul barely managed to get the warning out in time.

I threw myself back and down, landing hard on the two portable wooden steps leading up to the crumpled door. I'd blown a hole in the side of the trailer, and I shot the Ringmaster four times as he hung in the air over me, the crystal knob atop his cane ringing a high piercing note as a silverjacket bullet bounced off or past it, whining until it smashed into the side of his leering, screaming face. It even knocked his hat off.

He dropped straight down. My knees jerked up, I rolled backward down the steps. My shoulder grated hard and popped against straining wood, the edge of a step biting the back of my neck before I made a lunging, fishlike twist and was suddenly, irrationally on my feet but facing the wrong way, whirling and dropping to one knee as the whip flicked out. The silver flechettes tied to the end of its length jingled sweetly before they flayed flesh from the Ringmaster's wrist, and his cane clattered away, the crystal bouncing down first as if it was too heavy for the laws of physics.

The 'breed was bleeding, gushes of thin black ichor flooding out from every hole I'd blown in his tough shell. The roaches swarmed him, the pinpricks of red on their back dividing as they multiplied, and he screamed in Helletöng, a sound like the rusted sinews of the world groaning. The fabric of reality bowed around him in concentric circles, and the little insects burst, clattering shells puffing into sick green smoke as they hit the dust. The Ringmaster shouldered his way up out of the curls of vapor, his eyes dripping pumpkin hellfire, and snarled. The stairs splintered and groaned.

When you get to see under the carapace of beauty, the brain shudders aside from their alienness. A hunter who's been to Hell has seen this before, and it gives you a slight edge. You don't run screaming-insane every time they shed their human seeming and show the twisted thing underneath.

But it's awful close.

I remained on one knee, instinct fighting with cold logic. If he leapt for me, my chances were better here, where I was centered and had some clear space, than if I tried to get to my feet now. Training won out, and I stayed where I was, gun in my right hand and whip in the other, shaken free with a jingling sound. Saul was to one side, still growling but staying out of the way—just where he should have been.

A choked rattle echoed inside the gaunt silver trailer. My apprentice-ring cooled, a band of ice on my third left finger. The Ringmaster snarled and doubled over, falling to the ground with a wet writhing thump. Black ichor splashed, and the entire Cirque stilled, the faint ever-present calliope music skipping a beat. It limped and wheezed, gaps opening between the notes.

What the hell?

The Ringmaster screamed, and his cane quivered. The thin cry was echoed from inside the trailer, and I was suddenly sure that something else was happening I'd better take a look at.

I uncoiled, force pulled through the scar, and cleared the busted stairs and the Ringmaster in one leap. Landed on my toes, my center of gravity pulled up high and tight, and plunged into the trailer.

A pale shape lay, seizure bowing it up into a hoop, on the frowsty shelf-bed. It was the hostage, and just as I reached the side of the bed, wading through a drift of empty clicking shells and candy bar wrappers, the Trader began to rattle deep down in his chest.

Oh, fuck.

The hostage was dying. And if he shuffled off the mortal coil now, we were looking at a seriously fucked-up situation.

I dropped the whip, shoved the gun back in its holster, and leapt for the bed.

8

My hellbreed-strong right hand closed around Ikaros's throat, and I braced myself, knees on either side of his narrow rib cage. "Oh, no you *don't*," I snarled, and ripped the leather wristcuff free, one of the buckles breaking and hitting the side of the trailer with a sweet tinkle.

A razor-barbed mass of etheric energy pooled in my palm, slammed through the Trader's body. The ratcheting sound from his narrow chest peaked, and I heard the Ringmaster howl like a damned soul outside.

Get it, Jill? Like a damned soul? Arf, arf.

The air turned hard and dark, something alien pressing through the fabric of reality, hovering over the twisting body on the bed. I took in a harsh breath and *pushed,* the sea-urchin spikes of my aura dappling the inside of the trailer with aqueous light. The sudden welter of sensory overload from the scar's unveiling crested over me, my skin suddenly alive and my nose full of a complicated tangle of scents. Tears welled up hot and hard, my eyes coping with a sudden onslaught, every crack and wrinkle in the world visible.

The Trader hostage twitched and convulsed again, his teeth actually grinding. The collar's spikes bit my skin, blessed metal burning. I let out a short hawk's cry, the force of whatever was torturing the Trader giving me a short, hard punch in the solar plexus. It tasted like lit-up liquor fumes and hit the back of my throat, roared past me like a barreling freight train.

My free left hand jabbed up, two fingers snapping out, lined with twisting sorcerous flame. Banefire burned blue, hissing, but there was no helltaint for it to catch hold of.

The thing struggling to come through hit me hard in the face, my head snapping aside, and blood exploded from my mouth and nose in a bright gush, droplets hanging in a perfect arc for a long timeless second before splashing against the trailer wall.

So banefire wasn't going to work. Ikaros surged underneath me again, his body moving in weird angled jumps, like his bones were trying to turn themselves into rubbery corkscrews.

Goddammit, what the hell is going on here?

Fortunately, banefire wasn't the only trick up my sleeve. Intuition meshed with recent memory, and as he screamed so did I, our twinned voices rising in harmony again as my fingers tightened, the collar's spikes dragged at the meat of my wrist and forearm again, and I *pushed* with every ounce of sorcerous strength I could dredge up in an entirely different direction.

As if I was exorcising him.

The pressure built, excruciating heat behind my bulg-

ing eyeballs and under my stomach, the last bit of air
escaping me in a *huuuungh!* of effort. Ikaros rattled
again, but this time it wasn't the hideous *I'm-dying* type
of rattle. No, this time it was the inhale of blessed sweet
air, and my apprentice-ring gave another twinging pull.
He began to thrash with inhuman strength, but without
the corkscrewing weirdness.

The thing hovering over him snapped with a sound
like thick elastic breaking, a high, hard *pop!* that might
have been funny if there hadn't been a sudden gush of
green smoke and chittering legs. The roaches swarmed,
falling out of a point in thin air directly above us, and
both of us yelled in miserable surprise. The roaches vanished as they peppered us, more sickly pea-soup smoke
eddied and billowed, and the Trader surged up.

He had a lot of pep for someone who was just being
sorcerously strangled a few seconds ago. But I had the
upper hand and my booted foot on one of his wrists in
a trice, and I ground down with the steelshod heel, a
simple flexing movement. The collar slashed even more
cruelly at my wrist, but I ignored the pain rolling up my
arm, hot blood slicking my grip on the hostage's throat.
"Settle the fuck *down!*" I yelled. "Settle *down,* I'm trying to *help!*"

The irony of the situation—I was yelling that I was
trying to help a Trader—didn't escape me. He subsided
just a little, blue eyes rolling like a terrified horse's. I
waited until I was sure he wasn't going to thrash again
and eased up just slightly on his throat. He kept breathing in high harsh whistles.

I kept watching, loosening my fingers by increments.
They actually creaked, I moved so slowly. Harsh voices

babbled outside, a whirlpool of surprise, and I heard a werecougar's low thrumming growl.

That managed to get me off the bed, shaking out my right hand. Blood flew, dripping down from my scored wrist, and I was suddenly glad none of the blessed silver spikes had touched the scar. I'd had silver against the hellbreed kiss once before, and had no desire to repeat the experience.

Ikaros lay, his ribs flickering with deep heaving breaths, on the tangled bed. His eyes closed, heavily, and he curled into a ball as I backed away. I realized he was naked, light dancing and dappling his haunches. Old burn scars traveled up both legs, clasping his buttocks with angry rope fingers. I scooped up my whip without pausing, two strides kicking up a tide of candy bar wrappers. The green smoke began to thin, and the empty cockroach shells were vanishing with little crackling popcorn sounds.

The stairs were indeed shattered, and Saul crouched in front of them, one hand braced on the dusty earth. The trembling in his aura told me he was just on the edge of shifting, and his snarl rose steadily.

I didn't blame him. Because gathered in a loose semicircle, pressing close in an arc of sharp teeth and hellfire-glowing eyes, were hellbreed and Traders. The Ringmaster hooked his cane up with one clawed hand, the crystal spitting spark after agonized green spark and his entire tattered costume swimming and dripping black ichor.

It was going to hurt as he healed, the silver residue poisoning him. *Let's hope it doesn't make him crazier than he already is. Control the situation, Jill.* I cleared leather, pointed the gun up, and squeezed off a shot. The sound crackled through both Saul's growl and the rising noise coming from the hellbreed, a deep thrum of Helletöng like iron balloons rubbing together.

"Good evening, everyone." I paused for a breath. All eyes turned to me except Saul's, and the crowd of 'breed and Traders took in a collective breath. Silver hissed in my hair, the charms moving angrily. "Seems someone has a bit of a grudge against your hostage. I just saved his life." Another pause, this one taking a different tenor as the gun came down and swept slowly, leisurely, along the front of the crowd. "Anyone have a problem with that?"

There's a definite proportion of this job that is just plain theater. The little bitches don't take you seriously unless you act the part. I used to think Mikhail enjoyed the acting, but then I figured out he was really a fan of getting the job done in the shortest amount of time so he could move on to the next. It just goes more efficiently with the right proportion of fuck-you posturing.

The gun swept the front of their ranks again. Saul had stopped growling, but he still quivered with readiness. The Ringmaster straightened slowly, shook himself like a cat shedding water. Half his face was peppered with threads of damage. The black spikes of hair covering his head were plastered down, and thin foul-smelling ichor splashed free of his quick little movements. Little threads of white smoke curled up when the droplets hit the dust.

Silence stretched. Even the calliope was silent, the entire glass bowl of the Cirque holding its breath. If this went on much longer I'd probably have to actually kill someone to keep the peace.

My only trouble was figuring out where to start.

The Ringmaster hobbled forward. "Our hostage still lives," he rasped, and I tried not to feel relieved.

Watch him, Jill. He's a tricky little bastard. I hopped down, avoiding the broken steps. "Of course he does. He ends up dead and I have to kill every motherfucking last one of you. What the fuck are you up to out here?" *And where's Perry?*

"I do not," the Ringmaster husked, slowly, "answer to *you*."

I made a small beeping noise. The gun settled on him, my pulse cooling immediately. "Wrong answer, hellspawn. This is my town, you *do* answer to me. I am not having my city fucked up because you guys brought bad business with you."

"You blame this on *us?*" He actually bristled.

Yes, *bristled,* his hair standing up in ichor-stiffened spikes, his skin turning mottled and pinpricks of the shape underneath poking out through the skin. Each hole I'd blown in his shell ran with diseased orange foxfire.

An elegantly manicured hand closed around his shoulder and squeezed, grinding. Perry pushed the Ringmaster down, the thin 'breed's knees folding until they hit the dirt.

"Of course she blames you," he said conversationally, his eyes glowing gasflame-blue, a deep indigo inkstain threading through the whites. "I must confess I am halfway to blaming you myself, *brother.*"

The assembled 'breed and Traders drew away in a single coordinated movement. Perry twisted his wrist slightly, and ground his fingers in. It was a slight movement, and didn't look like much unless you know how horribly, hurtfully strong hellbreed are. A meaty popping sound—like bones crunching in a side of beef—cut through the breezy silence, and I heard another short cry from somewhere in the Cirque's depths. It was either a peacock's scream, someone dying, or a woman in full-throated orgasm.

Take your pick. The show must go on, I guess.

"Let me be exquisitely clear," Perry continued. Another one of those meaty sounds, and the Ringmaster turned the cheesy-pale shade of a mushroom in a wet cellar. I'd shot him in that shoulder, and I was suddenly sure Perry was grinding the silverjacket bullet—or whatever was left of it after it mushroomed in hellbreed flesh—in deeper. "Our hunter will follow this attack to its source. If that source connects with you in any way, if this is a bid for domination or spoliation of *my* territory, I will be exceedingly displeased. Do you understand me, carrion?" His tongue flickered out as he grinned, the cherry-wet redness of it gleaming. A low buzzing, like chrome flies in chlorinated bottles, filled the space behind and between each word. The popping of vanishing cockroach shells finally petered out.

The scar had turned to a hot pucker of acid. I swallowed, kept the gun steady. Saul's shoulders were rigidly straight, and I suddenly wished I was in front of him. He was between me and a whole fuckload of 'breed and Traders, and some of them were eyeing him instead of watching Perry and their boss.

Just be cool, Jill. No need to sweat anything. I eased

forward two steps, my coat whispering as warm redolent air caressed it.

"Understood." Great pearls of watery ichor beaded up on the Ringmaster's narrow face. He wasn't nearly as pretty now. The prickling hadn't gone away either. The thing that lived under his mask of humanity snarled and cringed.

"That's very good." Perry's gaze flicked across me. The urge to freeze warred with iron training; training, as always, won out. I took another single step, the scar twisting and burrowing, my pulse ratcheting up before I could force it back down. "Kiss?"

Don't call me that, goddammit. God, I wanted to say that to him just once and wipe that smirk off his face. But if I did, it would be blood in the water. Who could guess what he would come up with if he knew something so simple bugged the shit out of me?

It took an effort of will to lower the gun. "Something was definitely attacking the hostage."

"So I gathered." He simply stood there, as if he wasn't holding a cringing hellbreed like a mama cat will hold an offending, writhing kitten. "Who is the offender, avenging one?"

"Don't know yet." I paused, weighing the next sentence. "I'm fairly sure it wasn't 'breed, though."

It had the intended effect. Everyone, including Saul—and he had to twist halfway around in his lean easy crouch—stared at me.

All eyes on you, Jill.

"You are certain of this?" Perry didn't drop the Ringmaster, but his eyes narrowed slightly. His fingers still held the other 'breed immobilized, but some of the hurt-ful tension drained out of him.

"Fairly certain. Last time I checked, hellspawn don't use voodoo. Any reason why someone on the side of the *loa* would have a hard-on for a Cirque de Charnu hostage?"

If the silence before was glassy, the silence that fol-lowed was molasses-thick. It was broken only by the soundless buzz of my pager in its padded pocket. Bright eyes sparked in the gloom, the hellbreeds' with varying red and orange tones, an occasional yellow speckle; and the Traders' with their flat dusty shine.

Nobody said a fucking word. The trailer behind me rocked a little on its springs, and a faint groan slid from its depths. Ikaros was probably feeling a little better.

Saving a Trader's life was a novelty, and not one I liked.

"Someone had better start explaining things to me." I took perverse joy in using the same tone a teacher would with a class of young imbeciles.

Perry's fingers tightened again. The Ringmaster's pale face contorted, but he didn't make a sound. If this kept up we were going to have yet another Bad Situation.

"Ease up on him, Pericles." I dug for my pager, every nerve alert. It would take very little to turn this entire mob into a melee, especially with the way most of them were now shifting their attention, ever so slowly, toward Perry. And while I didn't particularly mind the thought of them tearing him apart in little quivering pieces, I minded the thought of dealing with the Cirque *and* a scramble for power among the hellbreed who jostled in

Perry's long deep shadow. "He's got the most to lose if the hostage bites it."

The number on the pager was familiar, and my intuition tingled. *Huh.*

"Voodoo?" Perry pronounced the word like he didn't know what it meant. Saul rose as soon as I took another step forward, gravel shifting under his booted feet. His was the only warmth in this place that didn't make me feel like slime was trickling over my skin.

"Yeah, voodoo. As in, the *loa* taking an interest in this, or someone who has enough credit with them to make a Trader uncomfortable. Nobody wants to tell me why anyone would have a grudge against the Cirque?" I don't think I could have sounded any more sarcastic. "Or why there were roaches crawling all over your sorcerously-being-strangled hostage not five minutes ago? Or something about this murder I'm supposed to be looking into?"

The bitter, rancid grumbling of Helletöng rose. It cut short when I swept my gaze over them and tapped at a gun butt with one bitten-down fingernail. "English," I said softly. "Good old-fashioned American English. None of this töng shit."

I couldn't even feel good about glaring a bunch of 'breed into silence.

Perry finally bestirred himself to speak. "One of the performers has been murdered." He let go of the Ringmaster, who crumpled and caught himself on hands and knees, ichor splashing and his cane making a soft chiming sound that sliced the stillness. "We shall examine the evidence."

Well, la-di-da. Of course we shall, Pericles. But

I didn't want to give him control of the situation just now. "Wait a second. First things first. Who died, who found the body, and who had the last contact with the victim?"

It was amazing to watch them move like quicksilver, exploding away from one tall male Trader who hunched, his eyes grown round and desperate. He wore a straw hat and suspenders, and looked vaguely familiar in the way all blond, dark-eyed men with ferret faces do. You know the type—the narrow-eyed, unreliably handsome, and just waiting to slip a thin knife between your ribs and *twist*.

Yeah. That kind. Especially in a frayed, worn linen button-down and a pair of gray pinstripe trousers that wouldn't have looked out of place on an Edwardian dandy. The flat shine of Trader on his irises looked weird for a moment, like two silver pennies.

Perry beat me to the punch. He sounded kind and avuncular, and the only thing more terrifying was the way everyone in the crowd shivered and pulled back further. "And just who are you?"

The Trader snatched at his hat, his silken thatch of hair damp with sweat. I suspected he'd look vaguely pretty in daylight, but here in the dim shifting light the pointed jaw became strong and his wide cheekbones merely masculine instead of pugnacious.

Then he opened his mouth. "T-T-T-Tr—"

He stammered.

I frankly stared. What kind of joke was this? Hell-breed don't usually Trade with someone so flawed, and Traders usually bargain for beauty as well as weird body mods. This guy must have something else to recommend him—smarts, or viciousness.

"Dear heavens." Perry made a mocking little moue, his lips twisting. "Were you a joke?"

"N-n-nosir. J-j-just a k-k-carny. I'm T-T-Tr-Troy. I w-was H-Helene's t-t-t—"

He kept going with the t's, his face contorting. Perry tapped one elegant wingtip, his shark's grin widening.

"*Talker*," the unfortunate Trader finally spit out. "H-Helene's t-talker."

This is going to take a while. I glanced at the number on my pager again, suppressed a sigh. Stuffed it back in my pocket. "Helene? 'Breed or Trader?"

"'Breed," Perry answered. "You would have enjoyed it, Kiss."

Enjoyed what? I didn't ask. "I do not have all night. You were the last person to see the victim?"

He simply nodded. Thank God.

"All right." I dropped the hand resting on my gun butt with an effort. Saul was still and quiet behind me. "Show me."

"What do you want done with him?" Perry gestured at the Ringmaster, who shivered again, more foul-smelling ichor splattering. "He will survive this night, if you let him. Unless the hostage is attacked again."

What a lovely thought, Perry. Thanks. "Leave him alone." I weighed the words, felt the need to add more. "I've just gotten used to his ugly face. I'd hate to have someone new to deal with."

9

The 'breed named Helene had died in a gaudy tent painted with screaming-red broken-open pomegranates and big stalks of green vegetable. After a few moments I identified the green stuff as leeks, and weird creeping laughter crawled up my throat, was strangled, and died away. "So what was this Helene's act?"

"Fruit seller?" Saul piped up, and a great scalding wave of relief went through me. He sounded okay.

Perry, a respectful distance away, actually sniggered. It was the sound of a popular kid in high school tittering in the back of the room. "Hermaphrodite."

Suddenly the leeks and pomegranates made sense. "A hermaphrodite hellbreed?"

His bland blond face split in a wide grin. "Hell has its freaks too. Here is where they prove their worth."

Which was another lovely thought.

Troy pushed aside the spangled curtain over the door-opening. "In h-here."

"A stuttering barker?" I had to know. "How did you—"

He half-turned, his dusted eyes glittering sharply. "*Step right up!*" His face contorted, and a thin thread of cold slid down my back. Instead of a piping stammer, what came out was a rich, seductive baritone. "*See the half-man, half-woman, all loveliness! Step right up, ladies and gentlemen!*"

I folded my arms. "That's what you Traded for?"

He shrugged. "H-Helene t-taught me. L-l-like s-s-s-singing. Sh-sh-she was n-n-n-n—"

Oh, my God, is he about to say "nice"? Now I've heard everything.

"Spare me your love song," Perry cut in. "What happened?"

For once I agreed with him, but I might've liked to hear more.

"It was a s-slow n-night." The Trader spoke very slowly, trying to enunciate each word clearly. "I w-was b-barking, b-but there were n-n-no t-t-takers. I w-was d-d-doing my b-best. F-first n-night's always s-s-slow—"

"Get. To the. Point." Perry tapped his foot again.

"Shut up and let him talk, Pericles." *This is going to take even longer if you keep making him nervous.*

"But of course, my dear. Anything for you." The indigo still hadn't left his whites, veining through like cracks in glazed porcelain. His suit fluttered slightly at the edges, white linen mouthed by the warm damp breeze redolent with the smell of fried grease.

"She s-s-sc-screamed." The Trader was pale as milk, his unreliable face twisting as he tried to get the words out. "I th-thought a r-r-r-rube was g-g-getting n-nasty.

B-but they d-d-don't usually. S-s-s-so I w-w-went in."
He shuddered, the movement rippling through his skinny
frame. Beads of sweat stood out on his forehead. "Th-th-
there were b-b-bugs."

Bugs? "Flies? Or mosquitoes?"

Hey, you can't ever trust them to tell the truth.

"R-r-roaches." Another shudder. His red suspenders actually creaked. "All over. W-with r-red spots." He
ducked into the tent and I followed, Saul behind me as
close as my shadow. I had a moment's worth of worry—
Perry was right behind my Were.

Jesus. This is getting ridiculous.

It certainly was.

The smell hit me between one step and the next. They
rot fast when they go, just like Traders. There was a
wide greasy stain on the small strip of planking serving as a stage. The rest of the place was scattered with
pillows and rugs, a bargain-basement impression of a
harem helped along by the rusted glass-and-iron hoo-
kahs scattered around. Each pipe was at least four feet
high, scalloped and decorated to within an inch of its
life. Frayed tassels hung everywhere, and behind the
stage hung a tapestry of trees and rivers that shifted, its
stitches running over each other with a faint sound of
needles against fabric.

"It looks like a whorehouse," Saul muttered, and I
heartily agreed.

"Have you been in one lately, cat?" Perry inquired
sweetly.

"Perry?" I checked the circuit of the tent, examined
the stage's raw lumber. Three red satin cushions were
covered in thin black gunk dried to a crust.

"Yes, my dear?" Silky-smooth, but he didn't look at me.

"Shut the fuck up." I inhaled deeply, wished I hadn't. Under the reek of sex, tobacco, and marijuana lay the rusted-copper tang of blood and a breath of . . . what was that?

Cigar smoke. Candy. And rum. It was very faint, fading even as I inhaled deeply again, trying to catch another whiff. *Now that's interesting.*

"I was only asking." Perry eased into the tent, his lip curling. "Such petty games played here."

"As opposed to the ones played out at the Monde?" It was my turn to inquire sweetly. "If you're not going to be helpful, you can wait outside."

His tongue flickered over white teeth, a flash of wet cherry-red. "I can be singularly helpful, for your sake."

Oh, I'll just bet. "Good. You're going to stay here and keep an eye on the hostage. I've got other business tonight."

"I might have business too."

The scar turned hot, and a spill of poisonous delight threaded up my arm. "Too bad. Now that you've seen the crime scene, you can run along."

"Dismissed by my lady." He sighed, but the scar tweaked.

So he was getting to the point of pulling my chain, was he? Hellbreed hate being outfoxed, and they hate being outfoxed by their own cleverness even more. If Perry hadn't been so eager to use a measure of what he thought was his newfound psychological leverage on me, he wouldn't have lost every bit of his hold—including the ironclad agreement to have me in every month. My time for his power; that had been the deal—and when he welshed, it was his power for nothing.

Except I had to step carefully, or I would get trapped again. And he would make me pay for every insult I offered him.

Still, that wasn't a reason not to twit him while I could. And I wanted him out of the way for the next ten minutes. The stuttering Trader looked ready to die from fright, and couldn't get out a coherent sentence.

I understood. I didn't sympathize, but I completely understood.

"I'm not your lady *or* your hunter, Pericles. I'm the hunter of Santa Luz and I'm telling you to keep a close watch on the Ringmaster and that hostage. You're responsible for their good behavior. And not so incidentally, for the hostage's continued survival." I was apparently staring at the stain on the stage. My attention was all on him, though. The Trader crouched with his face level to the planking, peeping up at the red satin pillows like a kid looking through the banister for Santa Claus. "Now be a good little hellspawn and run along."

The air tightened, and I wondered if this was going to be the time that Perry pushed it. It was getting more and more likely the longer this went on.

But apparently, he was just as invested in keeping the Cirque under wraps as I was. I was banking on that. So often, I was banking on the flimsiest things to keep him from seriously fucking around with me.

It is the woman, has the advantage in situations like this, milaya. *You just remember that.* Mikhail's voice, a memory equal parts pleasure and pain.

I was hoping, like always, that it was true.

"Very well," Perry finally said. "Happy hunting, my dear. I expect this . . . situation . . . to be resolved shortly."

"The longer you stand here jawing, the less likely that is." *Unless you've got some elegant little finger in this pie, which is very possible. I'm not ruling anything out.*

But still . . . voodoo. The one thing pretty much no hellbreed would be involved in.

Perry's presence leached out of the room slowly, like an invisible heavy gas. The Trader still crouched, peering up at the stage, and I sighed.

"So, this Helene. Did she have any enemies?" I was fully aware of the irony of the question.

"O-only th-the u-usual." The stammer *did* get better with Perry out of the room. The ferret-faced blond shot me a glance that could have meant anything. "You're n-not going to l-look for whoever d-d-did this."

"Are you kidding? Of course I am." I studied the stage again, and suddenly saw how Helene probably lay down—in a way guaranteed to show off the goods to the maximum number of people in the room. "Was she between showings? In here alone?"

"N-no. Th-there were r-rubes. Not very m-many." He was damn near peppy with Perry out of the picture, and I suddenly thought I liked him better when he was scared. The self-serving little weasel glint in Trader eyes always makes me want to reach for a weapon.

It's that same weasel glint I used to see in my mother's eyes when one of her boyfriends was on the rampage. A cold calculation—*how much can I get? How can I use something else to get out of this? What's in it for me?*

"Sh-she was just a 'b-b-breed. I know what y-you h-hunters are l-like."

You do, huh? Well. That's nice. "Is that so." There were tiny pinpricks dotting out from the stain in random twin loops—cockroach tracks. They stopped cold about two feet from the body.

Little skittering roach-tracks. Did they vanish in a puff of green smoke too?

"So what did the . . . the *rubes* see? Any of them still around?" *Did any of them get home safe, either?*

"D-d-don't kn-know. Was b-busy trying to g-get the b-b-b-bugs—" His face flushed. "Bugs. Away."

"Did the bugs do that?" I pointed at the stain. "Was she making any sound? Choking?"

"S-screaming. And th-they r-ripped h-her ap-p-part. N-n-not m-much l-left."

I questioned him a little more, but he either knew nothing or covered it really well. The way he crouched right next to the stage was unnerving, and the story was even more so. Bugs descending out of nowhere, and an invisible force ripping a hellbreed to pieces? Or strangling a Trader?

There may have been a time when I might've decided to let that pass. But if the hostage ended up biting it . . . it just didn't bear thinking about. The Cirque would explode out of its boundaries, and I'd have a hell of a time getting things back under control again.

Get it, Jill? A Hell of a time? Arf arf.

Whoever was doing this probably had a beef with hellbreed or the right idea. But they were going about it in exactly the wrong way.

10

"Thank God," Eva said as I muscled up through the attic trapdoor, her dark eyes widening with relief.

She says that every time I show up. It's kind of nice to hear.

She nodded at Saul, her tiny gold ball earrings flashing. She used to wear hoops until they almost got torn off her head five times in a row during exorcisms.

She's stubborn like that.

Eva's black bangs were disarranged, and her suit jacket was torn. It hadn't been any trick finding her here—the victim was still making enough noise to be heard on the street outside. Fortunately (or not), here at the edge of the barrio nobody paid much attention. It wasn't like her to look so mussed, though. She's usually neat as a pin. While Avery, Wallace, and Benito often go in guns blazing, Eva depends more on outsmarting and leverage.

When you're short even compared to me, I guess that's the better way to go. Of course, Mikhail probably trained me because I tend to go in guns blazin' too. Call it a character quirk.

Hey, when you've got a hellbreed mark, firepower, and a serious rage problem, leverage and tact lose a lot of their charm.

"What the hell do you have here?" I looked past her and saw something familiar—a human shape on a pair of stacked mattresses, writhing around under a sausage-casing of leather restraints. And babbling in something that sounded very familiar, too—not the grumbling of töng, but a lyrical rolling song.

"Guy's wife called 911, said he was going weird. The black-and-whites called me in, since he was holed up in the attic and chanting."

"It wasn't Jughead Vanner, was it?"

She gave me a look that could qualify both as *amused* and *what the hell?* "No, it was Connor and the Pole. I sent them both on and the wife's at her mother's. She asked if we could help him, I said I wasn't sure."

Safe answer. "Huh. Did he go to church?"

"Nope. She does. Sacred Grace. Rourke's her confessor. There are a couple of indicators, but not enough to red-flag our boy. I'm stumped."

Saul's lip lifted at the mention of Rourke. He was on the ladder leading up into the attic, his shoulders barely clearing the small entrance. He hadn't said a word since we left the Cirque. It was quiet even for him, and I suspected trouble.

First things first, though.

Huh. I still hadn't really spoken to any of the priests at Sacred Grace since the last incident with the Sorrows. I had decided, after much reflection, not to tear the whole fucking place apart to find anything else Father Gui and his happy band of priests was hiding from me. I hadn't *forgiven* Gui yet, but I hadn't stopped doing exorcisms for them either.

There was being justifiably angry over them hiding necessary information from me, and then there was being stupid.

"Does she bring home novenas?" I stepped past Eva, clearing the way for Saul to come up.

"Yup. There's a whole clutch of them on the mantel downstairs. The husband's supposed to be irreligious, which is a surprise. Part of why I called you. And Avery said—"

"Yeah, Avery. How are you two?"

"He's good." She didn't blush, but she did smile slightly, an ironclad grimace. On her pretty, wide-cheeked face, it was amazing. She has delicate fingers and a strong nose, and is built like a gymnast. It probably helps when she's wrestling Possessors. Of all of my standard exorcists, Avery comes closest to having the qualities necessary for a hunter, but Eva is the one who thinks fastest—and most thoroughly—on her feet. And she's also the calmest. She paints eggshells *a la Fabergé* to relax, I'm told. It's exactly the sort of finicky, delicate thing I'd expect her to do. "This doesn't feel like a Possessor."

It probably isn't. "Good call. Got a mirror?"

"Of course." She wasn't male, so she didn't bother with useless questions. She just dug in her black bag— exorcists favor the old medical bags, since they're just the right size and can be dropped in a hurry—and fished out a hand mirror. "The victim's Trevor Watson. Male,

African American. Forty-three, works as an orderly out at Henderson Hill. Likes beer, soft pretzels, and his wife. The marriage seems happy, the financial side stable but not luxurious by any stretch. *Scratchin'* is what the wife called it. She's Hispanic, thirty-eight, registered nurse."

"He works at Henderson?" That was interesting. Mental institutions can sometimes lead to cross-contamination in possession cases. Not as often as you think, though— plenty of people in institutions are indigent, and Possessors don't go for *that*.

"Yeah. The *new* one." It went without saying, but she said it anyway.

Our eyes met. I suppressed a shiver at the thought of the old asylum. It wasn't a nice place for anyone with a degree of psychic talent, and I'd chased an *arkeus* or two up into its cold, haunted halls. Nobody worked up at the old Henderson Hill but an old, half-blind, mute caretaker who didn't care what happened as long as he could sit in the boiler room with his quart of rye. He seemed more a fixture of the place than the old furnace itself, and I'd given up wondering exactly what he was, since he didn't interfere with any case that took me up there.

The man on the mattresses writhed and gurgled. "He chewed through a gag," Eva said helpfully. "I was worried until nothing happened."

Since Possessors—and *loa*—can snap curses at an exorcist with a victim's mouth, I didn't blame her. "Reasonable of you. How did the mattresses get up here?"

"I don't know. The wife said they never used the attic."

Curiouser and curiouser.

Saul lifted himself up from the steps. "Smells like the other one, Jill."

I stopped, gave him a quizzical look. "Really?"

"Cigars. And candy." He sniffed, inhaling deeply, tasting the air. "An orange-y perfume."

"Florida water?" I hazarded. It was a reasonable guess.

"Could be. But there's a lot of sugar. Like cookies."

Huh. Even with my senses amped up and the scar naked to the open air, I smelled nothing but dust, fiberglass insulation, and the remains of a recent fried chicken. "Well."

"*Bruuuuuja,*" the victim crooned. "*Ay, bruuuuja!* Come heee-eeere."

Eva actually jumped. "What the—"

I shushed her. *Jesus. This can't be what I think it is.*

"*Bruuuuuuja!*" A long, drawn-out sigh. The voice was eerie, neither male nor female, a sweet high piping. "We want to *talk* to you!"

"*Madre de Dios.*" Eva crossed herself.

Amen to that, I thought. "Leave your bag. Go downstairs and start saying Hail Marys. Saul—"

"Not going anywhere." Saul folded his arms as Eva brushed past him. She didn't even argue—another thing I could be thankful for. Sometimes a civilian will try to protest or object or something.

My mouth was dry. "If he gets loose, keep him from getting downstairs. Got it?"

He nodded, his eyes lighting up. I liked seeing that, and wished I had time to ask him what was going on with him. A good hour or so to worm out what was bothering him and maybe get somewhere would have been nice.

But duty always calls. I dug in Eva's bag until I came up with a taper candle and a mini-bottle of blessed wine. Father Gui blesses these tiny bottles in job lots, having a dispensation from high-up in the Vatican to perform some of the, ahem, *older* blessings.

It wasn't rum or tequila, but it would do. The victim started moaning again, and I uncapped the bottle. It was a moment's work to stare at the candle wick, the scar prickling with etheric energy bleeding down a vein-map into my fingertips, until the waxed linen sparked and bloomed with orange flame.

The attic *shifted* around me, turning darker. The shadows took on a sharper edge, hanging insulation moving slightly, though the air was dead still.

One of the oldest truths in sympathetic magic: *to light a candle is to cast a shadow*. If I didn't believe Hell predated humanity—having it on good authority—I'd think that human beings had created it. As it is, we do our bargain-basement best up here on Earth, don't we?

I wonder about that sometimes. Not enough to give myself the blue funks Mikhail used to withdraw into, but enough to make me question this entire line of work.

It's a good thing. Without the questioning I'm just another vigilante with a gun.

The taper's flame held steady. The liquid in the bottle trembled slightly, but that could have been the tension blooming in my midsection. This wasn't your ordinary exorcism, and things were beginning to take on a pattern. *Find the pattern, find your prey;* that's an old hunter maxim too.

"You want to talk to me?" I pitched my voice loud enough to carry. "Here I am."

The victim flopped against the restraints like a fish. I wondered how Eva had gotten him tied down. He looked to be twice her size.

But when a girl's motivated, miracles are possible.

I chose my footing carefully, my dumb eye on the candleflame and my smart eye soft-focused, scanning the etheric congestion over the mattresses. It still bugged me—the floor was dusty, no drag marks—so what were mattresses doing up here?

The flooring creaked. Veils of insulation shifted. It was still warm up here after the day's heat, and a prickle of sweat touched my forehead. It wasn't because of the temperature, though.

The candleflame wavered, but I was quick, shifting my weight just a half-step to the side. The strike slid past me, boards groaning, and I heard Saul skip nimbly aside. *Son of a bitch. You hit him with a curse and I will tear your face off, goddammit.*

The flame guttered; I let out a soft breath and it straightened. My smart eye watered. The mass over the bed was seething, trying to find a purchase. The safe path I was following twisted to the right just as the victim gave another chilling, childlike chuckle.

"Come a little closer, said the spider to the fly," it crooned, out through the man's mouth. "Come closer, *bruja,* and look into our eyes. We want you to see us, yes we do—"

You're about to get your wish, asshole. I reached the side of the mattress, kept my eyes on the flame, and tipped the wine-bottle up to my mouth. Blue light sparked in the fluid, whether it was the blessing reacting against the mark on my wrist or my intent flooding the alcohol I couldn't tell.

The thing inside the man's body chuckled wetly, smacking its lips, and I heard the groaning of leather as his body erupted into wild motion. But I was just a half-second quicker, and the wine I sprayed across the candleflame blossomed into blue flame just a fraction of a second before he would have smacked into me. I flung the taper too, shaking the flame out, and the sudden curtain of darkness gave me another critical half-second before I grabbed him by the throat and *shoved,* still dribbling blue-flaming wine from my lips.

It wasn't pure theatrics. There's not really enough alcohol content in cheap blessed wine to ignite, but sorcery helps—and the contact, mouth meeting flame or spit booze, is a symbol understood by the creatures in this man's body. It's what their followers do as an offering or a protection.

And it's hard for the body's natural protective reflexes not to trigger when there's a ball of blue flame coming straight at the vulnerable eyes. That reaction gave me a thin wedge and a chance to drive it home.

I was on the mattresses over him, my knees on his shoulders, one hand on his forehead, *pushing.* My aura sparkled and flamed, and the thing inside him exploded out with a shotgun's cough.

His screaming took on a harsher tone. I fell, hitting the floor with a thud, various implements in my coat digging into my flesh, and it tried to strangle me before my aura sparked again, sea-urchin spikes driving it away. It tried again, howling obscenities in a sweet, asexual child's voice, and I shoved at it with a completely nonphysical effort, screaming my own imprecations. The scar was a live coal, pumping sorcerous force up my arm.

There was a *crack,* the physical world bowing out in concentric ripples of reaction, and a weird ringing noise. The man on the mattress was still screaming, and Saul's growl spiraled up. Mixed into the noise, there was splintering wood and a sudden weightlessness.

I hit hard, narrowly missing clipping my head on a countertop, and little peppering noises resounded all around me. I blinked, chalk dust and splinters hanging weightlessly before descending in lazy swirls. The peppering noises were little bits of wrapped candy, falling out of thin air and smacking down around me with sounds like a hard rain.

Eva's face came into view. She was chalk-white, dark bruised rings under her eyes, and she frankly stared for a few moments.

Saul peered through the huge hole torn in the ceiling, his eyes shining green-gold. The sound of the victim's rubbery sobbing gradually overwhelmed the rain of candy. There's nothing like hearing a grown man cry like a three-year-old.

Especially when that cry is blessedly, completely human. But we weren't done yet, and I struggled against sudden inertia, my body disobeying the imperatives I was giving it.

"Well," Eva said. "*That* was impressive."

I blinked. Twice. It had knocked me right through the ceiling. "Shit," I muttered, and the world grayed for a moment before I came back to myself with Eva gasping and Saul suddenly *there,* his face looming over mine. *No,* I wanted to say, but I couldn't make my mouth work for a half-second, gapping soundlessly like a fish. *NO, go back up and watch him—*

It was too late. The flexing of the world completed, a hard snap with a thick rubber band. Or maybe it was leather peeling and popping free. The high-pitched, childish laughter came back, ringing, and more candy pelted down like stinging rain. Another rending, splintering noise, and the laughter was receding, along with a wet thudding sound, then light pattering footsteps.

Our victim, Trevor Watson, was on the lam.

11

This is getting seriously weird." I crouched on the cellar stairs, easily, running my smart eye over the candle-lit walls. "The wife had no idea?"

"She was adamant." Eva, behind me, was round-eyed. "I didn't think to look in the basement."

"Don't worry about it. You did exactly what you should have. There was no indicator the guy was into voodoo." The candles were arranged on an altar draped with green and gold, novenas flickering, a crudely done painting of the Trinity fastened to the concrete wall. A brass dish of sticky candy, a bottle of rum, and a few other implements, including wilted bunches of chrysanthemums. It was thick down here; the padlock on the outside door leading down to the cellar was new, and this whole thing was beginning to take on a shape I didn't like at all.

"Well, there was the chanting. But I didn't twig to it." She folded her arms.

I decided there were no traps lying under the surface

of the visible and rose, stepped down another stair, and crouched again, watching. "I said you shouldn't worry about it. This guy wasn't anything more than a low-level novice. Any serious practitioner would have some defenses down here." *Though I'm not sure yet. Slow and easy and by the book, Jill.*

Saul was outside smoking a Charvil. If Eva felt bad about not checking the cellar, Saul probably felt just as bad for letting the victim—or whatever was riding him, to be precise—get away.

To be even more precise, I knew *what* was riding our victim, but I didn't know *why.* I had a sneaking suspicion I'd find a connection to whatever was happening out at the Cirque, though.

I hate those kinds of suspicions. I moved down another stair, scanning thoroughly, but I found nothing that would tell me our victim was anything more than a secret follower. A complete and utter novice who shouldn't have been able to fling curses while under a *loa*'s influence—who shouldn't have even been able to be ridden.

It's called "being ridden." Like a horse. The *loa* descends on one of the followers during a ritual, and gains certain things from inhabiting flesh. Having it happen to a solitary practitioner isn't quite unheard-of, but it only happens where the practitioner has sorcerous or psychic talent to burn.

This guy had no markers of initiation, intuition, or sorcery. At *all.*

I stepped off the last stair, boots clicking and my coat weighing on my tired shoulders. *I really wish I wasn't getting the feeling these things are connected.* The

cellar was narrow, meant for nothing more than storing
a lawnmower or two, and the candles made it hot and
close. The guy was lucky his house hadn't burned down.
But if the *loa* were taking such a particular interest in
him, his house was probably safe.

They do take care of their followers, mostly. If you
can get their attention. But the trouble is, once you have
their attention, it's the scrutiny of creatures without a
human moral code. Capriciousness might not be cruelty,
but when wedded to power it gets awful close sometimes.

The altar looked pretty standard. Twists of paper and
ash half-filled a wide ceramic bowl, used for burning
incense for communications, or the names of enemies.
The only thing that didn't fit was a cup.

It was an enamel camping-cup, a blue speckled metal
number that looked easily older than I was. The blue
sparkled for a moment, something running under the
metal's surface, and my hand arrived to scoop it up with
no real consideration on my part. It was a reflex, and one
I was glad of, because one of the candles tipped over and
spilled flame onto the altar.

"Oh god*dammit,*" I yelled, and yanked the cup back,
tossed it into my left hand, and jabbed the right one forward. Eva let out a short blurting cry as the fire ate into
dry wood—he had his altar sitting on fruit crates, for
God's sake.

Smoke billowed. Etheric force pooled in my palm,
and the sudden blast of heat against my face stung both
smart and dumb eyes. "*Fuck!*" I yelled, and snapped my
right hand back *hard,* the scar singing a piercing agonized note into the meat of my arm as I yanked.

The flames died with a whoosh, all available oxygen sucked away. I backed off in a hurry.

"Jill?" Eva sounded about ten years old, and scared. Of course, producing flame is one of those things that tells a regular exorcist to call me in a hurry, but we weren't dealing with Hell here.

Or at least, we weren't dealing solely with Hell.

Huh. "Everything's cool, Eva." The cup was a big chunk, and my pockets were on the full side already. But I now had a good idea where I could go to find out more about all this. "We're going to clean up here, then I want you to go check on something for me, and I'm going to do more digging."

"More digging? Do I even want to know?"

Smart girl. "Probably not. I have to go out and visit the bitch of Greenlea."

"Great. I'll just let you do that, then. What am I checking on?"

"You're going to call Avery and check on another victim." *One that we've got in the bag, thank God.*

Greenlea is just north of downtown, in the shopping district. If you're really looking, you can sometimes catch a glimpse of the granite Jesus on top of Sisters of Mercy, glowering at the financial district. But Greenlea's organic froufrou boutiques and pretty little restaurants don't like seeing it. Sometimes I think it's an act of will that keeps that particular landmark obscured from certain places in the city, especially around downtown.

Saul waited until I set the parking brake. "I'm sorry."

"For what?" I peered out the window, scanned the avenue.

This district is just one street, with two high-end bookstores, vegan eateries, a coffee shop, and a couple of kitchy-klatch places selling overpriced junk. A few antique stores cluster down at one end, and a fancy bakery and two pricey bars at the other. It's the kind of well-fed, quiet little upwardly mobile granola enclave you can find in pretty much any American city. Sometimes you can find two or three of them in the same metropolis.

Two blocks off the main avenue—Greenlea itself—the crackerbox houses are pushed together behind their neat little gardens. They're old houses, on prime property, and people who have an address out here are jealously proud of it.

On the corner of Eighth and Vine, two and a half blocks away, is Sunshine Samedi. I'm sure some of the trendoid yuppies think it's a Buddhist term, too.

"He got away." Saul's face was shadowed in the half-light. "I thought—"

I didn't want him to keep going with that particular mental train. "Don't worry about it. He didn't come downstairs, right? We didn't have to peel him off Eva, and we'll find him soon enough."

"Still." He even sounded upset. I glanced at him. He looked haggard in the half-light, and I wished I had time to sit him down for a good talking-to. Only what would I say?

"Don't, Saul. You're my partner, and a good one. You did fine." Did he really think I was going to yell at him for being concerned because I'd been knocked right through the ceiling?

But it wasn't like him. He was my partner, and he knew better. Whatever knocked me sideways wouldn't put me out of commission; I was just too tough and nasty. He should have stayed where I put him.

But maybe he wasn't able to. Like he's not able to touch you anymore without flinching.

I looked away and unlocked my door, hoping he couldn't read my expression. "Come on, let's go see if she's in."

Of course she'd be in. She never left the house.

A little coffee-shop and bakery with carefully watered nasturtiums in the window boxes sat in a brackish well of etheric depression, congested like a bruise. It wasn't the congestion of Hell, but it was thick and smelled rancid—not truly *smelled*, but more sensed with that place in the very back of the sinuses where instinct lives. The closest I can figure is that the brain has no other way of decoding the information it's being handed, so it dredges up smells out of memory and serves them up.

In any case, it was more than strongly fermented here, just on the edge of turning bad. Etherically speaking.

The coffee here was horrible and the baked goods substandard, but that wasn't why people came. It most definitely was not why the place was still open, especially in a neighborhood where people were picky about their shade-grown espresso and organic-flour croissants.

Chalked signs writhed over cracked concrete, a ribbon of walkway and a naked patio holding only a terra-cotta fire-dish and chimney on three squat legs. To get back here, you had to lift the iron latch on a high board gate and wriggle past some thorny sweet acacia that hadn't been cut back. The smell cloyed in the nose, curdled and slipped down the throat, and I gapped my mouth a little bit to breathe through it. I'm sure Lorelei left the acacia there deliberately, and coaxed it into growing large enough to pick people's pockets—or rend their flesh.

The backyard was cool, holding only a ghost of the day's heat. There was no moon, and the porch light buzzed a little, illuminating nothing. The garden pressed close, far too humid for the desert.

Her water bill must be sky-high, I thought, just like I did every time I came here. Which wasn't often. Once every three years or so is often enough for me to keep tabs on the bitch of Greenlea, as Mikhail often called her. Lorelei kept her nose clean and wasn't directly responsible for any murders, so all things considered she was a minor irritant in a city filled with major ones.

I wish prioritizations like that weren't daily occurrences.

"Smells bad." The words were just a breath of sound. Saul wrinkled his nose.

I nodded. *This spider has the bad business in this whole neighborhood and a few others coming to her door. And I'm sure she helps it out quite a bit.* "Lot of people around here like to double-deal their neighbors. They come here for help."

"Hanging around with you always an—" He stopped short, his sleek silver-starred head coming up in a quick, inquiring movement. He looked more catlike than ever when he did that.

I heard it too. A skittering, like tiny insect feet.

Oh, shit. My left hand closed around the whip handle, my right touched a gun butt. Saul dropped back, melding into the shadows, and I *listened* intently. The scar turned hot and hard, and I wished I had a spare leather cuff. Still, superhuman hearing is far from the worst ally in a situation like this.

Skittering paused. The scar turned hot and flushed, a hard knot of corruption snugged into my flesh.

A small creak sounded from the hinges as a random breeze wandered through the garden.

The back door was slightly open.

Motherfuck. I eased forward, the gun slipping out of its holster and into my hand like a lover's fingers. The garden behind me exhaled, and I caught a thread of another scent, fresh and coppery under the reek of the acacia. *What the—*

I toed the door open, the hinges giving out a loose moan. Shadows fled aside, dim light spilling across yellow linoleum. Runnels of smeared blackness dragged their way down the back hall toward a shape in a blue housedress, pink fuzzy slippers decked with gore at the end of indecently splayed legs.

"Oh, fuck."

"What is it?" Saul, behind me.

"Lorelei's dead," I informed him grimly. "And I think—"

Whatever I thought was cut off as a living carpet of shining, multilegged things scuttled and swarmed from the gloom, their backs marked with pinpricks of red laser light, and raced toward me. It was a wave of black cockroaches, and the skittering of their tiny feet stabbed my ears as my smart eye pierced the etheric veil over them, catching a glimpse of a swirling, ugly intent.

Oh, holy fuck. The gun would be useless on a swarm like this. I skipped back twice, almost running into Saul,

who let out a short unamused sound and faded away.
The gun went back, the scar running with heat under
the wristcuff, and I jabbed my hand forward, two fingers
out. Etheric energy ran crackling over my fist, sorcery
rising to my lips, and the living tide of darkness scrabbled against my will.

It felt like tiny hairy feet running over my body, bris-
tly little things poking at my mouth and eyes, scrabbling
for entrance. My skin literally *crawled* before my aura
flamed, bright spikes jabbing through the darkness in
points of brilliance. A wet salt smell—ashes doused
with rum and stale cigar smoke—thudded down over us,
and the garden whispered uneasily to itself. Branches
rubbed against each other and the flood of acacia scent
didn't pierce the other reek.

The bugs imploded, darkness shrinking into tiny
red pinpricks that glowed like cigarette cherries before
green smoke puffed out of the place in the world they
had occupied. The vapor thinned unnaturally fast, leaving only acridity.

"Jill?" Saul's tone was neutral, leashed impatience.

"Goddammit." I let out a short, sharp sigh. "I think
we can cross normal homicide off the list for this one."

"You think?" Sarcasm turned to curiosity. "What *was*
that?" His eyes sheened with gold-blue briefly, rods and
cones reflecting differently from a human's.

"Don't know yet. Could have been one of Lorelei's
defenses." *Although it didn't do her much good, if that's
her.* "Could have been the same thing that tried to strangle the hostage." *Much more likely, but anything's possible.* I eased forward, my left hand still playing with
the whip handle. It was the equivalent of a nervous flinch.

"I'm gonna check the scene, then you can call Monty and have him get Forensics out here. I'll meet you at home—"

"No dice. I'm staying with you." He sounded like he meant it, too.

"I can't wait for Montaigne here. I've got other shit to do." I took another step forward, doing my best to avoid the claret spread on the floor. Blood looks black at night, even human blood. Hellbreed ichor is always black, but it's thin and doesn't splatter the same way human fluid does.

You have to see a lot of both before you can tell the difference with a glance, though.

"Goddammit, Jill." He sounded upset. It was so unlike him I paused and glanced over my shoulder. His eyes were orange-tinged; they get all glowy when he's excited, like a 'breed's. But Weres are as different from hellbreed as it's possible to be. "I'm not a cub."

You just look tired. I'm trying not to burden you more. "You're right, you're not. You're my partner, I need you here."

"Jill—"

I edged forward another step, every sense alert. "You can wait in the car if you're not going to help." *Might even be the best thing, the way this is going.*

It *was* Lorelei. Her black dreadlocks lay in fat limp ropes, soaked with clotted blood and daubed with bone beads and bits of glittering onyx. She hadn't been dead long, I was guessing. There wasn't much insect life.

Except for the cockroaches. Each with a pinprick of red light on its back, coming out of the gloom and vanishing into smoke.

This is not good.

She lay between the back hall and the kitchen. There was something bubbling on the stove. It didn't smell like spaghetti. In fact, it was a thin brew with nameless chunks of something stringy floating in it, and the remnants of sorcery popping and fizzing on the water's surface. I flicked the heat off, examining the brew.

Bubble, bubble, toil and trouble. I should have left it on, but who knew what would happen when it finished cooking, especially in a house full of forensic techs? And contaminating the scene was a small thing compared to the fire risk, especially when I was sure this was one of my cases.

How about that for ironic? If this was a regular garden-variety murder I wouldn't be touching anything.

I passed my right hand through the steam, greasy moisture scumming my palm. Sniffed deeply. It smelled like greedy obsession and musk, sex-drenched sheets left to rot in a dark hole.

Ugh. Nasty, nasty. What were you doing, Lorelei?

Three good Cuban cigars lay on the clean counter, next to a bottle of Barbancourt rum. The charms in my hair shifted uneasily. Right next to the unopened rum was a fresh bottle of Florida water and a jar of cornmeal.

She'd been preparing to do something, and the longer I waited the harder the traces would be to decipher. My right palm skipped through the steam once more, and yet more grease-laden steam touched my skin. My blue eye was hot and dry, the right watering from the smell. Cool air touched the rest of me, air-conditioning working overtime—Lorelei liked it cold as a tomb in here.

Get it, Jill? Cold as a tomb? It wasn't funny, and I'd given up wondering why people who liked it freezing had moved to the *desert,* for Chrissake.

Probably no shortage of people who wanted her dead, for one reason or another. But she hadn't survived this long as a black sorcerer by being careless or weak, and there was nobody I could think of with usable psychic talent and a vendetta against her.

And there was the slight matter of *loa* in a young man who shouldn't have them, the very same *loa* in an older man who shouldn't have had them so strongly, and a series of attacks on a hellbreed and a Trader hostage.

The commonality was voodoo, but I couldn't assume they were all directly linked—or could I?

Hunters are trained pretty thoroughly not to make assumptions. But we're also trained not to discount the thing that's staring us in the face. It's a fine line to walk.

My concentration narrowed. *One thing at a time.*

Poking, probing, my hand motionless in the steam, the rest of the world shut itself away. Saul had gone quiet and quiescent, watching my back. Intuition flared and faded, trying to track the traces of sorcery through a shifting mass of intention and weird, sideways-skipping dead ends.

It faded and flared maddeningly, and I came back to myself, exhaling a short dissatisfied huff of air. "God-*dam*mit."

"Nothing?" Saul asked cautiously.

"Nothing I can see from here. I'd have to go *between* to track this one." Goose bumps crawled over my arms as I said it, and I hurried to give him the last half of what

I was thinking. "Don't worry, I'm not planning on doing it unless it becomes necessary."

"It's not necessary?" He sounded dubious, but the relief of knowing I wasn't going *between* probably made him sound that way.

"Not at this point. I still have a couple other things to track down, like our other victim's other address. And I'm going to go see Mama Zamba. If it's a voodoo feud, she'll know about it. If it's not, she'll want to know someone's messing around on her turf, and she's far from the worst ally in a situation like this." I backed cautiously away from the stove. The surface of the water still roiled greasily, but the sorcery was fading. It hadn't been completed, so all the work and effort Lorelei had put in it was bleeding away, blood from a wound. "If nothing pans out with her, I'm going to have to go see Melendez. Jesus."

"You're not going to *either* of them without me." Flat and quiet.

I turned on my heel and opened my mouth to tell him I'd go wherever I had to, but the look on his face stopped me. Saul looked *worried,* dark circles under his eyes and his mouth a tight line. His hands had curled into fists—shocking, first because he was a Were, and second because he was always so even and steady. He was too calm to be believed most of the time, and I didn't realize how much I depended on that calm until he was gone.

Or until we hit a snag like this.

"What the hell's wrong with you?" I didn't mean it to come out so harsh. *Christ, Jill, his mom just died. Give him a break*. But the words spilled out. "We've got a couple of really serious problems here, and I need you firing on all cylinders. I *count* on you, Saul."

Great. Well, I suck at giving breaks. But Jesus . . .

"I know." His dark gaze slid past me, as if he couldn't bear to look. "I just . . ."

"You just what? I know—look, I really know you're suffering. Your mom . . . I mean, you're grieving, I understand. I'm trying to give you space, you know. It's just hard when I'm running to solve a case. I don't have a lot of time. I'm sorry." The tangle of everything I should have said instead—beautiful things that would help him feel better—rose to choke me, and I swung away from him, looking for a phone. "I'm going to call Montaigne. Take the car and go home, I'll wait for them to come secure the scene; I've got a couple things I need them to take samples of for me. Then I'm going to check out our first victim's address, and visit Zamba. I'll be home when I can and we'll hash this out."

He wasn't having any of it. "You think this is about my *mother?*" He sounded shocked. "So you've been—"

"Trying to give you some space. Which I'm going to keep doing. I've got shit happening here, Saul. If the hostage ends up dead or we're looking at a voodoo war, all fucking hell is going to break loose." *And I'll be on the front lines trying to deal out enough ammo to keep it from killing more innocent people.*

"Jill—"

I cut him off. I had to. "Saul. Go home. I'm sorry, I'm a hunter. That comes first. I love you and I'm going to give you the space you need to get your head clear. Go the fuck home." I took two steps toward the phone. They were hard—every inch of me wanted to turn back, grab him, and hug him and tell him it was all going to be okay.

But I had more than a sneaking suspicion that something was about to break over my city. If the hostage ended up dead, there went the Cirque's promise of good behavior, and I'd have a hell of a time getting another hostage out of them *and* making sure they didn't step outside their boundaries and go hunting instead of just luring the suicidal, desperate, insane, and psychopathic in to play their games. And if a voodoo war broke out at the same time . . . it didn't bear thinking about. There was only one of me, and a lot of uppity assholes to kill to keep the peace once chaos was on the loose instead of still mostly contained.

If the two things were connected, someone was making a lot of trouble for me, and I needed to get a handle on it *yesterday.*

"Jill—" Saul tried again.

"Go on." I didn't want to sound harsh. I really didn't. I tried to take a gentle tone. "Go home. Really. I'll be along when I can. I love you."

Lorelei's phone was at the end of the kitchen counter. I picked it up and dialed a number I knew by heart. Saul's footsteps were heavy. He headed for the back door.

Don't go. Come here and I'll hug you. Everything's going to be okay. I love you, I can love you enough to make the hurt go away. Come back.

"Montaigne," the phone barked in my ear.

Saul pulled the back door to but didn't close it. I *felt* him, each step taking a lifetime, sliding away around the corner of the house.

"Hello?" Monty bit the word like it personally offended him.

I came back to myself with a jolt. "Monty, it's Jill."

"Oh, Christ. What?"

"I've got a body I need taken care of, and I need a scene gone over. I also need Avery to meet me here." I gave Lorelei's address. "Get them here now—I'm on a schedule."

"When are you not?" He didn't ask any stupid questions, at least. "Are things going to get ugly?"

God, I hope not. The pressure behind my eyes wouldn't go away. Neither would the stone in my throat, but I sounded sharp and Johnny-on-the-spot. All hail Jill Kismet, the great pretender. "Time will tell. Get them out here, Monty. I'll be in touch."

"You got it." He hung up, and I did too. Thank God police liaisons don't question a hunter's judgment, even if they don't know what we're dealing with most of the time. Those that do know—and Monty had brushed the nightside once or twice—have a better idea than most, and leap to do what we ask.

The alternative really doesn't bear thinking about, but I'm sure they do.

I turned in a complete circle. I heard the Pontiac's engine purr into life outside. *Oh, Saul. Jesus. I wish I was better for you.*

I had work to do, not the least of which was sweeping the scene so I was sure it was safe for the forensic techs who were about to descend. Time to get cracking.

But oh, my heart hurt.

12

Avery arrived just as I was giving my forensics liaison the rundown. Piper is my very favorite tech. She didn't even blink when I told her what samples I needed. Lorelei's house was clear, her basement altar quiet, and the only problem was three live chickens brooding in wire cages downstairs. It's the kind of problem Piper's used to solving, and not much disturbs her serenity. She's got four kids and a husband who does house duty while she's out at crime scenes, and her sleek brown ponytail is almost never disarranged.

"Chickens?" She barely even raised an eyebrow. Behind me, they were photographing Lorelei's body.

"I don't care what you do with them, sell them or something."

She gave me a look that could only qualify as long-suffering. I'm sure she practiced it on her kids. "Okay. You want a file on the body, of course. Can Stan release it after the autopsy? Anyone likely to want it?"

"I have no clue. Don't release it until I give the okay."

"Is it likely to . . ." Both eyebrows *did* raise this time, slightly.

"If it was likely to sit up and start causing trouble I wouldn't let you keep it." I'd already taken care of piercing the palms and feet with long iron nails. "Have Stan do a full workup, but warn him not to take the nails out."

She didn't even blink. "Your wish is our command. Anything we need to be worried about?"

"Of course not. Take pictures of the altar downstairs, catalog the scene—the usual."

"Got it. Anything I should beep you if we find?"

Someone called her name, she raised a hand to let them know she'd be with them in a second. I mulled the question, shuffling priorities and evidence inside my head. "Nope. Just let me know when the file's done. See if you can find out if anyone visited her—check the phone and have the black-and-whites ask her neighbors."

She nodded. "Got it."

Technically I suppose I should have had a couple of homicide deets there to take care of the legwork, but I'd told Monty not to bother. This was so clearly one of my cases, and there was no reason for anyone to be brought in on call. It wasn't like I didn't know what had happened. "Great. Thanks, Piper."

She shrugged. "Yeah, well. You're *sure* this one won't. . . ."

"It won't come back to life, Piper. I promise. Just tell Stan not to take the nails out."

"Okay." A shadow crossed through her dark eyes, but

she shrugged again and went to work. Which officially finished up my job here.

Avery leaned against the hood of his Jeep, and I got a pleasant surprise. Eva was there too, perched on the hood like a Chrysler-approved pixie. The breeze stirred her dark hair, and I could tell just from the tension in her shoulders that she was still upset over losing Watson. Either that or something else, since Ave looked troubled too.

"How's our first victim?" I didn't bother with a preamble. Our second victim was still missing, or I would know about it.

"Funny you should ask." Ave's mouth twisted. "Had to sedate him and tie him down again. He was throwing himself all over the cell. I'm surprised he doesn't have a concussion. He was chanting again, too. It was hinky as hell."

Eva shivered. "It took three darts before he even slowed down. I don't know what we're going to do when he wakes up again."

Interesting. "Anyone there with him?"

"Benito and his bum leg. Wallace is out on a job. It sounded like a regular one," Eva added hurriedly, seeing my expression. "We've traded notes. Nobody's seen anything like this."

I nodded. "Care to come check out our first victim's other address? I want to eyeball it, and if there's anything there I'm going to have you two secure the scene while I go traipsing around following clues."

"Sounds like a good time." Avery grinned. "We were going to go to a movie but this is ever so much better."

Oh, I'll bet. "Bite your tongue. And give me your car keys."

That wiped the grin off his face, and Eva sighed.

"You're driving?" Avery dug in his jacket pocket, but slowly.

"We need to get there this century. Come on, Avery. I've never been in an accident in my life."

"It's not for lack of trying, I bet." But Eva looked angelically innocent when I glanced at her. "Seriously, Jill. You're not quite a menace, but you're close."

"Why does everyone feel the need to comment on my driving?" I held out my hand, Avery dropped his key ring in, and I motioned at them like a mother hen. "Come on, chickadees. Let's get going—Mama's in a hurry."

13

The address on Ricardo's food-handler's permit was a trim little one-story bungalow on Vespers. The place looked nice enough, despite the dying lawn. Still, we live in the desert, and not many people have the patience or the funds to drench sun-dried dirt regularly enough to make it bloom.

But that kind of bothered me. The lawn was dying, not dead. I sat in the Jeep, eyeing the house, and Avery groaned.

"I think I'm going to be sick."

"Don't be dramatic. You should take this beast in for a tune-up." I unclipped my seat belt, still staring at the house. *What's wrong with this picture?*

Sometimes looking at a scene is like that. Something doesn't jell, and it takes a few moments to make everything snap together behind your eyes in a coherent picture. I've given up wondering if the way hunters turn psychic is the sorcery or the science of informed guessing, or both. It doesn't matter. What matters is listening to that little tingling shock of wrongness as it hits right under the surface of conscious thought, and not ignoring it.

The hunter who ignores instinct is dead in the water.

"That was *fun*." Eva burbled from the backseat. "Damn, Jill, you should rent out as a cabdriver."

"People would drop dead of heart attacks." Avery *was* looking a little green. And he was sweating a bit. "Jesus."

"Come on, buck up." Eva ruffled his hair, and Avery grinned, blushing. The slow grin got him a lot of female attention, but it seemed a bit softer now. An internal happiness, rather than an external show.

He looked like a man in love.

Now I'd officially seen everything. And a sharp pin lodged itself in my heart. I ignored it.

I studied the house some more. *This really, really doesn't feel right. Lawn dying, but it was a nice one until recently. Ricardo worked as a dishwasher; why would he list this as his address if he was on the edge of poverty? And why does it give me the heebies so bad?*

The porch light wasn't on, though that probably meant nothing. It doesn't take a lawn a long time to yellow out here, especially in the autumn before the storms sweep up the river. But there was something else. The swirl of etheric energy over the whole place was congested, bruised. Strong negative emotion will do that, especially over time. But it's only one of the things that will.

"Jill?" Eva, again. Avery knew better than to talk when I went quiet like this. So did Saul.

Saul. Christ. I wish I could go home.

But there's never an excuse for leaving a job half-done. "Stay here."

"You got it," Avery said immediately. "Should we call anyone if anything, you know, happens?"

What, and have this place crawling with vulnerable people to protect? Still, he meant well. "No. If anything happens you should first drive away. Wait for me back at the precinct."

"What exactly do you think is going to happen?" Eva shifted uneasily in her seat. Both of them smelled healthy, with the darker edge of clean brunettes and her light feminine spice. Now the edge of adrenaline and fear touched both distinct scents.

"Can't tell yet." *I'm not even going to guess.* "Just stay here." I dropped Avery's keys in his lap and slid out of the Jeep, slamming the door with a little more care than I used with my own cars.

Quit thinking about Saul. Focus on the work at hand.

I went up the cracked driveway. That was another thing—no car parked outside. They had a garage, but the recent oil stain on the concrete led to the conclusion that a car was missing. I wondered if it was our victim's, discarded the question. It didn't matter right now, wouldn't until I figured out who belonged here—and who didn't.

The windows were dead dark. It wasn't early enough in the night for that, even though people in this neighborhood probably retired early. You had to work a full day to afford a house in today's economy, and this was the sort of half-depressed area that would slide right over into outright welfare warzone in a heartbeat. All it would take is one little crack house.

The front door was tucked back a little, the walkway running up along a quarter of the garage's length. My blue eye twitched and smarted a little; the concrete walk was littered with yellowing newspapers, rolled up and tossed higgledy-piggledy. Their delivery boy must've had a hell of a good arm.

Now I could see other rolled-up papers hiding in the straggled grass, hidden by the slight downward slope of the lawn. Whoever had been caring for the lawn had watered right over the top of them.

The place felt as deserted as a cheap haunted house the morning after Halloween.

I tapped on the front door with no real hope. Tapped again, toyed with the idea of ringing the doorbell.

The metal doorknob was cold under my fingers. A jolt of something went up my arm, the scar humming to itself greedily, a wet little pucker embedded in my flesh. I jiggled the knob, then twisted, and the wrong notes drowned out the whole fucking symphony.

The door was unlocked.

This is not going to end well. I ghosted the door open, listening hard. The scar listened too. I wished again for a fresh wristcuff to cover it up, drew a gun instead. Eased forward.

The house was soundless.

Well, not quite. There was a stealthy not-sound, a listening silence. I didn't think it was just my imagination.

The smell hit me a breath after I stepped into the front hall. The place was bare, empty white walls and a dead blank television in the living room, set on a wooden crate. The venetian blinds were half-drawn, and the kitchen was empty too. A plate in the sink had congealed, a thick rubbery mass on its surface.

The reek was thick and rotten. If you've even *once* smelled death, you know what it's like and how it clings in the nose, climbing down to pull the strings in your stomach.

The only question was, where were the bodies? There was no cellar, which is usually the first bet in a case like this. I turned down the hall, passed a bathroom, and headed for what was almost certainly two bedrooms, doors firmly closed.

Door number one, or door number two? Which should it be, Jillybean? Come on down, don't be shy. My boots whispered along thin, cheap carpet. It was warm in here, but not overly so. The windows weren't open, which meant there was air-conditioning—but it was set at an uncomfortably high temperature. Probably meant to save money.

Number one or number two, Jill? The one ahead or the one on the right? It makes sense to check the one dead ahead first.

It bothered me. The smell should be worse, if it was so nice and warm in here.

The stealthy non-sounds grew more and more intense, but I couldn't get a fix on them. There's a certain frequency where you can't tell if the sound is truly audible or just a mental echo of something else going on; it burrows under the skin and strokes at your eardrums with little hairy legs. A shiver of loathing went down my skin. My blue eye only caught the stirring of ambient energy, a slow lethargic swirl that told me nothing.

I debated reaching for the doorknob with my left hand or just plain kicking it. The first rule of any scene is to offer assistance to the living, but I was pretty sure nothing was left living in here. Still, if I went around kicking doors in . . .

Take it easy, there, Jill. Think for a second.

The smell was wrong. The silence was wrong. The newspapers, front lawn, blank walls, empty kitchen, and most of all the unlocked door were *wrong*.

My left hand flicked toward another gun just as all hell broke loose. The door crumpled and shattered outward, little splinters peppering me and the wall as a zombie lurched through, dry tendons screaming and half-eaten face working soundlessly. It was dripping with little bits of plated light—it took me a split second to determine the thing was crawling with roaches, each with the familiar little red dot on its back. But worst of all was the smell that belched out of the small close bedroom, and the zombie lifted its shattered arms and blurred forward with the eerie speed of the recently reanimated, roaches plopping off and scuttling for my boots over the cheap carpet.

I'd found Trevor Watson. And he wasn't alone.

The trouble with zombies is that the motherfuckers just won't stay *dead*. I stamped down hard, a short sound of disgust escaping tight-pursed lips, and the skull gave way under my steel-toed and -heeled boot with a sound like a ripe melon splitting. Zombie bones get porous after a little while, something about the body cannibalizing itself to provide enough chemical energy for their restless motion.

The roaches scuttled, but my aura flared, pushing them away from my feet. They ran with greasy green smoke, popping out of existence like Orville Redenbacher's ugliest nightmare. My fist blurred out, hellbreed strength pumping through my bones, and caught the fourth one in the face as well. It exploded, bits of rotting brain-matter splattering me and the walls liberally.

Guns won't do much good against zombies in close quarters. The ones whose heads I'd shattered were still scrabbling weakly on the carpet, sorcerous force bleeding away. Green smoke rose from the sludge their non-circulating blood had become. Identification of these bodies was going to be tricky—they were juicy as all get-out. But it explained why the smell was just awful and not truly, blindingly massive.

And I'd ID'd the first one before he'd tried to chew me into bits. He shouldn't have ended up here and dead, for God's sake. But I had other problems to worry about right now.

The roaches made little whispering sounds, puffing out of existence. Both bedrooms were awash with green smoke hanging at knee level, and a roving hand splatted dully against my ankle. I stamped again, felt flesh and sponge-bones give.

Two left, where did they go, spooky fuckers, they move so fast—I skipped to the side. When you don't have a high-powered rifle or particular ammo for headshots that will make the entire skull explode, you're down to fisticuffs and whip-work. Unfortunately, the area was too confined for the whip. Knife-work wouldn't do me any good.

I was wishing for my sunsword when one of the remaining zombies made a scuttling run, humping up out of the smoke and heading straight for the wall. I grabbed it, fingers popping skin and sinking into worm-eaten muscle tissue before, and broke the neck with a quick twist. That didn't do much—they're sorcerously impelled, not relying on nerve endings much—but it did slow it down long enough for me to take its legs out, get it on the floor, and stamp its head in.

Everything I'd eaten in the last twenty-four hours tried to declare mutiny, but I was too busy hunting around for the last zombie. It dodged out the door and I gave chase, wading through waves of roaches and spluttering, still-moving corpses awash in bloodsludge and green smoke.

Well, that answers that—the cases are connected. Hallelujah, but I hate to be right. I bolted down the hall, my left hand heading down for the whip.

It zigged around the corner and so did I, clipping the wall with my shoulder and taking away a good-sized chunk of it. Out into the clean, cold night air, where I saw two things—first, Avery was outside the Jeep, standing near the hood and staring at me.

Second, the zombie was scuttling straight for him.

If it reached him, it would probably tear his throat out. Just because I'm tough to kill doesn't mean regular humans are, especially if you're a spooky-quick, sorcerously engineered corpse bent on mayhem. A corpse just aching to do its master's bidding.

Then I'd have to deal with Avery's body too, and right in front of Eva.

I screamed and leapt, the whip coming free and flicking forward, silver flechettes jingling as it wrapped around one of the zombie's legs and almost tore itself out of my hand. The leather popped hard, once, like a good open-hand shot to the face or a piece of wet laundry shaken in just the right way, and the zombie went down in a splattering heap.

"Get in the fucking car!" I yelled. Then I was on the

thing, its foul sponginess running away as I broke its neck with a louder crack than the other ones. *This guy must be pretty fresh, too.* I balled up my right fist, my knees popping foul, slipping skin and sinking through muscle turned to ropy porridge.

I *punched,* pulling it at the last second so my fist didn't go through the head and straight on into the dying lawn. Newspapers ruffled in a sudden burst of cold air and the smell of natron. The wet splorching sound was louder than it had any right to be, and brain oatmeal splattered. The body twitched feebly.

No, they don't rely on nerve pathways much. But the head as the "seat" of consciousness carries a magical meaning all its own, and the symbol of breaking the head breaks the force the zombie is operating under.

I just wished it wasn't so messy. You'd think I'd be used to it by now, though.

I considered retching, but Avery was already doing enough for both of us. He was still gamely trying to make it around the car to the driver's side. Eva stared out through the windshield, her mouth ajar and her eyes wide enough to turn into plates.

Bits of dead zombie plopped off my coat as I rose, heavily. Shook myself like a dog heaved free of an icy lake. More bits splattered.

"J-J-J—" Avery was trying to get my name out through retches.

"Get in the car!" I yelled at him again. The scene wasn't safe, for Chrissake.

"Behind you!" Eva screamed, but I was already turning, hip swinging first, skipping aside as the whip sliced air. The silver jangled, bits of rotting flesh torn free,

and it hit the zombie I hadn't counted before full in the face.

The thing did an amazing leap, dead nerves trying like hell to respond, the same kind of unholy quick reflex motion a small, partially crushed animal makes as the body dies. It jittered and jived there on the lawn, and I was on it in a heartbeat. When it was finally twitching out its last, I cast a quick glance back at Avery, who finally managed to make his legs work and scurried around the front end of the Jeep. I turned back to the house, waited until he was in the car and had the engine going before taking another step toward it, senses quivering. The whip had transferred itself to my right hand, and my left fingers found my largest knife. It would brace my fist and I could probably lop a hand off if the zombie was old enough.

The sudden wash of sensory acuity turned me into a mass of raw nerve endings. I exhaled, made sure of clear play on the whip by shaking it a little, listening to the flechettes jangle. *Christ. Wish I had my sword. Or that Saul was here.*

But wishes didn't get the job done. I had a whole house to check, and who knew how many zombies to deal with.

I eyed it. One-story, no cellar unless it was hiding around the back, and I'd already cleared out two rooms with two zombies each. Where had the last one come from?

Lord God above, I thought, *I hate attics. Almost as much as I hate basements.*

I got to work.

14

Piper wasn't happy about bodies spread out in fast-decaying bits, but she took my word that they wouldn't rise again. I'd cleared the whole house and found three more wet ones—not up in the attic or in a surprise cellar, but in the small crawl space underneath. It made sense—they like dark spaces. It was hard to believe so many people had lived here, but the kitchen held dry goods and the bedrooms had mattresses as well as two altars. It was clear the altars were where all the money had gone. They were elaborate three-story affairs, candles burned down, dishes of flyblown sticky candy and bottles of Barbancourt, cigars that cost as much as the television. Whoever lived here was serious, though the wide bloodstain in the weedy backyard under a canopy was probably chicken or goat instead of human. They even had a firepit to grill things, and I wondered how many "barbecues" they'd thrown a month.

Still, the rest of the house was too empty. "It looks

like a front," was Piper's only comment, and I didn't
have to tell her how right she was.

It was the empty fridge that convinced me, actually.

Piper loaned me her cell phone, too, and I called
Avery's desk number. It was a relief when he picked up.

"You okay?" I tried not to sound sarcastic, or too
relieved.

He let out a gusty sigh. "Kind of. Jill—"

"The next time I tell you to get in the car, Ave, you
do it."

"Christ, Jill, I *know*. Don't rub it in. Listen, I—"

"You shouldn't have been outside. If that thing had
caught you, Eva would be very unhappy."

"Will you quit? Ricardo's gone. Tore a hole right
through the door—the cell is a mess. The circle in there
is broken. Something ground the concrete up and broke
it, made a gap."

My knees didn't falter, but it was damn close. Bright
lights were on inside the house, starring the night. The
neighbors didn't come out to check, and I wondered
how many of them had an idea about the backyard at
this place, and the drumming that would go on all night
sometimes. I could have had a homicide pair out here
at this scene too, but really, what was the point? I knew
where I had to go next.

"He's gone?"

"Completely AWOL."

*Goddammit. What do you want to bet he won't end
up a zombie too?* "All right. See what you can do about
getting the room repaired."

"I *hate* contractors," he muttered. "Jill, I'm sorry. I

was trying to get around into the driver's side to get us away if we had to. I was just about to go."

That's what I thought. I took a deep breath, watching the shadows of forensic techs in the living room, played against the bright golden windows. "Everything's copacetic. First encounter with a zombie?"

"Yeah. You know, no matter how many times you see weird shit, it always knocks the wind out of you."

Don't I know it. But I didn't really agree. It's amazing what the human mind will accommodate, given a strong enough framework. And the training helps.

Training made me think of Gilberto on my front step again. What would Saul do if the kid was still there? Ignore him, hopefully. And more hopefully, maybe the little gangbanger would have gone on his merry way.

Still, he had the look. Which meant he was a problem I would have to solve soon.

After, of course, I figured out who was attacking Cirque performers and strewing zombies all over. And after I figured out what Saul was—

"Jill?" Avery sounded uncertain.

"It certainly does," I agreed. "See what you can do about that room, and if anything looks hinky during *any* exorcism, buzz me. Don't even go on a call if it feels weird. Make sure Eva and the rest know that, too."

"Okay. Any idea what's going on?"

"Do you really want to know?" I took his silence for a negative answer and smothered a laugh. "I'll be in touch."

I flipped Piper's phone closed. It was time for God's honest truth.

I might not have looked very hard for the perpetrator

if it had just been a couple Cirque performers dead, or just Lorelei. If black sorcerers and hellbreed were looking to off each other, it made my life a little easier. It was the chance they took when they signed up for their kinds of fun and games.

But the hostage? If he ended up biting it, the Cirque would be stunned for a little while—and then the guarantee of their good behavior would be gone. And that was bad news for everyone. Even Perry, but while I could *probably* bank on his territorial jealousy, I couldn't bank on him not deciding a certain level of chaos was a good thing for his plans.

Whatever those plans were.

And *zombies,* for Christ's sake. Nobody needed to be unleashing carnivorous corpses on my city. I just hate that.

Especially when it looked like the corpses were people being fed to *loa* in return for something big.

I returned Piper's phone, assured her again the bodies wouldn't reassemble or otherwise even twitch, and realized I was there without a car. *Oh, dammit.*

Fortunately, one of the black-and-whites could give me a ride to the barrio. I ignored the paling of the rookie's face. It was the unfortunately-named Judy Garland, a smug trim blonde with a wide smile and a *summa cum laude* from the police academy. She would probably shape up to be a good administrator one of these days.

After I finish their orientation, very few of them actually want to interact with me in any way. The slide show takes care of most of it, and the demonstrations—I used to do other things before Saul was around to change and show them something their brains couldn't wrap around—did the rest. Most people's interest in the paranormal only stretches far enough to cover a thrill or two, or some white-light bullshit.

"Chesko, right off the freeway," I told her. "Turn your lights on and get me there yesterday."

"Yes ma'am." She sat bolt upright in the driver's seat. It was her bad luck, partnerless for the night and showing up to help secure this scene. I tapped my fingers on my leather-clad knee, suddenly remembering how bad I must reek.

Nothing like a zombie to clear the sinuses.

"You can open a window if you need to." I tried to sound a little gentler. "I must smell bad."

"It's okay," she lied, but cranked down her window halfway anyway. The night rushed in, full of city, concrete, and river. Red and blue strobes dappled the silent streets as we raced through over them, the shocks groaning. She was a good driver, but too slow. "Does this . . . this sort of thing happen a lot to you?"

What, you mean zombies, or smelling like death and goop? "Often enough."

"You were bleeding."

I'll bet I was. But it had stopped by now, or I would have used some healing sorcery on it. Another benefit to a hellbreed mark on my wrist. "Yeah, that happens too."

"Can I ask you something?"

"Fire away." *Only, how much do you want me to tell you?*

"We—I mean, some of us at the station, whenever your name comes up—" She was still pale, took a deep breath, and rushed on. "Why do you do this?"

Well now, isn't that an unanswerable question.
"There's nobody else to do it," I said, and left it at that.
I didn't tell her what Mikhail said, and I didn't tell her
what I really thought.

Idiots, Mikhail had often sneered. *They think we do
this for them. Is only one reason to do,* milaya, *and that
is for to quiet the screaming in our own heads.*

He was right as far as it went—he always was. But
sometimes, in the long dark reaches of the night when
nothing much is happening and I patrol looking for trouble, I follow the logic out a bit further. I think becoming
a hunter was preordained for me, but not in any Calvin-
ist way.

There was no grace to save me from these works.

I slouched in the seat, weapons digging into my flesh
as I shifted, and watched the city go by. She was doing at
least thirty over the limit, and it was too goddamn slow.

When I say it was preordained, I mean that there was
nothing else for me to do but die in a snowbank, and I
wasn't ready for that. I'd reached the end of my normal
life, and I was taken over the edge and into the nightside
by Mikhail, for no reason I ever heard him explain. I
never even considered doing something else, or taking
the other bargain he offered me—therapy and a fresh
start. The bargain offered to every apprentice.

No, as soon as I figured out what he was doing, I
wanted in. Or maybe not precisely. I just wanted to do
what would make him proudest of me. I wanted to please
him.

I wanted to be worth whatever had made him pull me
out of that snowdrift.

I had probably been moving toward him—and this—

all my short unhappy life. I could have taken a detour anywhere, I suppose. Free will means as much.

But there's free will, and then there's being made in such a way that you can only do what you must. There's no law against choosing a different path, and I suppose you could if you wanted to—but that isn't how you're made. It isn't how you *are*.

If the clay cuts the potter's hand, who is to blame— the clay, or the Great Potter who created it? It was an old riddle, and one I was no closer to solving. I was as I'd been made, and I was doing what I was made for.

It was as simple as that. And she wasn't anyone who needed more of an answer from me.

Maybe Saul does. We haven't fought over this in a while. Maybe he's just waiting for me to bring it up. He's probably waiting for me to bring something *up.*

We hit the freeway. It would take less than five minutes to get me to the Chesko exit, and then poor Judy could go back to her rounds. It would take me a short while to work around one edge of the barrio and get to Zamba's, and the night was getting old.

"Can I ask *you* something?" I stared out the windshield, watching traffic slide easily aside, pulling over. It was so much easier with a set of red and blue lights, instead of the usual intuition-tingling run through the streets.

"Shoot," Garland said, and probably wished she hadn't.

"Why do you do what you do?"

I caught her momentary half-shrug. Was she wishing she hadn't opened her mouth, or was she shrugging because she hadn't thought about it?

The road zoomed under the car. We were only a few feet above the concrete. Such a small distance.

"I guess it's what I was supposed to do," she said finally. "There's all sorts of reasons why people work this job. Too many for each person. Otherwise we'd be doing something else." The exit loomed, she braked, and we began the long slow bleedoff up the hill. The barrio pulsed, and her radio crackled, squawking at us.

The light at the head of the exit was green. She rolled to a stop, the reds and blues dappling the run-down gas station and the arching soar of the overpass. This far down Chesko she wouldn't have to worry about her car getting shot at, and she could get right back on the freeway. It all worked out.

"Exactly," I said, and bailed out of the car, slamming the door behind me. I was already two blocks away, the scar tingling as I pulled etheric force through it, by the time her engine roused again. I didn't look back.

Exactly.

The queen of the voodoo scene in Santa Luz lived in a ramshackle split-level on the edge of the barrio. The houses on either side were abandoned—nobody would stay in them long enough to pay rent *or* a mortgage. I often wonder if real estate agents have a clue why certain places don't sell.

The house had a three-car garage, an overgrown jungle garden full of spiny, smelly plants, and a zigzagging, cracked concrete walk up to the spindly porch, concrete stair-slabs laid in an iron framework that looked far too frail to hold them.

I stood across the street, in the shadow of a closed-down convenience store with blind, boarded windows. The area hadn't been so depressed and run-down last time I'd been through, but the edge of the barrio is a no-man's-land. It was a wonder everything hadn't been closed down before, but Zamba's presence had given the place a facsimile of liveliness.

Which brought up, again, the question of just what the hell was going on here now.

The shadows drew close. The night was getting too old, and the streets had no cover. Even the barrio was winding down, its pulse taking on the tired thump of the long dark shoal of three to five A.M., when the old or the critically injured often slip over the edge into deeper darkness. When the parties are winding down, the bars are closing up, and people just want to get home.

Of course, there's also the people who just want to fuck someone up this time of night, too. But they're easy to avoid, and if they haven't caught anyone by this point, they're probably not going to. This is the time when nightly fun and games switches over to alcohol- and fatigue-related traffic fatalities and code blues, instead of domestic free-for-alls or substance-fueled fights.

This is the time of night when the scar always turns hot and full, and I wonder if Perry's thinking of me.

It's anyone's guess.

High wispy clouds scudded over my city, and the swelling moon played peek-a-boo. I watched Zamba's house and thought about all this, breathing slowly, my pulse smooth and deep, silence drawn over me like a quilt. It smothered the little sounds that could give away my position—jingles of silver charms, the creak of leather, the subliminal sough of oxygen being taken in.

That silence is the first thing an apprentice learns, and the most thoroughly applied lesson imaginable. Sometimes you'll be deep in thought, and look up when you realize you've been making someone else uncomfortable. The quality of stillness in a hunter can verge on the uncanny.

It never bothers Saul, though. And really, cats can be just as still.

That was a distraction, and I didn't need a distraction inside Zamba's walls. That was officially a Very Bad Idea. The only Worse Idea was being distracted when dealing with Perry.

It's just a night for thoughts we'd rather not have, isn't it, Jillybean. I breathed soft and easy, considering Zamba's house. The peeling white split-level was completely dark. Blind windows watched the empty street.

I checked the moonphase again. No festivals in this particular part of this particular month, at least none that I could pin down off the top of my head. There was no reason for Zamba's house to be lit up, but there wasn't any reason for it to be dead dark either. And she wouldn't be a very good voodoo queen if she didn't have an idea that something was going on and I was likely to show up.

Then again, the sorcerous ability of a hunter usually means that you don't see us before we show up to knock you on your lawbreaking ass.

But I'd asked Galina to give her a ring.

It was the umpteenth time tonight I was feeling hinky

as hell. Either the successive shocks were making me jumpy, or it was thirteen o'clock around here.

Although it's *always* thirteen o'clock around Zamba. She's been around as long as Mikhail has, and she's always been the big power on the voodoo scene. If someone had taken her out and was messing with the Cirque as well . . .

I eased out of cover. Crossed the street, trying not to feel like the house was watching me approach.

Trying not to feel *lured*.

The last time I'd been out to visit her, Saul had been with me. We were digging to the bottom of a case involving two particular black sorcerers who just happened to be her devotees. Zamba hadn't been too happy about how that turned out—I got the feeling she'd been invested in their little rape and extortion stable, not to mention a profitable side-trade in the body parts for some of the, shall we say, less wholesome brand of sorcery you can tap as a *bocor*, the voodoo version of a black magician.

I used to get all twitchy about the less-positive side of voodoo until Mikhail pointed out it wasn't any different from people double-dealing each other in offices. The ambition of a *bocor* who sacrifices his friends and family is the same ambition that makes a workaholic cubicle-farmer double-deal his officemates and ignore or abuse his family. They're the same thing; the only question is one of *degree*. I just deal with the people who leave broken bodies and souls instead of broken careers in their wake. Lives are ruined just as surely by either brand of troublemaker.

And a good, fast, smart black sorcerer of any type can rise in the hierarchy of such things just like a conscienceless asshole can become a CEO. All it takes is the drive and the luck.

Zamba hadn't ever *overtly* gotten her hands dirty, and I hadn't been able to press the point. But this was an entirely different piece of pie. If someone was operating without her knowledge, it was a threat to her primacy. I was hoping it was that—if she had a vested interest in keeping her position, this would go a lot easier. She was a scumbucket, but she was a useful one, and less dirty than Perry by an order of magnitude.

If, on the other hand, the trouble started with her or one of her followers, we were looking at some serious unpleasantness. Best to get started on making it more unpleasant for her than for me.

The concrete walk unreeled under my gliding feet. The rickety stairs didn't move when I tested them, remembering the slip-sliding motion necessary to get up them without the rusted metal groaning and rubbing against the concrete slabs.

I did tell Galina to give Zamba a call, tell her I'd be by to see her. So why is the house dark?

I was too uneasy to ignore the way my nerves were twitching, pulled tight against each other. The sudden double sense—of being watched, and of ugliness about to happen—scraped me down to rawness in less than a second. I eased my right-hand gun out of its holster and breathed in, a long shallow inhale, poised on the steps.

Wait a second. The sense of being watched was coming from behind me, not from the dark windows.

I weighed the cost of looking over my shoulder. Was this a fakeout, or was something going on inside Zamba's house? Since Lorelei had just bit it, Zamba could be next. Or Melendez, or any of the larger fish in the Santa Luz voodoo-or-Santeria pool.

This makes no fucking sense. I think that so often before a case jells, it's a constant refrain. It just meant I wasn't seeing the pattern yet.

Between one blink and the next, I leapt forward, body stretching out. The stairs gave one howling groan as I pushed off, concrete squealing against iron framework, and my boots hit the door. Blue sparks crackled, an etheric strike as surely as a physical one, and the steel-reinforced door busted off its weakened hinges. I rode it all the way down, hitting with a hollow boom on the landing.

Up or down? But the decision had already been made, because something was moving. I leapt up and to the side, catching a banister and propelling myself over, one boot-toe pushing and my left arm doing most of the work. This swung me neatly around, and I hit the ground in the living room, rolling. It was *dark;* she had blackout shades on the windows or something, for fuck's sake.

I hit furniture—felt like the edge of a couch—and something that ground under my coat, sharp edges slicing. One whole wall of Zamba's living room was, if I recalled correctly, a multitiered altar to Ifa and several lesser *orisha,* built around a rock-walled fireplace. Drums should have been stacked against one wall, and the rest of the room should have been lined with furniture—two couches against the window, a long line of cushions for the lower-ranked devotees, and Zamba's thronelike recliner with its back to the altar, wheeled in by a couple of strong young men at the beginning of every court-holding session.

It was there, rolled to a stop on the floor with my eyes straining to pierce absolute blackness, that I remembered Zamba had a close personal relationship with the Twins. They had a whole quadrant on her main altar, and a private altar in her bedroom.

Don't ask how I know what's in her bedroom. Like I said, last time I was here, things got iffy.

My blue eye could get only confused images through a heavy, oppressive screen of etheric bruising. It was thick in here in more ways than one, a stench I was beginning to find all too familiar painting the back of my throat as I waited, full-length on the floor, hearing something shamble around in the living room.

And hearing the tapping skritches of thousands of little insect feet flooding up the stairs. The darkness came alive with tiny red dots blanketing the soaked carpet, and I was suddenly very sure that whether or not Zamba was involved, I'd find nothing living in this happy little split-level.

I was pretty sure I'd find plenty dead and moving around, though.

15

Fighting in the dark, especially when every footstep crunches with little moving bodies underneath, is no picnic. I couldn't tell how many there were—*a lot* was about all I could think, hearing them shuffle and close in on me. The roaches made little creaking sounds, a dry insect thrumming. My fist crunched through slippery flesh, I hooked my fingers and pulled, a gelatinous eyeball popping and running. Wet splorching hands fumbled at my waist—I kicked back, heard the splutter of contact and the crash as it flew back, hitting whatever was left of Zamba's altar.

And still they crowded me. What a welcoming committee. Either they had orders to kill whoever entered the house, or Zamba had fallen prey to something, or—

My aura flamed, sea-urchin spikes boiling with blue sparks. That was better and worse. Better because the shifting illumination gave me visuals to work on, instead of straining my other senses to place the opposition. Which meant I could afford to unlimber the whip.

But it was worse because it meant the atmosphere in here was boiling, and not about to calm down anytime soon. And the gloom only got more intense, clotting and thickening. A spiritual hematoma.

Bug guts slimed underneath, ground into the carpet. The roaches clattered and chattered, and the sound of dry tendons stropping each other as the zombies lurched around me.

The fighting art of hunters is a hodgepodge. Almost any martial art you can name, from *savate* to esoteric *t'ai chi*, is in there somewhere. You can never tell what move will save your ass, and every once in a while you have to run through everything you know just to keep it fresh. Of course we all have our *favorite* moves, but pulling something out of your ass in a fight is a good way to put your enemy down.

But for this—close combat in a dark space, with things pressing in on every side, more than I could comfortably count because I was too goddamn busy—I fell back on the fighting style Weres teach their young, relying on evasion, quickness, and grace. Whether or not I'm graceful is an open question, but evasion and quickness?

Yeah. Especially with the scar on my wrist whining a subvocal grumble as it spiked etheric energy through me, granting me a measure of inhuman speed.

Hellbreed speed.

These were new, juicy zombies dripping with roaches. Their reek clogged the throat, and if I hadn't had it drilled into me to *breathe, goddammit, breathe* by Mikhail endlessly I might have held my breath and passed out.

That wouldn't have been good. I splat zombies when

I'm going fast enough, but a helpless body on the floor wouldn't be so lucky. It would be pulled to pieces.

Step back, swing, fist blurring out to crunch through a rotted leering face, roaches dripping, a high tinkling childish laugh bouncing off the walls as the air thickened to paste, darkness *pressing* down as if I were the thing to be exorcised from this house, boots slipping and skidding in muck—

One leapt on my back and I got free, my legs tangling together. *Goddammit, too many of them, Jesus*— The scar chuckled wetly, pinging the nerves in my arm, sawing them like dry violin strings. The thing on my back exploded away with a wet popping sound, and right before I went down under a crushing weight of bodies I heard a coughing roar and the mechanical popping of a handgun. Sounded like a .22.

What the fuck—

Teeth crunched against my elbow, worrying at the tough leather. I struck out with fists and feet, something hit me behind the knees, and I starfished again, trying to get them *off* me, roaches skittering, little insect feet probing at my eyes and mouth—

Crunch! The weight suddenly lessened, and the roar became a steady snarl. I *knew* that voice, even though it held no relation to humanity. The world whirled into chaos, ripping and wet splorching noises, foulness gushing out. I was spattered with hot fluids, and the density in the air fled before the clean sound of my Were's battlecry.

I thought I told him to go home! I surged up, fighting for air and life, and they exploded off me.

It *was* Saul. He blurred between man and cougar, the

roar changing as his chest shifted dimensions. He didn't pause, either, sliding into cougarform and stretching as his claws took out an abdomen; he blurred up into humanshape, collided into another zombie with ribsnapping force and dropped gracefully back into catform again to avoid a strike. Seeing a Were fight is like seeing a tree bend itself to the wind, leaves fluttering. Every motion is thoughtlessly deliberate, beautifully precise. They never pause between humanshape and animal form, but the glimpses of unhuman geometry between the two are heartstopping in their beauty.

The popping of a handgun sounded again, and a high boy's voice, breaking as he cursed.

I launched myself, my hand sliding greasily against the balustrade, and hit the landing. Broke one zombie's neck, put it down, and ripped the other one off a supine human form. *Goddammit! Civilian.* The priorities of the situation shifted—I reached down with my hellbreed-strong right hand, grabbed a handful of flannel shirt, and tossed him unceremoniously out the door, not hard enough to bruise.

Or so I hoped.

Who the hell is that? I had no time to figure it out, because I heard Saul roar again and bolted up the stairs. A living carpet of roaches was trickling down the first two steep drops, the dots on their backs glaring at me.

Saul feinted, then reversed with sweet and natural speed. Another zombie exploded, foulness spattering both of us, and I leapt, meeting the next one with a crunch that rattled my teeth.

From there it was sheer instinct, fighting, with Saul at my side. We've done this so often—and I knew better than to ask him what the hell he was doing *here* until after things were under control.

There was a popping sound and the smell of wet salt and natron again. The roaches began to puff up into green smoke, and the zombies milled, losing their mass mind for a few crucial seconds. We waded into them, porous bones snapping like greenwood sticks and noisome fluids spraying and spattering.

Forensics was going to have a hell of a time with this place.

The roaches were popping out of existence, green fog knee-deep, and I hoped like hell there weren't more zombies downstairs. Whoever I'd dumped on the porch would be a prime target.

Saul's claws reached out, his fingers blurring between paw and hand, and sheared the last zombie's face clean off at the same moment that I hit it, double-fisted, and snapped ribs like matches. A few more moments' worth of work, and we were done here.

"Hey, sweetheart," he said as I stood panting and collecting myself.

Wouldn't you know it, even spattered with zombie goo he looked too good to be real. And now that the air was no longer paste-thick, ambient light was creeping around. It was no longer darker than midnight in a mine shaft.

I got my breath, ribs flickering. "Hey yourself." I turned on my heel and headed back down the stairs. My glutes were sure getting a workout from this case. "Civilian?"

"Kid," Saul said behind me, understanding immediately. "Gilberto. Says he heard you were coming out

Chesko way on the police scanner, figured you were heading for this place."

Oh, great. "For Christ's sake." But it showed promise, and intuition. Neither of which were going to help him once I got my hands on him.

After I secured the scene.

"Seems like an okay kid." That was as far as he would go. "You okay?"

"Fine. Just ducky." *I thought you were at home.* I glanced out onto the front porch.

Gilberto crouched, his eyes huge in his thin, sallow face. His hair was mussed, free of a hairnet for the first time and falling lank across his pimpled forehead. He held the .22 like it was his personal holy grail.

"Happy now?" I didn't have time to say much else. There was half a house that could be crawling with more zombies. "Watch him," I tossed over my shoulder, and plunged down the stairs.

The basement smelled bad but not overwhelmingly so. This used to be where Zamba kept a couple pit bulls all year, and a few goats inside during the autumn rains. The chickens had their own coop in the back yard, but as soon as my eyes adjusted I saw ragged bundles of feathers scattered over the concrete floor.

I hit the light switch. There was nothing living down here.

The dogs were shapeless lumps of fur. The feathers were chicken corpses, strewn around as if there had been some sort of explosion. In the middle of the basement, a chalk-and-cornmeal circle writhed. The lines were moving sluggishly as the sorcery in the air bled out, whispering with a sound like a kid drawing on pavement, a dry hollow whisper. The meal was scattering, bleeding away from the thin lines.

Inside the circle, the three goats were twisted together, their legs stiff with rigor mortis and their bellies bloated. The floor was awash with sticky, almost-dry blood.

This isn't real voodoo. Nobody even made an attempt to cook these, or to kill them kindly. My gorge rose, I pushed it down. Why was it that zombie-smell didn't make me puke, but the dead helpless bodies could?

No, the animals had been killed with sorcery. They lay twisted in agony, their throats ripped open. No self-respecting practitioner would do this. Not even a *bocor* would waste lives this flagrantly.

I examined every part of the scene I could see, gun in one hand, whip in the other. There were no teensy-tiny track marks in the blood here. My blue eye caught the fading marks of etheric violence, souls ripped from bodies.

The explosion of energy when something is killed is one form of food for the *loa;* it is the offering the practitioners use to make bargains or payments. Cooking and eating the animal afterward is a sacrament. Even a *bocor* won't waste good meat that often. But this kind of wanton death bore no relation to voodoo. It was destruction for its own sake—the destruction of souls, which carries its own price and its own charge of dark energy, like jet fuel. This was more like the work of the Sorrows, those soul-eating carrion.

The Church holds it as a point of doctrine that animals don't have souls. I know better. I've *seen* better. It's only one place where we differ, the Holy Mother Church and I.

There are plenty of others.

Oh, God. The basement was clear. I headed back up the stairs. Saul met me on the landing. "No more of them. Some bodies in the bedrooms, though."

In a minute. I nodded. Half-turned. Gilberto was still crouching on the porch, the wreck of the shattered door creaking as I stepped on it. He looked up at me, and before the walls behind his eyes could go up I caught a glimpse of what he must have looked like before whatever had made him into what he was.

The first time I'd met this kid, I'd known he was a killer. Strength, size, and speed are all useless without the willingness to do serious harm; someone smaller with the ruthlessness to hurt can take on a giant and come away a limping winner. The dead-eyed gangbanger had that willingness in spades. We recognize each other, those of us who have come out the other side of decency and settled for survival.

And sometimes, something just gets left out of people, and they don't see anything wrong with killing. That's one of the tests of taking on an apprentice—finding out if they're willing to hurt someone if they have to, or if they're just sociopaths.

You have to be sure. A hunter is a deadly thing, and that deadliness *has* to be disciplined. Otherwise you're no better than the things you put down. You're worse than a Trader, even.

"I told you to go home." I didn't have to work to sound unwelcoming. "Did you not hear me? I said go home, and leave the night alone."

"What was those?" He rose slowly, the gun dangling in his right hand. "Right out of a fucking horror movie, eh, *bruja?* And him, he's *el gato. Lobo hombre, gato hombre.*" He was breathing so fast his narrow ribs flickered. That smell was on him—desperation, wanting so hard the teeth ache as if under a bad load of sugar.

"You're not listening." I glanced at Saul. "He was already here?"

"Yup." Saul's eyes glowed orange for a moment. He stood easily on the stairs, his back to the entire upper portion of the house, and I suddenly wanted to check every single room and cupboard.

It was ridiculous. He said he'd checked, and I trusted him to tell me when part of a scene was cleared. That was the whole idea behind having a partner, wasn't it?

I trusted his judgment, didn't I?

Of course I did. I swallowed hard, prioritized. "And you came out here because . . ."

"Galina called. She got no answer when she dialed Zamba. Figured you might run into some trouble." One corner of his mouth curled up. "Besides, I like seeing you."

My own lips stretched into a grudging smile. How did he do that, make me feel good with five little words? "Flatterer."

"Hey, whatever works." In this light he didn't look nearly as tired. And no doubt about it, he'd pretty much saved my bacon. I would've survived, but still. "Where's Zamba?"

"Don't know. Any blondes in the wreckage?"

"Not that I saw, but the bodies are a little . . . well, you'll see."

I looked back out onto the porch. Gilberto was following our exchange. He wasn't pale or in shock. He was just as he'd always been—sallow and dirty-looking. His eyes were a bit wide, but that was all. He seemed to be handling this well.

It could've been an act. Gangs are big on face, and he probably had a lot of practice in not looking scared. But usually, when someone encounters the nightside for the first time, there's more trouble. Screaming, fainting, puking, rage—I've seen it all. The initial reaction doesn't mean much. It's how people deal with having the rationality of the world whopped away from under them over the long term that matters. After a brush with the nightside some retreat into rigid logic, a bulwark against something their upbringing tells them shouldn't exist. Others get increasingly loud and nervous, ending up wearing tinfoil hats and screeching about conspiracy aliens.

Some of them get really, really quiet, go home, and eat a bullet or some pills. It all depends.

On the other hand, in the barrio they know about Weres. Enough not to mess with them, at least.

Gilberto just looked at me, his chin coming up a little. Stubbornness made him look mulish, especially when he hunched his thin shoulders and peered out under strings of hair. *What's it gonna be,* that look asked. *What you gonna do with me? Because I ain't going home.*

I stared at him, trying to make a decision. It's not like snap decisions aren't a part of the job—some days, it's nothing *but,* and you have to make the right one in under a hundredth of a second. But this wasn't a decision that would or could be made without a lot of thought.

Then again, the students come along whether a teacher

is ready or not. The world was just full of on-the-other-hand answers today. "You got a car, Gil?"

He shrugged. Even the shrug was right—equal parts stray-cat insouciance and hesitation.

"All right. Here's the first thing: *don't* steal any fucking cars. From now on you don't break or even bend the law. Go back to my house. There's a key under one of the empty flowerpots stacked on the east side. Go inside and don't touch anything, unless you're getting yourself a snack. We'll talk when I get home, and I don't know when that will be. You got me?"

He nodded. The hunted look didn't go away, but at least he straightened a little.

"I mean it," I persisted. "Don't steal a car. Don't break the speed limit. If you have a gun, clean or not, ditch it before you step in my door. You come in clean, or I won't have anything to do with you."

"I'm not stupid." The sullenness returned.

"Prove it by being clean when you step in my door. Stay inside, don't leave until I talk to you. Go on, now."

He shrugged. His slim brown fingers loosened, and he dropped the .22. It made a heavy sound when it hit the porch, and I winced internally. *He's going to be a live one.*

I watched him go down the sobbing, squeaking steps. He headed across the street and vanished into the darkness. I hoped he made it, and I hoped he listened to me.

Then I shelved that hope, scooped up his .22, and got back to the problem at hand.

This was not looking good at all.

"What just happened?" Saul still stood on the stairs, watching. Bits of zombie glop still clung to him, dripping off the fringe of his jacket. It was going to be a job and a half cleaning the suede up. Thank God he believes in Scotchgarding everything. It doesn't do much good with the rags my clothes end up as, but it works wonders for his.

"I don't know yet." *I might have an apprentice, that's all. We'll see.* "Best to keep him out of the way until I do." I checked the pistol, made sure the safety was on, and wondered if it was one I'd seen him use before.

The thought of that case was uncomfortable, to say the least. And Saul still hadn't asked any questions about it. And there was a grave up on Mount Hope, with a good cop sleeping under a green blanket. The people responsible had been mostly cleaned up—but not all of them.

Prioritize, Jill. Get back up on the horse. "When did Galina call?"

"Just as I got in the door. I came out here. Was wondering what the hell the kid was doing here when I heard the fight." He shrugged, stuck his hands in his pockets. "Any idea what's going on yet?"

"Not much. Other than these cases are connected somehow. And if Zamba's not a body here, she might be involved."

"Great." He sounded as thrilled as I felt about that. "What does she look like again?" As if he wouldn't remember her, but he was being sure. Checking. It was a partner's responsibility to check.

"Blond dreadlocks. Tall. Bad legs, but a good smile." I tried a smile on my own face, but it felt like plastic. This was going south fast. "Show me the bodies. Let's get this wrapped."

"Sure thing." But he just stood there, looking at me, for a long moment. "I'm glad I came out."

What do you want, a tickertape parade? But that was uncharitable of me. I could just chalk it up to nerves, couldn't I? "Me too, catkin. Let's see those bodies."

"Are you really?" It wasn't like him to persist. "You sure?"

I exaggerated rolling my eyes, just like a teenager. I'll never see the sunny side of thirty again, but sometimes eyerolling is so satisfying I don't care. "Of *course* I'm glad. Jesus, Saul, what's up with you?" *And can it wait? I've got a city about to blow sky-high here, and a pattern I don't like the looks of underneath.*

"Nothing." He turned gracefully and led me up the stairs. "There are bodies in the bedrooms, nothing in the kitchen but a pot on the stove. Smells like the other place, a little."

"But no blondes? Blond dreadlocks, waist-length?" Wide face, big nose, bad skin, rotting teeth rimmed with gold making a bright-starred smile, and those dreadlocks. Zamba was tall and almost breastless, and I'd sometimes thought she was in drag. Nowadays you can't tell, and dealing with 'breed on a regular basis will wallop some of your assumptions about gender pretty hard.

"Come and see."

Goddammit. But he was right not to tell me, I suppose. I might not have believed it, if he had.

It was nine bodies, all told. I recognized an ebony-skinned trio, male and female, who had been Zamba's longtime acolytes. There was a small, compact Hispanic male—Zamba was truly catholic in her choice of trainees—and a taller, Grecian redhead. A double-gemini of husky dark-haired males completed the sets. They were three to a room, her inner circle all naked and twisted together like the goats in the basement. The beds had been scattered with chrysanthemum petals, and their throats had been ripped out.

They probably wouldn't rise as zombies, though I would nail the palms and feet before Forensics got here. There wasn't enough etheric residue in them to power that kind of motion, though. Zamba's devotees had been *eaten*. And either someone had brushed aside Zamba's protections and killed her followers and her, or . . .

Jesus.

In the kitchen, a pot on the stove was long cool. A stringy brew of something that smelled vaguely similar to Lorelei's still-bubbling concoction rested under a thick scrim of clotted grease. The kitchen was otherwise spic-and-span, the attached dining room where Zamba fed her acolytes holding a long table, chairs ranked neatly, and an altar on the wall under the window that looked out on the side-yard and the wall of the abandoned house next door.

"What do you make of this?" Saul asked quietly. He stood by the sink, arms folded, looking at the bottle of dishwashing liquid and scrubbies, neatly placed in a chrome rack.

"I don't like that we can't find her body." *That's just one of the things I don't like about this.*

"Any chance she could be the one behind all this?"

Trust him to say what I was thinking. "More than a chance, catkin. Still, I suppose there's always room to hope she's not. I'd like it better if the bitch was dead."

"Now there's something I don't hear you say often." He peered out the window. "It's almost dawn."

No shit. This has been a long night. I spotted the phone, hanging at the end of the counter. "If Zamba's behind this, it's bad news. If she's just disappeared it's bad news too; it means we might have another body site." I let out a sigh. The smell was bad, the situation was worse, and I had the idea I wasn't going to spend today sleeping, either. "I've got to call in and see who they can spare to come out and process this site too. No rest for the wicked."

"Amen to that." His shoulders went down a little. Had he been bracing himself? For what? "What's our next step?"

I thought about it. "Calling someone to come out and take care of this site. Seeing if I overlooked Zamba's body downstairs or in the back yard. Going over this place with a fine-tooth comb, then going through the files—" I tapped the counter with bitten-down nails, my fingers drumming. "This has all the earmarks of a serious fucking tangle."

As usual, Saul put the question in reasonable terms. "If Zamba *is* behind this, what does she have against the Cirque?"

"I don't—" I straightened, suddenly, and stared at the pot on the stove. "Huh."

Saul kept quiet, looking at the sink, and let me wander around inside my head. It was good to have him there—he served up the right questions, and knew when to keep his mouth shut so I could *think*. I found myself studying the lines of his fringed jacket, his jeans splattered with zombie, the edge of the stove, his boots, my own boot-toes. Eyes roving, snagging on the linoleum as I pursued the line of thought to its logical end, found it wanting—but not wanting enough.

"If a better theory comes along, I'll snag it," I decided out loud. "Call this scene in, I'm going to check the back yard and the houses on either side."

"I'm coming with you." His jaw jutted, stubbornly.

Oh, for Chrissake. "Of course you are. *After* you call."

16

*P*iper was still processing the last scene. This time Foster showed up, his own brown ponytail slick as ever. He surveyed the stinking goop starred with porous bones that had been zombies and sighed. "Busy night. Anything else?"

I almost hated to tell him. Foster always reminds me of an otter—brown, sleek, with a cute little nose and quick clever fingers. "The bedrooms. Don't take the iron nails out of the corpses. And there's animals downstairs."

"Well, shit." But he motioned his team past, Carolyn holding the door log in front of her like a holy grail, Max with his camera, Stephanie and Browder with their matching smiles and bags of gear. "*Beaucoup* overtime."

Behind them, Sullivan and the Badger showed up. The Badger negotiated the stairs with her mouth set tight and turned down, her gray hair pulled back into its usual bun, the white streak down one side glinting, since I'd flicked the porch lights on. Sullivan, scratching at his coppery stubble, gave me a weak grin. He looks like dishwater even on a good day, but that pale, nervous exterior hides a sharp, inductive mind.

The Badger looks like a cookie-baking, kitten-sweatshirt-and-mom-jean-wearing soccer mom—a particularly cuddly and harmless one. She'd added a pair of steel-framed glasses to her round florid face, and moved carefully. I wasn't fooled—for such a rotund woman, she was light on her feet when it counted. And they don't call her the Badger for her hair.

No, she gets that name by being tenacious as hell. She does it in such a nice, unassuming way that people forget her namesake has teeth *and* claws.

Rumor has it she went a couple of rounds with a sex offender once, and busted him up bad by the time backup arrived. The perp thought one plump lady cop would be easy to bowl over. He spent three weeks in the hospital and another couple months in physical therapy, I was told.

I'd lay odds it's true.

"How many fucking scenes you going to give us tonight?" Sullivan said, blinking. He patted his breast pocket, where a pack of Marlboro Lights peeped up at me. For someone who looks so washed-out, he certainly has a big strident voice.

"As many as I've got. Hi, Badge."

She grunted, heaved herself up onto the porch, and eyed me. "Thought you didn't want a team tonight."

I shrugged. Silver tinkled in my hair, falling over my shoulders. "With bodies mounting up like this, I need backup." *I'm glad it's you two.*

"Huh. Should we check the other scenes?" It's amazing, the way her soft, modulated voice can slice through a hubbub. One of the forensic techs was laughing—shrill laughter with that edge of disgust you hear so often at homicide scenes.

It's not disrespectful. It's because sometimes you have to laugh to keep from screaming, crying, or throwing up. "Might as well. This turned out bigger than I thought it'd be. I thought I could save you guys some work."

Sullivan wheezed and the Badger chuckled. "You kidding?" she got out, between snickers. "If we wanted less work we wouldn't have chosen *this* job."

"Very funny. Make sure the techs don't take the nails out of the hands and feet. See if you can get any IDs on the messy bodies; the less-messy ones will be easier but I already know who they are. Find out where they were last seen, see if you can trace the animals—"

"Animals?" Sullivan's pale face twisted up. The short buzz of his coppery, receding hair glittered again as he hunched his shoulders. "Shit."

"Sorry." And I was.

"Well, you didn't kill 'em." He stuffed his hands in his pockets. "Should we go over Piper's scenes too?"

I nodded. Saul moved briefly behind me, a restless movement utterly unlike him. "Please do. Oh, and see if you can dig up who this house actually belongs to. I'd like a legal name, DOB, everything." *I don't know nearly enough about Zamba. That's going to change.*

"That means you have a hunch." The Badger nodded. "Don't worry, I won't ask—I know I don't want to know. I'll page you as soon as we have something."

And bless her thoroughgoing little heart, she would

have the full report from chowder to cashews—or as close to it as it was humanly possible to get. "Good deal. Thanks." I eased past both of them—the Badger stood stolidly and Sullivan flinched back. He covered it well, though, turning to look down at the garden.

"Huh," he said. "Go figure."

"What?" I glanced down at the belt of jungle greenery, uncomfortably reminded of Lorelei's backyard.

"Plants are dying. Looks like someone did a lot of work on the yard, though. You'd think, a place like this, they wouldn't have stopped watering before they died. Or are the bodies old?"

"Not *too* old." *Especially the ones that were trying to kill me about half an hour ago.* But they didn't need me to lay that little thought in their heads. "See you."

Sullivan sighed. "See you, Jill. Try not to trip over any more dead 'uns tonight."

"Shut up, Sully. It's our *job*." The Badger sounded long-suffering, as usual, and she herded him inside the house.

What a pair.

Saul drifted beside me as I made my way down the cracked, zigzagging walk. "Car's this way."

I nodded, let him take the lead. Sullivan was right, the garden was just in the first stages of dying. Plants were drooping, but not browned and crispy yet.

I stopped, turned, and looked back at the house, its windows blazing with golden light now. A hose was coiled up next to the porch's listing sneer.

Hellebore. Feverfew. Foxglove. Wormwood. Mugwort. Bindweed. American ginseng under a rigged-up canvas canopy. Some succulents, but not many, and the rest of the plants were useful, in one way or another, to a rogue herbalist or kitchen witch.

Or a voodoo queen.

The zombies were relatively fresh. So were the bodies. Rigor mortis doesn't last *that* long. Bellies were distended on the goats downstairs, but that happens . . . I'd need an autopsy to be reasonably sure of time of death.

But the garden, though. Things wilt fast out here in the desert, but if things were normal out here at Mama Zamba's—if normal could be the word applied to the biggest wheel in the voodoo community in my town—the garden should be in tiptop shape for a little while after she was dead.

So what had kept her so busy her garden didn't get watered? She had people to do it *for* her.

But those people were dead.

The zombies were too juicy and the human bodies were too fresh. It just *didn't add up.* Unless the reigning queen of the voodoo scene had had something more than gardens on her mind lately—and on the minds of her followers.

Her newly dead followers.

"What are you thinking?" Saul finally asked as I stood staring at Zamba's garden like I was hypnotized.

"I don't quite know yet," I admitted. "It's more and more likely Zamba's involved instead of a victim. I think we should get some breakfast, since dawn's coming up."

"And then?"

I tested the hypothesis in my head. I just didn't know enough to see if it explained everything. "And then we're going to visit Galina again. If she hasn't gone through her diaries yet, I'll wait while she does. I've got a theory, but I can't figure one thing out."

"That one thing would be?"

"Why a voodoo queen has it in for the Cirque. You'd think if she hated hellbreed she'd find some closer to home to murder."

17

Micky's on Mayfair was just the same as it always is around dawn—almost deserted, clean as a whistle, and staffed with Weres. Some of the waitstaff are humans, true, but the greater percentage including the owner are from the Santa Luz prides, packs, and flights.

Amalia, a lioness of the Norte Luz pride, greeted us at the door. "Jill, nice to see you. Dustcircle." She nodded, and Saul nodded back. "A table? Or is it business?"

I must have looked grim, and realized I was dirty and disheveled. They do usually see me in this state, but I'd been thinking so hard even my nose had shut off.

"A table," Saul said as I cast around vainly for something to wipe off with. "Does Theron have any towels lying around?"

"I'll check." She grinned, her broad, high-cheek-boned face lighting up. I suddenly felt even more dirty and mucky, snuck a peek at Saul. He was just the same as ever, his essential difference shining out from under weariness and zombie muck, and I felt myself deflate like a punctured balloon. It wasn't fair. They're so much better than we could ever be, the Weres.

No wonder humans hunted them, during the bad old days of the Inquisition. The only thing humans hate more than ugliness is actual beauty.

Theron, a lean dark Werepanther, actually came out from the bar to greet us, wiping his hands on a white cloth that had seen much, much better days in the bleach bucket. His long fingers danced with it, refolding it so the holes didn't show. "Hey, Saul. Glad to see you back."

"Theron." Saul gave him an answering grin. "How's bartending?"

"Good work if you can get it." Theron's dark gaze flicked past to me, and his forehead furrowed. "Jill."

"Hey. Sorry, I smell. Got a spare towel?" As usual, I sounded more truculent than I really was. They were just so pretty. Amalia's face was flawless, not a pore in sight, and neither of the two males would ever lack for female attention.

It made me wonder what the hell Saul was doing with me. Not for the first time, and a question I was mulling over more and more lately.

"You bet." But Theron stayed where he was, looking first at Saul, then curiously at me, the line deepening. "Um . . ."

"She's hungry." Saul folded his arms, and a hint of gravel poured through the bottom of the words.

It was so unlike him my jaw threatened to drop. But Theron just shrugged, Amalia tipped me a wink and a salute, and both of them disappeared, leaving us to seat ourselves.

"What was that?" I poked him on the shoulder when he didn't respond. "Saul?"

He gave me a single dark glance, hitched one shoulder up, and dropped it. I sighed and considered folding my arms, but Saul set off for our regular booth along the back wall and Theron showed up again, carrying a stack of damp washcloths.

"Here you go." The Werepanther gave me a meaningful look. I raised my eyebrows, my hands full of warm, sopping wet cloth. "You guys want a beer?"

"Might as well." I wiggled my eyebrows and pointed my chin at Saul's retreating back. *What's up with him? Help me out here.*

Theron just looked confused, a blush sliding along his high-arched cheekbones. His dark hair fell across his forehead, curls and waves damp with sweat. It looked like Micky's had seen a heavy night; he was just cleaning up before dawn.

The liquor laws in Santa Luz kind of don't apply to the nonhumans. Hellbreed and Trader bars go the same way, only they rollick far harder than any place the Weres run.

In *both* senses of the word. Harder, dirtier, and far, far fouler.

"What's wrong?" I mouthed, wishing my eyebrows would go up higher and that my face could communicate the complexity of the question I wanted to ask.

Theron spread his hands helplessly, spun on the balls of his feet, and set off for the hall running alongside the kitchen. It actually looked like he was *retreating*.

What the hell is going on here? The washcloths— they were bar towels, soaked and smelling of bleach and fresh laundry—dripped in my hands, rapidly cooling. Nobody was likely to give an answer. I heard one of the cooks in the depths of the kitchen off to my right swear, and the hiss of something hitting the grill.

Yeah, sometimes when you go into Micky's around dawn, you get what the cooks think you should eat instead of anything on the menu. It's always good, and you should never look a Were's gift in the mouth, so to speak.

I shook my head, silver clicking in my hair, and headed for the girls' room. I'd probably feel better about all this once I was a little cleaner.

Then again, I thought, clutching the washrags, *maybe I won't.*

Saul slid the file across the table at me and tucked into his fried-eggs-and-ham. I took a long pull off a bottle of microbrew Theron had slung on the table and eyed the steak-and-eggs combo, hash browns cremated the way I like them, extra bacon, and toast slathered with butter. It probably had enough calories in it to keep me fueled through a long night of chasing evil. I wondered if it would fuel my brain enough for me to figure out the pattern behind the murders.

Once I started eating, I realized how hungry I was. This led to a good quarter-hour spent in silence, just the clinking of forks on plates and an occasional slurp. I finished my beer and another arrived. So did more toast. Amalia simply plunked down a fresh plate of it and raised an eyebrow—about the closest she'd get to telling me I'd better eat it all.

Weres. It's only one of the ways they show they care.

I cut a strip of steak, sliced it up, and was grateful it wasn't rare. Now that the first edge of hunger was past I could slow down and enjoy the taste. There had to have been at least five eggs on the plate.

Fighting off the undead and Hell's citizens all night does work up a girl's appetite. Sorcery can only do so much, and I wasn't as young as I used to be. I used to be able to go for days without eating, running from one thing to the next, writing checks my body cashed without complaining too much.

Not anymore.

Go figure.

I finally looked up from my plate to find Saul chewing slowly, watching me. His eyes were dark and fathomless.

I swallowed a mouthful of steak, glad Micky's was empty. My skin twitched under the sensory overload from the unveiled scar, every noise and photon amped up exponentially. "Hi," I said finally. "Good to see you."

A small smile lifted the corner of his chiseled mouth. "Hi, kitten. Nice to see you, too."

Is it? Or are you just saying that? "This is looking like a huge problem."

"Isn't it always." But his tone was reflective and amused, faintly sarcastic. "You think it's connected?" One lifted eyebrow could have meant that he agreed, or that he wanted to give me a chance to get my thoughts in order.

I ticked them off on my fingers. "Those bugs. Each with a red spot. The green smoke. Voodoo practitioners dead, zombies everywhere, possessed people that shouldn't be, one of them ending up as a zombie, and Zamba missing. The Cirque's hostage attacked, and another Cirque performer dead. Both Zamba and Lorelei had something cooking on their stoves . . ."

"If it looks like a duck, swims like a duck, quacks like a duck—"

"—it's certainly not a zebra," I finished. "So, they're more than likely connected, all these things. I just don't know *how* yet." I forked up another load of eggs. "What possible connection could the Cirque have with any voodoo practitioner?"

"I don't know."

I took another long swallow of beer. It went down nice and easy. Wrestling zombies gives you a powerful thirst. "Voodoo and hellbreed don't tangle. It's just one of those things."

"They must mix sometimes," he pointed out practically.

I shook my head. Silver shifted and chimed, and some of my curls were stiff with gunk. "The *loa* are jealous, and hellspawn don't like anything interfering with their games either."

"What about . . ."

I watched him, fork paused in midair, but he merely shrugged.

"No," he finally amended. "I got nothing."

"And then there's this." I yanked the plastic-shrouded straight razor out of my pocket, laid it on the table. Next out was the enamel cup.

Put together, they looked shoddy. The straight razor crouched in its swaddling, and the cup's chipped sides reflected fluorescent light.

"A razor? And a cup." He set his fork down. "Huh."

"Yeah. My instincts are all tingling, but I don't know what they're saying."

"Tingling instincts?" He might have looked bland and interested, except for the wicked twinkle in his eyes. "I hear they have creams for that."

A chuckle caught me off-guard. "They're not *burning*. Just tingling. Anyway, and then there's zombies. It takes work and effort to create one with voodoo. Now all of a sudden they're crawling around everywhere—and the Twins are taking an active interest in everything."

It was a huge pileup of events. The more I sat back and considered, the more it seemed like one thing.

"What?" Saul speared a piece of fried ham. "You look like you just thought of something."

"I did." I applied myself to clearing my plate, but I also hooked the file a little closer and flipped it open. There might not be anything in it, but it was best to check.

"Well?" He didn't quite fidget, but he did shift on his side of the table, his long legs stretched out until his boot-toe touched my calf.

"Nothing solid yet, catkin. Let me think." I scanned the file, flipping past Xeroxed pages and paperwork filled in with Avery's neat scrawl. Lucky boy, our first victim, Mr. Ricardo. A green card and everything. Avery, bless his little heart, had even pulled the application for me. I'd bet anything Juan Rujillo, our local FBI contact, had facilitated that little search as a favor. Dear old Juan, a joy to work with. Not like the last Feeb we had.

Hmm. That's interesting.

Ricardo even had a sponsor. The little click of a puzzle piece sliding home sounded in the middle of my head, and I took a long draft of beer. "Hey, Saul. Guess what? Ricardo had a green card."

"Mmmh." He had a full mouth. He was busy slathering even more green Tabasco on the remainder of his ham. "Mmmmh?"

"Guess who his sponsor was."

"Mrph?" He jabbed at his plate and shrugged.

"Lorelei." I slapped the file closed as his chewing stopped and his eyebrows went back up in surprise. "As soon as we finish here, we're heading for Galina's. I'll bet your ham and my entire plate she knows something about this, and she's had a chance to go through her diaries by now."

18

Dawn came up in gray streaks, followed by rose and gold. Once the sun heaved itself up over the rim of the world, I let out a half-conscious sigh of relief. My pager stayed quiet, and—true to my guess—Galina had spent all night with not only her own diaries but the records of the Sanctuary before her. Huge leather-bound books, each cover stamped with the seal of the Order, stood in stacks on her butcher-block table.

She was covered in dust, her hair held back with a red kerchief, and as ill-tempered as I'd ever seen her. Which was still pretty damn polite.

"Lorelei's dead?" A line etched itself between her winged eyebrows. She swiped at a smudge on her cheek. "And zombies at Zamba's? Christ. Try saying that ten times in a row."

"Tell me about it. No, wait. Never mind. Tell me about the problem Sloane had with the Cirque." I folded my arms and leaned against the wall. Saul was fiddling with the kettle and her stove. Gray dawn filtered through the skylight and the big box window, touching his shorn hair and wide shoulders.

"I've been going back through the records." She spread her hands. "I was wrong. It wasn't Arthur Gregory. The trouble started with Sam."

"Rosehip tea?" The kettle started to chirp, and Saul looked over his shoulder.

"Oh, yes. Yes indeed." Galina dropped into a straight-backed wooden chair, swept the kerchief off. Her marcel waves were disarranged.

"Coming right up." Saul didn't ask if I wanted tea.

I stifled a burp. Now that I'd eaten, I was beginning to realize how tired I was.

No rest for the wicked, though. "Sam?" I prompted.

"Samuel Gregory. Arthur's younger brother. Arthur came to Sloane needing help—his brother had disappeared. The Cirque was in town, and Sloane suspected them, but he couldn't find the boy. Arthur kept following Sloane around, pestering him. He didn't get what he wanted, so he went elsewhere."

"Elsewhere?" It could mean just about anything.

"He apparently decided that since Sloane couldn't help him, he'd make a deal with someone who would."

Not too bright of him. But sometimes civilians make that sort of mistake. "Hellbreed?"

She shook her head. Her earrings—little peridots in marcasite—swung. "Voodoo. Or so I heard. Sloane suspected Lorelei. She wasn't Lorelei then, she was Abigail Figueroa. It was in the seventies that she switched over to—"

"Hold on." *This may be connected, but* how? I dropped

down into a chair myself, my brain buzzing. "This Arthur. He had a hard-on for the Cirque?"

"I don't know. I do know Sloane suspected that was where Samuel disappeared to, and dug pretty hard to find him. Arthur disappeared, and Sloane went looking for him too. He came across some of the Cirque folk running a game on the side—something to do with child-slaves, I think, though he never said—and put them out of commission. He tried to find either of the Gregory boys, but neither of them ever showed up. He was still working that case, off and on, when the outbreak happened."

Yeah, that would put a dent in working a case or two. "So it never got wrapped up. And it's only vanishingly likely it's connected to what we have going on now. Was there any proof at all that this Arthur kid went to voodoo? Or did Sloane just suspect?"

Of course, a hunter's suspicion is sometimes good as gold. But you can't move without proof, or you turn into what you're hunting. It's just one of those things.

"The last place Arthur was seen was going into Lorelei's old shop. She used to be down near Plaskény Square instead of on Greenlea; I can't believe I'd forgotten that. Anyway, Sloane had a witness who placed him there before he disappeared. There was something else. People who knew the boys turned up dead."

"Like who?"

"Their father, for one. A real winner—the kind who likes to use the strap. He ended up torn in pieces and scattered around his rooming house cot, blood all over the walls. Another man—he'd apparently been their mother's other pimp." She glanced at me, then swiftly back at the table. "It was a different world then, Jill."

I wondered what my face was saying. "Not so different. So the 'father' was a husband, and she had another pimp?" I knew that game, I'd seen it played before, up close. A woman desperate for any kind of attention, selling herself to and for the man who promised to protect her while she nursed bruises from the other man—and when the first one beat her again, she'd go back to the second. It was a vicious cycle.

"Bounced back and forth between them. Poor kids." Galina's eyes were dark and troubled. "There were others. A few police detectives—ones on the take, Sloane said—and a schoolkid who hung out with the Gregory boys, was apparently a bit of a bully."

"That's a high body count. They can't have been unrelated."

"Life was cheap back then, Jill. This was a mining town and a riverport. I remember when you didn't dare go outside at night if you were a respectable female. At least, not without a man and a gun." For a moment she looked much older, her mouth pulled down and her cheeks sucked in. "Anyway, the deaths were all the same. Torn into tiny pieces, lots of blood."

Life is still cheap around here, Galina. At least, if you're brown-skinned or poor. Gold leached in through the skylight, taking on the tenor of daylight.

I rolled my shoulders back in their sockets, trying to ease a persistent ache. "Huh. I wonder . . . I should still have some of Sloane's records. Can you write down the dates for me?"

"I can do that." She looked, in fact, relieved to be

given a concrete task. I didn't blame her. Digging through old records can be deadly boring, and for a Sanctuary it was probably even more so. They drive their roots in deep and live a long time, but the things they trade for it . . . you don't make a bargain like that without wondering if it's worth it.

Or at least, that's what I think about every bargain. The world keeps asking you to peel bits of yourself away, just to keep breathing.

The kettle whistled, Saul flicked the stove off and poured. And as usual, he asked the right question. "So is someone settling scores?"

I stared at the leather-bound books. She must have been excavating all night. "Possible. But why try to kill the hostage? That won't damage the Cirque. It will remove the constraints that make them behave. And Helene . . ."

I hate that feeling—when you think you have a lead, and all you get is more questions.

"It was a long time ago," Galina said softly. "Long and long."

"Do we have any pictures of either of the Gregorys?" There wasn't much hope.

She sighed, a flicker of irritation crossing her round face. It wasn't with me—although heaven knows Galina usually has enough reason. "No, unfortunately. This is so *frustrating*. I feel like there's something I should be remembering." She stared at the books as Saul handed her a mug.

I blew out a long breath. "Well, it was almost a century ago, Galina. It's not like forgetting what you had for lunch yesterday."

"It kind of is, though. This is important. It's just on the tip of my brain. But I should have noted it, and I've been all through my official diary and the private one. It feels unfinished."

"Life is full of unfinished things." I glanced at Saul, who stretched his long legs out. *This is all very historical and interesting, but it sounds like a dead end. There's nothing to tie an old case to what's going on now, unless it's Lorelei. And she had her fingers in so many nasty pies, it's not very likely she was just now killed for something that happened almost a hundred years ago. No, the connection's probably elsewhere. Which means I'm right back where I started—except I have a missing voodoo queen, zombies, dead hellbreed, and a situation that could get Very Messy Indeed.* The exhaustion came back, circling like a shark.

Prioritize, Jill.

I took it out loud, so I could think it through better. "The attack on the hostage was voodoo. Perry's supposed to stay and make sure the hostage doesn't bite it. In any case, it'll be nightfall before someone can try again." *One problem that doesn't have to be solved immediately.* I stared at the leather-bound books heaped on the table, breathed in deeply. Galina blew across the top of her tea. "I've got voodoo practitioners dropping like flies, spirits in people who shouldn't have them—though if they're believers, it changes the equation a little—and one of them came down with a bad case of zombie. *And* Zamba's missing in action. She could quite possibly be needing protection, or she's part of this. Either of which is equally unprepossessing. I've got Forensics collecting evidence, and Sullivan and the Badger doing some digging."

It took me a couple more seconds to piece everything together.

"What's up next?" Saul, as usual, gave the right question.

"Going home and getting cleaned up," I decided. "Figuring out what to do about that kid. Then the next step."

"Which is? And what kid?" Galina took a gulp of her tea. Maybe she needed it to wash the taste of history and dust out of her mouth.

"The kid who's been following me around. And the next step is visiting some *botanicas*. Zamba wasn't the only game in town, just the biggest one." I pushed myself up to my feet and almost regretted it. Aches and pains twinged all over my body.

"An apprentice?" The Sanc looked at me like I'd just expressed a desire to take off my clothes and howl naked in the street. "When did this happen?"

"It hasn't happened yet." I pushed my chair in. The sunlight strengthened. It looked like another beautiful day. "Right now I just want him kept out of trouble."

"That's funny." Galina's tone suggested it wasn't funny at all. "That's just what Sloane said about Arthur Gregory. I remember *that* much, at least."

For once, I observed the speed limit. Saul turned the radio's volume knob and lit a Charvil, and dawn traffic was light. Santa Luz sometimes looks washed out, the sun bleaching buildings and dirt, the dust haze putting everything in soft focus. The greens are pale sage, the whites turn taupe and buff, and any dab of brightness gets covered with a thin film before long.

It's different in the barrio. Bright blocks of primary color are a little more cheerful in the daylight—but a little more carnivorous at night. Even well-tended lawns look anemic under the first assault of morning light. It isn't until the richness of twilight that things take on that mellow gold tinge, like waking up from a siesta with the world scrubbed clean and a little brighter.

It could just be me. But things seem tired in the morning. The day has risen, wearily, from the bowl of night. It's when I get to go home, because the nasty things mostly stick to darkness to do their dirtiness.

They don't call it the nightside for nothing.

And this morning seemed a little darker than usual. The windows were down and the radio was off, early coolness rising from the river and a promise of scorching later, but I thought I heard something else under the purring engine and the rushing air. The scar had been uncovered almost all night, and the sensory acuity was beginning to seem normal. The noise resolved itself into notes from a steam-driven calliope in the distance.

A bright, cheery tune. That "Camptown Races" thing again, but with a darker edge. And the shadows were wrong this morning. Just by a millimeter or two, but they were at strange angles, and darker than the usual knife-sharp morning shadows. Gleams flickered through them—pairs of colorless gleams, low and slinking.

It wasn't precisely against the rules for the Cirque's dogs to be out running—but it was strange.

Stranger than someone with a grudge against both

voodoo practitioners and hellbreed? Or stranger than Zamba disappearing and her entire household laid waste?

Stranger than Perry doing exactly what I tell him to?

The more I thought about it, the more my brain just went in circles. Even intuition wasn't any help; it just flailed and threw up its hands. I was too tired, and getting dull-witted. Fatigue is a risk during cases like this.

"Goddammit," I sighed, and Saul exhaled a long tobacco-scented sigh as well.

"Jill." He sounded serious.

"Huh?" *The thing that troubles me most,* I decided, *is not finding Zamba's body. That slippery little bitch wouldn't have let anyone kill her closest followers. That was her power base, the ones that ran herd on all the others.*

Always assuming someone *else* had killed them.

"We need to talk."

Oh, Christ. Not now. "What's up?"

Seconds ticked by. I braked to a stop on Chesko. We'd turn and go up Lluvia Avenue. The engine hummed to itself, a familiar song.

The light turned green. Saul still said nothing. "What is it?" I prompted again, touching the accelerator. We moved smoothly forward, and no, it wasn't my imagination. The colorless eyes in the shadows were following us.

Great.

"I love you." He tossed the half-smoked Charvil away. It somersaulted in the slipstream and was gone. I checked the rearview. *Just wonderful. Jesus.* "You know that, right?"

"I do." *That's not the problem. The problem is that you can't stand to touch me now. And there's a bigger problem right now, too. It has to do with those eyes in the shadows. The ones watching us right now.*

Why now? Nighttime was their time.

There was another long pause, like he was waiting for me to say something. I kept checking the mirrors. *Is this trouble? Why would they wait for daylight?*

"Are you—" He tapped another Charvil up out of the pack. Held it in his long expressive fingers. I checked to make sure his seat belt was on. Of course it was. I pressed the accelerator a little harder. "Are you listening to me?"

"Of course I am." The needle climbed, slowly but surely. The shadows were thickening, and I got a very bad feeling. "You said you love me. I said I know. You asked—"

"Jill. There's something . . ." He twitched, looked out the window. "Is something following us?"

"Hang on." My fingers caressed the gearshift. "Half a second."

"Goddammit. There's never a minute alone with you."

"You're alone with me right now." The shadows were growing blacker, their crystalline eyes reflecting daylight stripped of all its warmth.

I mashed the accelerator. Tires chirped, and the Pontiac leapt forward obediently.

We roared down Lluvia, the shadows keeping pace. They circled as we bounced over the railroad tracks and down a long sun-drenched stretch of road. Here the sun hit a wall of warehouses dead-on to my left, and there wasn't a shadow to be found—except the shadow of the Pontiac, running next to us with its own loping stride. The tires made low sounds of disapproval, I skidded into a turn and jagged right on Sarvedo Street, working the turn like threading a needle in one motion. Saul grabbed at the dash, breaking his Charvil and giving me a single reproachful look.

My warehouse was about ten blocks down, and even from here my smart eye could see the layers of protection on my walls waking in bursts of blue etheric flame.

Oh, holy shit. There's a civilian in there. I sent him in myself.

I jammed the accelerator to the floor and prayed I wasn't too late.

19

I bailed out in a blur, Saul right behind me, and I didn't have to break my own door down. The entire warehouse was tolling like a bell in a windstorm, and there was a gaping hole where the front door used to be. Green smoke billowed out, thinning in the morning breeze, and there wasn't a shadow to be found.

The fume was acrid, tasting of rotten pumpkins and stale cigar smoke. Down the short hall, bursting into the living room—couch overturned, floors awash with greasy knee-deep smoke—I flashed through, boots pounding, into the long, wood-floored sparring room.

The mirrors along one wall were all cracked, the ballet barre splintered, the weapons hanging on the walls scattered except for one long quivering shape under a fall of amber silk. Gilberto Rosario Gonzalez-Ayala was in a crouch, a Bowie knife flat against one forearm, feinting at a shape made of smoke and nightmare. He was bleeding—a scalp wound, I thought, since his face was covered with blood. His left arm hung, flopping queerly, at his side, but his face was alive.

His eyes damn near *shone.*

I'd never seen Gilberto light up before, and now wasn't the time to pay attention. Still, the computer in my head took note. I hurled myself forward, heard Saul's coughing roar right behind me as he changed, and hit the shape of green smoke with both physical and etheric force. The scar blazed under my skin, vibrating wetly, and my right fist pistoned forward, smashing into the lattice of evil intent.

A ringing sound hit the pitch just under "puncture-an-eardrum," then broke in a cascade of splinters. Just like the smoke, which solidified into breaking crystal shards, raining for the floor. I hit the ground and whirled, boots grinding in the wreckage, and saw Saul, dodging the shambling fingers of a zombie. Four more crowded behind it, all with their jaws working, and just as his claws sheared the face off the one he was dancing with I lurched forward again, fingers unlimbering the whip.

"Six!" Gilberto yelled. *"Seis!* Six!"

What the hell? But then I realized he was telling me how many enemies we had loose inside the warehouse, or at least how many he'd seen.

Well, at least he's got his wits about him. How long has he been in here with them? The whip cracked, silver flechettes thudding home in rotting flesh, and the smell exploded. *Goddammit, and I was looking forward to getting clean, too.*

It was short work putting the zombies down. These ones were old and fragile, porous bones and worm-eaten flesh. Five of them, and I was looking for the sixth when

it blundered around the corner, arms outstretched like a
bad B-movie villain, and snarled.

The whip hit, my fist arrived a few moments later, and
I was struck by just how *satisfying* making a zombie's
head explode can be. If only all problems are as simple as
setting your feet, uncoiling from your hip, and smashing
a hellbreed-strong fist right through something's head,
then shaking the gobbets of flesh from your fingers.

But, of course, I have to spoil all that enjoyment by
thinking about who the hell would send zombies *into
my fucking house.* Just when I was looking forward to a
shower and a little bit of rest.

I stood still for a moment, panting, head down. Saul's
growl petered out. He cocked his head, still in cougarform, tail lashing. Then the blurring enveloped him, his
form running like clay under water, and when it receded
he was there again. It's an amazing thing to see, and
the fact that I can *see* the strings under the surface of
the real world responding with my smart eye, see the
quivers of energy as thermodynamic laws are violated,
doesn't make it any less amazing.

The human mind can compass an awful lot, but it
isn't comfortable even when you're used to it.

"Dios mio." Gilberto coughed behind me. It was the
first time I heard him sound anything other than bored.
"Madre de Dios."

*Yeah, kid, calling on God is a good thing to do in a
situation like this.* I let out a long slow breath. "Jesus
Christ. What the hell?"

Saul glanced at me, then turned on his heel and strode
back to Gilberto. "What happened?"

"Doorbell rang." The kid winced as Saul touched his

left arm, but he didn't let go of the knife. I recognized it—an antique Bowie, with a plain hilt and a blessing running under the metal's surface.

It had belonged to the first Jack Karma, one of the hunters in my lineage. *Why am I even surprised?*

"His arm's broken," Saul said over his shoulder. "Jill?"

"Get it set and find out what happened. I'm going to sweep the house."

"I don't hear any more." But he nodded, and crouched easily next to the kid. "This is going to hurt a bit."

"*Chingada,* man, just get it over with." Gilberto sounded very young. "There was a blond bitch at the door, but I think she left."

Wait a second. "Blond?"

"Dreadlocks, *bruja.*" He was sweating as Saul probed his arm more. "Right down to her ass. Tall, too. Dressed like *mi abuela,* for fucksake. Flower muumuu and everything."

"Greenstick. Humerus." Saul looked up at him. "Brace yourself."

"*Ay de mi,* just fucking—"

Saul made a swift motion, Gilberto spluttered and sucked in a breath. He turned the color of cottage cheese under his brown skin. It was amazing—he actually looked yellow. The acne scars stood out, like the cratered surface of the moon.

Tall. Blond dreadlocks. And I wonder if he's talking about a blue caftan embroidered with orchids. "Hold that thought," I said, and swept the rest of the warehouse.

Someone definitely had an agenda. They went straight

to my bedroom, where the bed stood away from all four walls and three filing cabinets against one wall were busted open and ransacked. Paper fluttered, and I stood for a few moments staring.

What the hell?

There was nothing in those cabinets except bills and invoices for things like custom leather work, ammunition, artifacts bought—necessary for tax purposes.

Hey, even a hunter has to file. Death and taxes are immutable laws for us, too. I generally end up getting a refund, though. It's the least Uncle Sam can do for me.

All the really revealing personal papers, like Mikhail's birth certificate and mine, files on cases closed or unclosed, immunization records, school records, anything that might give an enemy a foothold or a piece of insight, were locked up in a concrete vault under Hutch's bookstore. After Mikhail's death and Melisande Belisa's rifling of his personal papers, it seemed like a good idea, and I was never so glad as right now.

Sloane's papers are there too—whatever survived the fire in '38, that is. Huh.

I holstered the gun, coiled my whip. The warehouse was fracked-up but clean of zombies, and the shadows were only shadows. Someone had quickly but thoroughly torn through the filing cabinets. I strode out to the kitchen. Someone had opened all the cabinets and torn open the filing cabinet at the end of the breakfast bar. Police and federal contacts, files on protocols for requesting funding from different municipal, county, and state (not to mention federal) contacts—all pulled out and scattered. This was potentially more damaging, so I crouched and searched quickly through the papers, checked the drawers. Each file was labeled in either my spidery handwriting or Saul's firmer copperplate script.

Nothing immediately appeared to be missing. A few files had been yanked out and scattered. That was it.

What the hell?

"Jill?" Saul appeared in the doorway to the living room.

"Someone went through my papers." I rose, surveyed the kitchen. They hadn't pulled the dishes out, but the fridge door was ajar. *Jesus. Wonder what she was looking for?* "How's his arm?"

"I'm going to cast it. Need anything?"

I spread my hands. Silver shifted in my hair. "Just one thing, and it's nothing anyone here can help me with."

"Huh." His shoulder slumped as if he thought I was talking about him personally. "Really?"

Shit, Jill. Sarcasm is *a deadly weapon.* "Not really. You're going to help me find something out."

"Like what?"

"Like what Mama Zamba was looking for in my fucking filing cabinets. And why she's alive if most of her inner circle is dead." Frustration threatened to knot my hands into fists. "And what the fuck is really going on here."

"Oh." He didn't look happy, but who would, faced with that news? "Sure it was Zamba?"

"Tall? Long blond dreadlocks? A bunch of zombies and green smoke? Sounds like Zamba to me. The only things missing are the cockroaches."

"You know, that doesn't comfort me as much as it should. You okay?"

I nodded. Silver shifted and tinkled. "Frustrated as all hell. But okay."

He opened his mouth, shut it, then plowed on. "All right. I'm going to get the kid put back together. Is anything missing?"

"Not that I can figure out." I looked down at the papers, and this time my hands curled into fists despite my deep breathing. I'm just like anyone else—I *hate* having my house broken into. "Get the kid something to eat, too. He's thin as a rail."

"He fought off six zombies." Was that actually *grudging admiration* in Saul's tone?

Wonders never cease.

"Or he was smart enough to stay away from them. Six of one, half a dozen of the other. Get him fixed up."

He shifted his weight back, paused. "And then?"

I struggled with my frustration, kept the words even and calm. "Then we're going to get cleaned up, board up the front door, and get going. We're dropping the kid off at Galina's, where I know he'll be safe. After that we're paying a visit to Hutch's."

"I thought Hutch was out of town."

He's vacationing in the Galapagos. Just when I need him too. "He is. But Zamba was after something. It's a safe bet that whatever-it-is is in the vault. Go on, Saul. Time's a-wasting."

He vanished down the hall, and I heard Gilberto swearing in a high unsteady voice. The kid had some potential. He was also goddamn lucky Zamba hadn't unseamed him from guts to garters. She must have been in an awful hurry.

My pager went off as I stood there, thinking. Zombie-stink rose from my clothes, and we were going to have a hell of a time getting the house back together. I dug in my pocket and brought the thing out, still staring at the scattered papers.

The number was unfamiliar. I snagged the phone, dialed, and was rewarded with a click and two rings.

The connection went through, and my breath froze in my throat. I could tell who it was just by the slight static behind his breathing and the rumble under the words.

Perry's voice crawled into my ear. "My dearest Kiss. I presume you're well?"

Don't FUCKING CALL ME THAT, you goddamn hellspawn. I swallowed, reached all the way down to my toes for patience.

It was a long reach. I settled for my best fuck-you tone. "Why is the Cirque sending its dogs after me, Pericles?"

"That isn't the Cirque, my dearest. It was me, and they are to watch over you." He paused for maximum effect. "Another performer is dead. Your presence is requested."

Oh, for Chrissake. . . . I took a deep breath, forced myself once again to prioritize. My weary brain rebelled. "Who's dead? Trader or hellbreed? And when?"

"Before dawn. One of my kind. A fortune-teller, I believe you would call it. Moragh."

Moragh. The name meant nothing to me, especially with all my other irons in the fire. *Before dawn* meant that Zamba'd had a busy night. "And the hostage?"

"Safe and snug, and under my *especial* protection and supervision." A low, silky laugh. "Fear not for him, my dear. Come see the latest death and destruction. It has a certain symmetry."

"I'll be there when I get there. And Perry?"

"Yes?"

What was I going to tell him? *Fuck off* was what I wanted to say, but it would just give him an opening. He also hadn't done anything to deserve it—at least not lately. "Take care of that hostage." *If he bites it, this entire city's going to have a very bad night. You don't want that either; it'll interfere with your own games. Don't think I don't know it—and don't think I'm not betting on it.*

"I told you he's safe." Now he sounded irritated. Score one for me. "Why do you make me repeat myself?"

"I just like to make sure you *understand*," I informed him sweetly, and slammed the phone down.

20

Hutchinson's Books, Used and Rare, was painted on the window in fading gold—but Saul and I parked four blocks away and slid up to the back door under a punishing wave of sun and heat. Midmorning, and it was already a scorcher. The shadows teemed with shapes, far darker than morning shadows had a right to be. I kept seeing the little glimmers of colorless crystal eyes and twitched for a weapon.

Saul didn't mention it. Whether he was magnanimously refusing to comment or he didn't sense them was an open question. I was willing to bet on the former.

I blinked the exhaustion out of my eyes and touched the doorknob. A thin thread of sorcerous energy slid off my fingertips, stroked the locks I'd built. They eased open, tumblers clicking with thin little sounds.

Saul crowded behind me. Gilberto was dropped off at Galina's, wide-eyed and with a fresh cast on his arm. Galina, bless her, didn't ask a goddamn question, just took one look at my face and clucked and cooed over the gangbanger, promising to get him into fresh clothes and get some healing sorcery on that arm. Technically I suppose I should have charmed the bone before we left the warehouse, but I had other things on my mind.

The whole time, Gilberto clutched Jack Karma's knife. I didn't ask him to let go of it. I guess that answered *that* question. I had a new apprentice. To add to all my other problems.

The door ghosted open. Paper, dust, and air-conditioning closed around us as I swept it to and re-locked it. "Zombies," I said for the third time. "In our *living room*. What next?"

"Well, at least we didn't have to kill them in the kitchen." Saul sighed heavily. "That kid . . ."

"He's got the look."

"Great." Saul didn't sound in the least excited. "Another person to get a slice of your time."

"Is that what this is about?" I checked the shop. Books sat quietly on their shelves, leather-bound tomes stacked on chairs and on Hutch's massive mahogany desk, shipwrecked in a sea of papers. A PC that hadn't been there last time crouched on one corner of the desk, a shipshape new Mac on the other corner. The two laptops were in their traveling cases, tucked out of sight under the desk.

Pity he hadn't taken his phone. The whole point of his vacation was to get him out and away from temptation, the little monster. The deal was, he hacked only when the local hunter needed him to, and the local hunter kept his ass out of jail.

Unfortunately, sometimes Hutch just couldn't help himself. He's small and beaky and a Cowardly Lion, but a challenge in cyberspace? Suddenly he's Superman, six feet tall *and* bulletproof. And completely without any goddamn self-control at all. I had to wait until things calmed down and the local FBI liaison, Juan Rujillo, finished smoothing the ruffled feathers before Hutch could come back.

Saul sounded angelically innocent. "What *what* is about?"

"You." I turned past the small kitchen where Hutch heated his lunches, opened an EMPLOYEES ONLY door. "And whatever it is you're sitting on."

"I'm not sitting on anything."

Yeah, that's why you can't touch me anymore. That's why you flinch whenever I get a little frisky. "Okay. When you want to talk about it, fine." The small room was lined with bookshelves, and even the dust in here vibrated with secrecy. Ordinary people wouldn't even *see* the door we'd just ducked through. Though precious few people came in here; this place was kept afloat because of the hunter's library. Hutch got a stipend and dispensation for when he occasionally went breaking a few electronic-surveillance laws in service to whatever case I was working at the time; I got a research library and an extra pair of eyes to go digging through dusty tomes whenever the end of the world drew *too* nigh.

"We never have time." Did he actually sound *sulky? Jesus.* "You're kidding, right?"

"Do I sound like I'm kidding?" He let out a sharp sigh. "Work comes first. I know. I just have to talk to you sometime."

"So talk to me." I pushed aside the conference table, a big wooden thing suspiciously clean and neat now that Hutch was out of town and I hadn't been bothering him to look things up for me. Saul bent down and lent his strength, even though I was already handling it. The legs scraped across cheap industrial carpet, and it fetched up against one of the overloaded bookcases. A copy of Luvrienne's *Les Chateaux de Chagrin* teetered on a shelf; I prayed it wouldn't fall. There's only six of the copies he produced in existence, and it's one of the best all-around books about the Sorrows to have been written in the last four hundred years.

Nobody knows you like your own. Luvrienne had barely escaped the fate that stalks every male in a Sorrows house, lived to write about it—and they track down and destroy every copy of the book they can find. Just like they tracked him down and took him back.

Fortunately, Hutch scanned it into a digital archive and emailed it to every hunter's library we had addresses for. He gets orders from other libraries for printed copies. The digital age is a wondrous thing.

However, I don't want to touch the damn book if I don't have to. I know too fucking much about the Sorrows to want that.

I snagged the loop of denim sewn into the carpet and yanked up the cutout square. The concrete underneath was smooth and featureless, its expanse broken only by a recessed iron ring. I grabbed the ring, set my legs, and let out a breath while *heaving* up.

A hellbreed-strong right fist helps when you have to lift a concrete slab. But you still have to lift with your legs, not your back. Ergonomics for hunters—a bad back is a liability. Saul kept out of the way—there wasn't enough room for him to help.

I keyed the code into the climate-control pad and

slid the glass panel aside. A few items Galina keeps for me; I learned my lesson when that Sorrows bitch stole Mikhail's talisman and rifled all his personal stuff. But the papers are here. All the salvageable vitals on the hunters of my lineage, down from the first and second Jack Karmas. Before the first Jack, we don't know anything.

This isn't the kind of career that lends itself to leaving evidence in the historical record. The day world, the real world, doesn't want to know. Hunters sometimes rely on sheer outrageousness to slide by unnoticed. A regular civilian's reaction to a genuine paranormal event is usually screaming and running in the other direction.

Emerson Sloane's files were very thin. The big Santa Luz fire of 1938 had eaten most of the records he'd left, one way or another. A bare triple-handful of manila folders labeled in a round Palmer script, some with notations in Mikhail's broad firm hand with its Cyrillic notations followed by English translations.

I flipped through them. About twenty had no connection to anything remotely resembling the current clusterfuck we were looking at. My pager went off; I dug in my pocket and pulled out the other thirteen files that looked promising.

I gave my pager a cursory glance. It was the Badger. Maybe she had something for me.

"Do you still want me?" The words just burst out of Saul and hung in midair.

It was like being punched in the gut. I sucked in dust and paper-laden air. The dead quiet of the bookstore closed around the sound, and my hands went nerveless for about half a second. I almost dropped the files.

"Of course I do," I told the hole in the floor. "I always have. What the fuck?"

"My family's gone." It was a simple statement of fact. "My mother's dead. Billy Ironside killed my sister. My mother's sisters are . . . well, I'm not theirs. They have their own cubs. If I didn't have a mate, it'd be different. But . . ."

"But there's me. And I'm not a Were." There it was, half the dysfunction in our relationship laid out in plain words. The other half didn't need to be spoken. *I'm tainted. I've got a hellbreed mark on my wrist and a serious rage problem. I'm not a nice person, Saul. I'm not even a* good *person, despite your thinking so. I'm a hunter. End of story.*

"I don't care what you are," he answered quietly. "You need me, Jill. You'd kill yourself over this if someone wasn't reminding you . . ."

"Reminding me of what?" I flipped through the first file, scanned it. No connection. The second, too. My eyes were hot and grainy, and I was hoping I wouldn't miss anything. My heart was a lump in my throat, the words had to squeeze around it.

Five little words. "That you're worth a damn."

Mikhail was the only man who ever thought I was worth a damn, I'd told him once.

Not the only one, he'd told me later. Tit for tat, we were even, except we weren't.

We would never be even. Not while I was still breathing. Only it wasn't the kind of debt you could repay, or even anything that could be called a debt at all.

I didn't know what it was, except maybe love. Or something so huge it could swallow me, something that

terrified me when I thought he might not want *me* anymore. Mischa thought I was worth plucking out of a
snowdrift and training, but he left me behind. I wasn't
worth enough for him to stay. And that little voice inside
my head, buried under a hunter's iron.

*You're not worth anything. You're ugly. Too ugly for
anyone to love.* Even my mother, the bitch, had said so.

And, I mean, come on. Just look at the man. Even
gaunt and grieving, he was Native American calendar
beefcake, broad-shouldered and dark-eyed.

Who wouldn't want him? Who wouldn't feel their
breath catch every time he looked their way?

The third file fell open under my numb fingers. I
blinked back hot water and what felt like rocks in my
eyes. The little tingle of intuition ran up my arms and
exploded under my breastbone. A puzzle piece fell into
place with a click so loud I was surprised it didn't knock
over a few books.

"Holy shit," I breathed.

There, clipped to the inside of a folder probably older
than I was, a singed, faded black-and-white photo glared
at me. Saul approached, but I kept staring.

The jaw was the same. So was the blond hair, the
sculpted lips, and the straight thick eyebrows. And the
glint of gold around the teeth. And the bad skin, but
underneath that . . .

All this time I'd thought she was just an ugly woman.
Funny how beauty mutates according to expectation.

My Were bent down, and his warmth touched my
back. "Huh." The faint ghost of zombie clinging to us
both faded under the good smell of him, male and fur.
"Is it Zamba's brother?"

"I think it's Zamba." I moved my hand so he could see what Sloane had written on the mat, the fountain pen marks digging hurriedly into the yellowing fibers.

Arthur Gregory, missing, presumed dead. I flipped the file closed. "Jesus."

"Huh. She didn't *smell* male."

"It can't just be a coincidence." I handed him the file and leaned forward, jammed the others back in vaguely where they went. "Right under my goddamn nose all the goddamn time. I *hate* that."

It took under a minute to get the vault closed up. I tugged the carpet square back over the cover and smoothed it down, turned sharply to find Saul just standing there, a line between his dark eyebrows, staring at me.

The urgency of a case heating up bit me sharply, right in the conscience. *Goddammit, can't this wait?*

But no, it couldn't. I braced myself and met the problem head-on. "Don't worry about me." There it was again—that sharp tone, the grating whine underneath it. "I did this job before you came along, Saul. If you're aching to get back to the Rez, you can go. I wouldn't hold it against you. God knows nobody else has ever been able to fucking put up with me."

Jesus. I meant to say something gentler. Like *I love you, don't leave me.* Or even just, *I need you too much. I don't care.*

I *did,* though. I cared that the dark circles under his eyes were getting bigger, that his ribs were standing out sharply, and that his shoulders were hunched. Those were only the first few things in the long list of things I cared about when it came to him. It all boiled down to him maybe not wanting to keep banging his head on the steel wall I couldn't figure out how to drop. The place in me where I'd been broken and remade, beaten until I turned strong. I'd figured he knew the way through the wall without my having to tell him. It was there every time I woke up next to him and my heart hurt because he was next to me, warm and breathing.

Because he *knew* me.

"Do you want me to?" His mouth pulled down at the corners, bitterly. "What did I do?"

Huh? I searched for a handle on my temper, didn't find one. The rock in my throat turned into sharp ice edges. "You? You didn't do anything, goddammit. If you're trying to figure out how to gracefully get rid of me, Saul, don't worry about it. It's okay."

I was lying. It wasn't anywhere near okay. But I would say it was. For him.

"Jill . . ." He made a helpless motion just as my pager buzzed again. "I'm sorry."

I had a sudden, violent urge to grab my pager, throw it across the room, and shoot the motherfucker for good measure. "Don't be sorry. Look, I know something's wrong. It's been wrong since you came back. *I'm* sorry. I should have known it was too good to be true."

"What the fuck are you talking about?" There it was, a spark of anger. It was a relief—when he was angry, the twenty-pounds-underweight-and-unhappy-too wasn't so visible.

I grabbed the file. He didn't resist. "You don't have to make any excuses to me," I informed him. "No promises, no deals, no bargains. You said that the very first night. If you can't stand me anymore, it's okay. I expected it.

Just go ahead and go. Find a nice tabby and raise a litter or three. God knows you're domestic enough."

"Are you *insane?*"

Holy hell and hallelujah. He'd actually *shouted* at me. No more moping; he was now officially pissed off.

I closed my eyes, the massive mental effort needed to think clearly dragging at every inch of my body. The shaking had me in its jaws and wouldn't let go.

Zamba, Arthur Gregory. Some kind of beef with the Cirque, and his brother? Who knows? He found a bargain somewhere—probably voodoo. And the Twins, they specialize in androgyny. It would make sense, it would make a whole lot of sense.

He went to Lorelei, Lorelei brokered a deal. Now that the Cirque is back, Lorelei was a liability, and her death would serve as fuel, and payment for the loa *too. As well as the deaths of Zamba's inner circle. The possessions could be aftershocks or for some other part of Zamba's plan.*

And once the possessed had died inside their violated bodies, they were easy meat for reanimation, *and* payment for the *loa*. Zamba was mortgaging herself to the hilt for this, whatever it was. Revenge?

Probably.

There were things I had to do. I opened my eyes, found I was staring at the ceiling. The acoustic tiles all but vibrated until I realized my goddamn eyes had fucking flooded. I couldn't blame it on the dust in the air. Everything shimmered as I blinked, trying to get them to reabsorb the water. "I'm not crazy. I'm just saying that if you can't bring yourself to touch me anymore, something's obviously very wrong. You're torn up over your

mother, I know. I *understand*. But don't kill yourself
staying with me because you think you have to. If you
have to cut me loose and go back to the Rez, if this isn't
what you need or want, you're free as a fucking bird. I
can't keep you, Saul. I *won't* keep you."

My pager quit buzzing. I tipped my chin back down
and got a good look at him.

Saul stared at me as if I had indeed lost my mind.
His mouth opened, then closed. I clutched the file to my
chest like a schoolgirl with her books.

"I've got to go," I finally said. It sounded very small
in the stillness. "I've got to figure the rest of this out.
Any moment now it could blow sky-high." Knowing
pretty much who I was dealing with gave me more to
work with. The other big question—*why*—could be attacked now, and wrestled to the ground. Not to mention
pistol-whipped and shot, if the occasion called for it.

I was so tired it didn't even sound like a relief.

"Jill—" Saul had finally found his voice.

If he was going to tell me that he wanted to go back to
the Rez, I was going to start screaming. I couldn't afford
to lose it now.

People were counting on me. A whole city full of
them. My people, in my city.

"Save it." The words were a harsh croak. "Do what
you're gonna do, Saul. If you're going to leave me in the
dust, make it quick and clean. If you ever loved me, do it
that way. Don't drag it out."

I stamped past him, every string in my body aching
to stop and touch him, throw my arms around him, and
maybe engage in some undignified begging. Screw the

entire city, screw *everything*. I didn't care as long as he stayed with me. As long as there was a *chance*.

But. One teensy-tiny little *but*.

I'm a hunter. It's that simple.

If Zamba-Arthur or whoever it was kept killing Cirque performers, things were going to get sticky. There's very little a really motivated voodoo queen can't do to you, and she'd already hit the hostage, too. Perry was there, but if she found some way past him—or if he decided it was too much trouble and some chaos served his ends—well, it would be party time for the entire Cirque *and* I'd have Perry and a renegade fucking voodoo queen to deal with.

Big fun.

It meant a lot of innocent people dead or maimed. It meant hellbreed thinking they could slip the leash and make trouble in my town. It meant years of steady work keeping things under control wasted.

It meant more victims.

And there was just no fucking way I was going to stand for that.

No matter *what* I stood to lose.

21

When the Badger gets her teeth in something, she doesn't let go. "It was a job and a half to find out who holds title to that goddamn house." Behind her, another phone rang, and I heard Sullivan's big voice raised. He was probably cussing at his coffee. The way Homicide bitches about the coffee, you'd think someone would have brought in some decent beans by now.

Other than that, it sounded like a cubicle farm on speed. Which is to say, a usual morning in Homicide.

"Huh." I closed my eyes. It was easier that way, with the outside world shut out. "In what way?"

"I had to go rousting." She sounded almost indignant. "It wasn't in the usual databases. I had to go down to the tax assessor's office, they sent me to some goddamn basement. Had to pull records from 1930, can you believe that? They haven't got around to putting that slice of the city in the databases, he said. Weird, since every other district is."

Well, isn't that interesting. "And the winner is?"

"Someone named Ruth Gregory. Utilities, phone, garbage pickup, all under the same name—there were bills in the house. But here's some other weirdness: Ruth Gregory doesn't exist."

"If she gets bills, she must exist."

"That's the thing. None of her information's anywhere we can find it, no DOB, no nothing. But she got bills and paid them. Has a bank account, but if it wasn't for paper statements we wouldn't know, her bank doesn't have her on electronic file. There's not even a listing in the phone book. This woman just came out of nowhere, and she doesn't show up in the databases."

That's voodoo for you. The electronic stuff is easier for the loa *to affect than paper. Dammit.* Ruth Gregory. "What's her middle initial?" It was a small question, but I needed something I could feel good about anticipating.

"Ruth R. Gregory. Why?"

Ruth R. Arthur. A little fuck-you from Mama Zamba. Just like a supervillain. "I don't suppose you've found any hints of other houses?"

"I ran a check. Guess how many Ruth Gregorys there are in the good old United States."

How the hell should I know? But it was just like her to run it into the ground. "Thousands?"

"Less than four hundred. Four in our state. None with the middle initial R. And no hint of a separate identity, though it's a good bet that if she had one we wouldn't be able to find it electronically either. It could take us weeks of sifting paper—"

We don't have weeks. "That's not necessary. If any scrap of another identity comes up from processing the house, let me know. Otherwise, just keep identifying those stiffs. Okay?"

"All right." She sounded almost disappointed. She would run Zamba into the ground over weeks if she had to. Months. Or years.

"Good work." And I meant it. "Did you get everything you needed out of the house?"

"Boxes of paper. She was a real pack rat, our Miz Gregory. We left everything not needed for Forensics there and closed it up. Should we go back?"

No way. "No. God, no." I didn't mean to sound horrified. "Stay away from there. Just keep processing that paper and buzz me if anything else tingles your weird-o-meter, okay?"

"You got it."

"Any ID on the other bodies yet? Other than Trevor Watson?" *At least, the zombies that weren't Zamba's followers?*

"Not yet. They're pretty spludgy."

Well, that's one word for it. "Okay. Thanks." I dropped the phone in the cradle, considered screaming and shooting something.

Prioritize, Jill. Get your head straight.

It was a good plan. I just wasn't sure I could do it.

What next? Come on, what are you going to do next?

There was only one thing to do. And it wasn't going by the Cirque, thank God, or standing around yelling at Saul. I looked up, but the bookshop was deserted. Nothing but empty aisles faced with stuffed-full bookshelves, boxes on the floor, the antique cash register sitting stolidly, gathering dust. "Saul?" The word quivered. Was he gone?

Oh, fuck. I stood there with my hand on the phone, my hip against Hutch's desk, and my heart twisting itself like a contortionist inside my chest. "Saul?"

I checked the kitchen and the EMPLOYEES ONLY room. I even checked the goddamn bathroom.

He was gone. I hadn't even heard him leave.

God. I swallowed something hot and nasty, paced through the entire shop one more time. Blinked several times. My cheeks were wet.

This is one less thing for you to worry about. Get back up on the horse, Jill. Do your job.

It was time for me to visit Melendez.

22

If Zamba was the reigning voodoo queen, Melendez was the court jester. Don't get me wrong—anyone who bargains with an inhuman intelligence is suspect, and just because I hadn't heard of Melendez doing anything even faintly homicidal or icky didn't mean he didn't dabble.

But it didn't mean the little butterball was harmless, either. Any more than the mark on my wrist meant I was a Trader.

Only I was, if you thought about it a certain way. And while Melendez didn't go in for the theatrical horror and power games Zamba did, he also didn't go out of his way to make things easier on people. *Live and let die,* that was probably the closest thing to a motto he would ever have.

Saul had left me the car. Awful nice of him. I told the sharp spearing ache in my heart to go away and made time through midmorning traffic, brakes squealing and tires chirping. The shadows leapt and cavorted in my peripheral vision until I began ignoring them, even the colorless crystal eyes and the glass-twinkle teeth. I caught the flow of traffic like a pinball down a greased slide, all the way across town to the northern fringe of the Riverhurst section.

A nice address, all things considered, clinging to rich respectability like cactus clings to any breath of moisture. The houses are old, full of creaks, fake adobes and some improbable Cape Cods. They had bigger yards than anything other than the rest of Riverhurst, and most of them were drenched green. I even saw some sprinklers running, spouting rainbows under the heaving, cringe-inducing glare of dusty sunlight.

Melendez didn't hold his gatherings in his home. He owned a storefront on the edge of the barrio, with a trim white sign out front announcing the Holy Church of St. Barbara, nonprofit and legitimate under a 501(c)(3). His own private little joke, I guess. Seven nights a week you can find drumming, dancing, and weird shit happening on the little strip of concrete that had pretensions of being Pararrayos Avenue.

Mornings, though, he could be found here. It's a good thing the streets are wide even on the edge of Riverhurst, because his followers usually come out for consultations, filling up his driveway and the street for a block or two. Quarter-hour increments, donations optional— nobody leaves without paying *something*—and results guaranteed.

You don't last long in that business unless you have the cash to back the flash.

Today, though, the street was clear and I parked right near the front door. Melendez's faux-adobe hacienda sat behind its round concrete driveway with the brick bank in the middle, holding still-blooming rosebushes, a monkey puzzle tree, and a bank of silvery-green rue. Lemon balm tried its best to choke everything else in the bed, but aggressive pruning had turned it into a bank of sweetness.

I was relieved to see his tiny garden was tiptop. The fountain—a cute little chubby-cheeked cherub shooting water from his tiny wang—was going full-bore. I wondered if there was a homeowners' association in this part of town, and what they thought of his choice in lawn decorations. Not that there was much lawn to speak of. The largest part of his lot was out back with the pool.

The heat was oppressive, a bowl of haze lying over the city. A brown smudge of smog touched downtown's skyscrapers, and high white horsetail clouds lingered over the mountains. I couldn't wait for the autumn rains to move up the river and flash-flood us, just for a change of pace. Hunters are largely immune to temperature differentials, it's right up there with the silence, one of the first things an apprentice learns.

I winced at the thought of apprentices, opened the car door and stood for a few seconds, looking across the Pontiac's roof, sizing up the place. My smart eye caught nothing but the usual stirrings and flickers, an active febrile etheric petri dish.

I wonder if I'm not his first visitor today. Well, no time like the present to find out.

The wrought-iron gate was open, as usual. The courtyard was just as lush as it ever was, smelling of mineral hosewater and the sweet orange tang of Florida water. The splashes across the threshold, where the concrete stopped and the red-brick paving began, were still wet.

Well, Melendez. You've been keeping your house neat and clean, haven't you. I stepped over the barrier, a brief tingle passing over my body. The silver in my hair sparked and chimed, oddly muted. I wanted to touch a gun butt, kept my fingers away with an effort.

He had a fountain in the middle of the courtyard too, a big seashell with a spire rising from the middle of it. It was bone-dry. Masses of feverfew, more rue, a bank of bindweed . . . and the red-painted front door, open just a crack.

Gooseflesh rose hard and cold on my arms and legs. I wished Saul was behind me. Right now he was probably back at the warehouse, packing. Or maybe he'd already blown town. He traveled light, sometimes just a duffel, most times not even that.

Focus, Jill.

I wanted to kick the door open and sweep the house. Instead, I stood on the front step and rang the bell. The sweet tinkling chimes of—I shit you not—the chorus to Fleetwood Mac's "Dreams" sounded, leaking out through the open door.

The air changed, suddenly full of listening. No matter how many times you get to this point as a hunter, it never gets any easier.

I toed the door open. "Melendez!" I tried to sound nice and cheerful, only succeeded in sounding like Goldilocks saying *hello* when she walks in the door and smells porridge. "Señor Melendez, *una clienta para Usted.*"

The entryway was red tile, full of cool quiet and the smell of incense. Lots of incense, in thick blue veils. My blue eye smarted, filling with hot water. There was a sound of movement, and my hand leapt for the gun, fell away.

"*Ola, bruja*," he said at the end of the hall. "Come in. Been expecting you."

Melendez lowered himself down in a straight-backed leather armchair behind a massive oak desk cluttered with paper and tchotchkes. He called this room his study, and it was full of bookshelves holding leather-bound books—nothing Hutch would get excited over, these were just for decoration—and other, more useful tools of his trade. An empty fireplace, clean as a whistle, seemed just a set piece for the crossed rapiers hung over it. Both fine examples of Toledo steel, and worth more than the house itself *and* probably the neighbors' houses as well.

I surveyed the choices available. A padded footstool that would put me below him, literally, like I was a third grader. An overstuffed armchair that would swallow everything up to your neck. A penitent's chair made of iron, with a faded red horsehair cushion.

I elected to remain standing, and Melendez's broad brown face split in a yellow-toothed grin. He settled his ample ass deeper in his chair, his potbelly brushing the desk's edge. "Been a while."

"No murders traced to any of *your* followers lately." I folded my arms.

"You here about Ruth?" His dark eyes gleamed.

Well, there's either a very lucky guess, or he knows something. Guess which. "I'm here about Arthur Gregory. And the Cirque de Charnu."

"You here because Mama Zamba is calling in all her favors. She got an old feud against the devils, older than yours." He steepled his long, chubby brown fingers. In a blue chambray shirt and jeans, a red kerchief tied around his straight black hair, he was in that ageless space between twenty-nine and forty if you went by his round, strangely unlined face. It was only the way he moved, with a little betraying stiffness every once in a while, and the distance in his gaze that gave him away.

The *loa* can hold off age just like a Trader's bargain can. They cannot grant immortality, but it gets awful close.

"If she keeps killing Cirque performers there's going to be trouble. I don't have a lot of time to dance around." Impatience boiled under my breastbone. I shelved it. "What do you know?"

"Oh, *bruja*." He laughed. "You need a better question, you gonna expect answers from me."

The urge to whip out a gun, squeeze off a shot for effect, and put the barrel to his forehead and then *expect* answers from him leapt up like a flame in the middle of my head. I took in a deep breath, fixed him with my mismatched stare, and told myself firmly I was not going to be shooting anyone unless it was necessary.

The trouble with that is, all of a sudden you can think it's necessary when it's not. Especially when you're deconstructing under severe stress.

"Melendez." I tried to sound patient. "I've got a city that could explode at any moment and a voodoo queen looking to cause a lot of trouble. You fuck around with me and I just might decide to look too hard at this sweet little deal you've got going for yourself. Besides, with

Zamba out of the picture soon you're looking at being the reigning king of the scene around here. If, that is, she doesn't show up and do you like she did the bitch of Greenlea. It didn't seem like Lorelei had an easy death."

"Ah, Lorelei. She was Zamba's godmother. Seems like Zamba cleaning up loose ends." He looked down at the desktop, ran one blunt finger along a glossy strip of varnish peeking out from behind papers.

"Are you a loose end?" It was worth a shot.

"I belong to Chango." All jolliness dropped away, and his broad moonface turned solemn. "The Twins, they have no hold on me. My *patrón,* he whip their asses if they come near me. I in *strong* with Chango. And you got some help too. Ogoun just waiting for you to come around."

My mouth was dry as desert sand. "I didn't think you had any truck with Ogoun."

He shrugged. "The spirits come when they will. You know. You called on them in the beginning of this. Papa Legba and Ogoun both watching you."

Well, training in dealing with possession has to take these sorts of things into account. I suppressed a shiver. The first time I'd brushed up against voodoo was during a ceremony devoted to Ogoun, Mikhail by my side. There was a skip, like a needle lifting from a record, and the next thing I knew I had a mouthful of fiery rum, Mikhail watching me very carefully, and the followers were drifting away toward the dinner table. He never would tell me what exactly I'd done when the drums lifted me out of myself. Broken glass had littered the floor of the peristyle, and there were curls of cigar smoke in the air. It had taken me a while to wash the smell of cigars away.

After that, Mikhail was very, very careful to teach me how to build an exorcist's hard etheric shell. I'd never had that problem again, thank God, but still. You never can tell when dealing with shit like this.

I fished the two Ziploc bags out of my coat. Straight razor and enamelware cup, both of them almost quivering with readiness. "What do these have to do with Zamba?"

He eyed my hands, then went pale under his brownness. *"Ay de mi."*

"Are we going to start talking, or are you gonna try yanking me around some more? Because I have to tell you, *señor,* my temper's getting a little thin." *Understatement of the year, isn't it?*

He was still staring at my hands. His eyes unfocused, brown irises sheened over as if with cataracts, a thin gray film spilling over his gaze. The air tightened, a breeze from nowhere riffling the papers on his desk, touching the leather-clad spines, and fingering the sheer curtains over the French doors looking onto the backyard's wide green expanse.

I braced myself.

When he spoke next, it was a different voice. His mouth moved, but the sound came from elsewhere, a mellow deep baritone crackling at the edges. *"Ay, mi sobrina. Bienvenidos a mi casa."*

The goose bumps rose again, hot this time instead of cold. My hair stirred, the silver chimes shifting, and my blue eye caught little dark shapes moving through the charged, heavy atmosphere that had suddenly settled inside the study. *"Buenos días, señor. Muchas gracias por su atencion."*

Hey, it never hurts to be polite.

Melendez's face worked itself like rubber, compressing and stretching. His mouth worked wetly. "You come here seeking knowledge, eh? What you give to Papa Chango?"

How about I don't rip you out of your follower there? How about I leave this place standing instead of burned down as a lesson in not fucking with me? I kept control of my temper, but just barely. It was getting harder and harder. "You wouldn't ask me if you didn't have something in mind already."

"Es verdad. Me and the Twins, we have a wager. They think their little *puta* is a match for the devils and for you. She pay them well, she always have."

I'll bet she does. There's all sorts of death lately she's been paying them with. "Payment isn't everything. There's more at stake here than just revenge. What does Arthur Gregory want?"

"I tell you what, *bruja. Mi hijo* here, he tell you all he know. In return, you owe me *una bala.* He lie, or he tell you nothing useful—and you put that *bala* through his *cabeza,* eh?"

Oh, for fuck's sake. "Why should I strike a bargain with you?"

The thing inhabiting Melendez's body laughed, a chortle that struck every exposed, shivering surface and blew my hair back. I smelled ozone, and rum. And cigar smoke, drifting across my sensitive nose. My eyes stung, smart and dumb alike.

"Because otherwise, *mi sobrina,* you ain't never

gonna find that tick dug itself into the city's skin. She gonna bloat up with blood and strike the one she aimin' for, and you can't let that happen, can you? No. And this little *caballo* of mine know not just the *who* but the *why*. That what you wantin'. You just like every other *macizo;* you always sayin' *por que, por que?*"

It chuckled, moving Melendez's lips like ripples on the surface of a pond. "So what you say, *bruja grande de Santa Luz? Una bala, por la razon,* for the great *por que.*"

Jesus Christ. It always comes down to this, doesn't it. What part of myself am I willing to mortgage to get this case over and dealt with? "Deal." The word was ash in my mouth. Cigar ash. "But if you double-deal me, *señor,* this *caballo* is wormfood and you're on the outs within the borders of my city."

A good threat. I couldn't bar a *loa* from the city, of course—but I could make it hell on his followers. If I had to.

If it became *necessary.*

It laughed again. Chuckled long and hard, Melendez's hands jerking like brown paper puppets on strings. "We like you, *bruja. Mi hermano* Ogoun and me, we got a wager on you too. We be watching."

And just like that, it winked out. Melendez sagged, coughing, in his chair. A long jet of smoke spluttered through his lips, and his face hit the desktop with a solid thump.

It looked painful. He coughed, and more smoke billowed up. I swallowed a sarcastic little laugh. *If this turns into a case of spontaneous combustion, we're going to have a problem.*

Yeah, just add it to all my other problems. I stayed where I was as Melendez hacked, and the smoke gradually thinned.

When his bloodshot eyes swiveled up and he pushed himself upright, I sank my weight into my back foot, prepared to go any direction.

"Kismet." He coughed again, but without the smoke.

"Melendez." I sank down, coiling into myself like a spring. Just in case.

"I need a beer," he muttered. "Then I tell you *todo*."

"Sounds good." I didn't relax. "Does Chango smoke every time he rides you?"

"*Chingada,* no." Amazingly enough, the round little man laughed. "Only when he mad, *bruja*. Only when he really fucking mad."

23

I left his quiet little house a half hour later. I paused only once, standing on his threshold, to look back at the courtyard and the dry fountain. I was cold, and not even the white-yellow eye of the sun could warm me.

It was the damndest thing, but the Cirque's dogs didn't come up Melendez's driveway. Instead, they clustered up and down the street, each piece of knife-edged morning shadow full of writhing slender shapes and winking colorless-glowing eyes.

The Pontiac's door slammed and I stared at the steering wheel. Measured off a slice of it between my index fingers, bitten-down nails ragged, my apprentice-ring gleaming on my left third finger. Tendons stood out on the back of my scrawny hands, calloused from fighting and sparring, capable work-roughened hands.

Jesus.

When all else fails and you're looking at a huge clusterfuck, sometimes you just need a moment to sit and collect yourself before you start running the next lap toward the inevitable.

What came next?

The Cirque. Get out there and take a look at the newest body. Chances are you'll be able to triangulate her position from the traces, now that you know what she's doing and how they're linked. If you can get to her before she gets what she wants—

But there was another consideration. If Mama Zamba, *née* Arthur Gregory, was out for vengeance against the Cirque, she had a right. Sloane had been working the case, which meant it fell to me to tie up loose ends and finish the job.

Helene took the brother in, and the fortuneteller—Moragh—had something to do with it. The Ringmaster too. That's who Zamba blames, at least. Reasonable as far as I can see.

But what about Ikaros? Why does she want to kill the hostage?

I reached over, grabbed Sloane's file from the passenger seat. Saul should have been there with me. He would be looking at me right now, his head tilted slightly and his eyes soft and deep.

The pain hit me then, gulleywide sideways. I blinked back the tears rising hot and vicious. *Shut up*, I told myself. *Shut up and take it. You can take this.*

I hadn't really thought he would leave me. Well, I *had;* it was the song under every thought of him, the fear under every kiss. But I'd hoped.

That great human drug, hope. It makes fools of everyone, even tough-ass hunters. And I was so *tired*. When was the last time I'd slept?

"Goddammit," I said to the glaring-hot dash, the burning steering wheel, the flood of sunlight bleaching everything colorless-pale. "Do your *job,* Jill."

It was left to me. It was always left to me. That's what a hunter is—the last hope of the desperate, the last best line of defense against Hell's tide. No matter what shit was going on in my personal life, it was up to me to see that the entire fucking house of cards didn't fall.

My pager buzzed again. The goddamn thing just would not shut up. I fished it out with my free hand, glanced at it, and swore.

Perry, again. Which could only mean trouble.

I flipped the file open. Past the picture of Arthur Gregory's young, heartbreaking smile to the précis of the case.

Brother disappeared. Last known contact was outside the Carnaval de la Saleté. Suspects: Helene, hellbreed of the lesser type. Moragh, hellbreed of the higher type, refused to give information when questioned. Henri de Zamba, hellbreed of the higher type. Also refused to give information.

Holy shit. There it was—Arthur Gregory's gauntlet thrown down. *Zamba. I'll be damned.* It was there, staring me in the face. Another piece of the puzzle fell into place, clicking hard.

Maybe she wasn't trying to kill the hostage after all. Maybe she's been after the Ringmaster all this time, and it's just echoing through the bloodbond since the Trader would be his weak point. Jesus.

I slapped the file closed, dropped it on the passenger-side floorboard, and twisted the key in the ignition. The

Pontiac roared into life; I didn't bother buckling myself in.

Come on, Jill. Get this done, and you can rest.

It sounded good. The trouble is, as soon as this was done something else would come along.

I'll deal with that when it comes up. And if it does, that will mean I don't have to think.

There's something to be said for drowning your sorrows in work.

I parked on the bluff and locked my doors, then took the path down to the parking lot. The cars were hooded with dust, the paint already looking weary and sucked-dry. There were a lot of them, and the empty spots looked like knocked-out teeth. It was barely noon and the calliope was going full-bore, a souped-up version of "Let Me Call You Sweetheart" punctuating the air. The reek of cotton candy, animal shit, and fried fat painted the heavy motionless air. I checked the sky—over the mountains hung a dark smudge.

Rain, finally. Which would mean flash floods and misery, wet boots and cold hanging out on rooftops, steaming mornings and dripping against every surface. It would also mean old-fashioned hot chocolate, Saul's signature hash browns, and chili.

I pushed the thought away.

There were only two or three shufflers outside the ticket booth. The same Trader was on duty, her rhinestones sending back a vicious glitter, sweat-sheen greasing her pale skin as she kept as far as she could in the shade. I didn't pause, just strode straight past and jumped the turnstile. She gave a high piercing cry, but I paid no attention.

During the day, the Cirque did look shabby. Holes in signs, tawdry glitter, most of the booths deserted. The murmuring of Helletöng spilled under the surface, plucking at the visible world with flabby fingers. Dust rose in uneasy curls, and the calliope belched, missed a beat, caught itself, and went on.

Where is everyone?

I was cold, despite it being in the high nineties under the sun's assault. The alien scents of the Cirque swallowed me, teased at the inside of my skull. It was a few degrees cooler inside the Cirque's borders, but not enough to be a relief. Just enough to pull out some humidity and make every surface cloying and sweaty.

I heard a low wet chuckle and spun, steelshod heel grinding in dirt. My coat flared like a toreador's cape, the pockets weighted down.

Nothing but the shadow-dogs, crowding close. One slid a smoky paw out into the fall of sunlight and snatched it back, an angular curl of dust rising and dissipating on a breeze I didn't feel.

Something is very wrong here.

Another eerie cry went up, somewhere else in the Cirque. A thin, chill knife ran through my vitals.

They boiled out of the shadows, the dogs smoking with violet fumes, the hellbreed cringing and flinching, and the Traders hissing as they closed on me. The sun was suddenly my best ally, and my hand flashed for my whip just before the first one reached me.

24

Adrenaline spiked through me, the taste of a new copper penny laid against my palate. The dogs clustered, hissing and smoking in the flat white glare of sunlight. They bled gushing gray smoke, their unskin bubbling. One crouched and sprang, hitting a Trader with a bony crunch. The Trader—long, skinny, walnut skin clustered with tufts of hair—screamed and went down, bleeding bright red tainted with black.

I'd already killed two 'breed and three Traders. The bodies lay twisted, hellbreed flesh stinking and simmering with thin black ichor running from its rents and breaks. The Trader bodies were jerking and twisting, contagion eating at the tissues, foulness simmering. My breath puffed a vapor-cloud as if it was subzero instead of scorching, and the silver in my hair rattled and buzzed.

The dogs pressed close, seeming not to notice the roasting on their surfaces. Blisters popped and oozed, and little black specks crawled over them.

It was a serious *what the fuck* moment, even for me.

The Cirque performers pulled back. Sharp glittering teeth, body paint, tawdry shimmers from rhinestones and glass paste. The skinny plague-dealer I'd seen at the entrance to the bigtop crouched in front of the dogs, his knees obscenely splayed under burlap breeches. His antique top hat was stove in, and his eyes glittered madly, dripping hellfire.

Daylight scored each flaw in their beauty, burned it deep, and put the twisting on display. The Traders writhed, caught between the desire to fling themselves at me and the snarling of the hounds.

Jesus, Mary, and Joseph. I tracked the front line of twisted faces, turning in a complete circle, one gun out, the whip jangling in the dust. *Do you suppose it's my cologne?*

The scar blazed with sudden acid fire, pulling on every nerve in my right arm, and every single humanoid form circling me, Trader or 'breed, fell face-first.

He picked his way through them, a mincing step and a tight-drawn mouth. The air peaked behind him in two turbulent whirls, and the breeze turned clotted, full of spoiled honey and dry sand. The whites of his eyes ran with trails and vein-traceries of indigo, his white-blond hair was standing up in soft spikes, and Perry looked *pissed*.

The shadow-dogs whined and cringed, the blisters on their hides smoking furiously.

I straightened, leveled the gun. "That's close enough." My ribs heaved with deep hard breaths.

"Oh, not nearly." His teeth glimmered, sharp and perfect white. Two more mincing steps, his polished wingtips picking delicately between tangled arms and legs. "Here is better." One more. "Or here."

The hammer clicked back as I put more pressure on the trigger. "Come on, hellspawn. Test my patience." *I fucking dare you.* It was an effort not to add the last four words.

"Now, now." But he stayed where he was. "It seems I did well, in insuring your life." A graceful sketch of a motion indicated the dogs. The 'breed and Traders whined, digging themselves into the dirt.

The last time I'd seen Perry in sunlight he'd looked almost transparent, and extraordinarily unhappy. Right now he just looked furious, his eyebrows drawn together and dust swirling into two high peaked points behind him. A ripple passed through all of them, and I had the sudden, not-unwelcome thought that if I could just keep all of them in the sunlight long enough, they might all implode like vampires in bad B movies and save me a lot of trouble.

Sunlight is deadly to a lot of things, but it looked merely *uncomfortable* to Perry. Just my luck. "Don't break your arm patting yourself on the back. What the fuck is going on here?"

He tilted his head to the side. A ripple ran under the surface of his skin, a quick blemish gone as soon as the seeming reasserted itself. "Oh, my dear. Didn't you receive my messages?"

"I've been a bit busy chasing down whoever has such a hard-on for the Cirque performers since I last talked to you." But a sinking sensation thudded into my stomach, and I was suddenly not very happy about what he might say next.

There were any number of things that could make the Cirque performers angry or stupid enough to attack me. Perry didn't let me linger in suspense, though.

"You mean you haven't heard?" His face twisted up in a facsimile of dismay. Then he went and said the most horrible thing he could have at that point. "My darling Kiss. The hostage was attacked again, and lies near death."

Oh, shit. I braced myself. "I'll get to that in a minute." *And here I thought they were pissed because I didn't pay for a ticket.* "What about Moragh?"

"She is dead, eaten by the same monster. What more can concern you about her?" False interest brightened his blue eyes. The rippling under his skin increased, like a pond rippling once a stone's thrown in.

I gathered myself. *All right, Jill. Play this one very carefully.* "I should take a look at whatever's left of her body, Pericles. And if you're a really good little hell-spawn I'll tell you who killed her."

I swear to God, he looked *disappointed.* Perry eyed me for a long few moments, his fingers dangling at his sides, the dogs whining and a low rumble of Helletöng rising like steam from the 'breed plastered to the dusty ground. The Traders twitched in ways no human body should as his will passed over them, a tightening of corruption my blue eye could see all too well.

"Are there likely to be more deaths?" He cocked his head, buttery sunlight turning cold and cringing when it touched his pale hair and his linen-clad shoulders. The dogs growled, a rising note of unhappiness.

Four or five different things slid together in my head all at once. "Of course there are. Unless you get off your hellbreed ass and start helping me control the situation instead of trying to play it like a harmonica. It would be very upsetting to be second fiddle to the Ringmaster in my town, wouldn't it?" *Even temporarily.*

There. Not bad for a toss of the dice. I stared right at the bridge of his hellbreed nose, the naked scar on my arm running with soft wet fire, and wondered if I was going to have to kill them all. Or at least, take as many of them with me as possible.

That's the trick to staring down an unblinking hell-breed—just like scaring the shit out of a human being. Focus on the nose and your gaze grows piercing, a lot of their little glamours and fiddles don't work, and any move they make is generally telegraphed. Peripheral vision is a lot better at picking up that sort of twitchy almost-movement; that's what it's for.

Stare or not, though, even I might have some trouble with the entire Cirque *and* Perry on my ass.

The first consideration was that Perry needed a rea-son to be on my side—and *no* reason to let the Cirque run wild to gain some leverage on me. The second con-sideration was that if he was here, he wasn't watching the hostage.

The third was that I needed him if I was going to hold off the Cirque. I did not want to let them run riot through my city until someone else got a handle on them. Leon down south in Ridgefield or Anya over in the mountains had their own problems; this one was mine.

Last of all, I had to figure out what Perry knew and what side of the fence he was playing. As usual.

"You know what is causing this?" Did Perry sound, of all things, *tentative?*

Wonders never ceased.

"I haven't just been sitting on my fucking thumbs, Perry." I kept the gun steady, sharp hurtful gleams twinkling off the barrel. The sunlight was still so cold my shoulders were tight as bridge cables, and my head hurt. My eyes were dry and full of brambles. *Come on. Can we just have one time without a huge fucking production?*

No, of course we couldn't. These were *hellbreed,* for Christ's sake. Nothing was ever simple or easy. It was all a game, and you constantly had to stay a few jumps ahead.

Perry weighed me for a long moment. The dogs slunk back, smoking and bubbling. Their crystal eyes were tinted red now, veined through with cracks of magma. They vanished into the shadows, and the chill lessened a little. The smells of the Cirque didn't break, but the spoiled-honey-and-flies stink lessened.

The 'breed and Traders still writhed and jerked around us, as if a bomb had hit and we were the only unwounded. The scar sawed away at the nerves in my arm, Perry's attention moving slow and jelly-cold over me. I wished I'd thought to scoop up a fresh leather wristcuff to cover the goddamn thing.

"Then tell me, my dearest one." His tone was a numb-razor kindness. "Tell me who is responsible for this. I will kill him, and we will all be happy."

I almost laughed again, caught the sound before it could reach my throat.

Ha. Nice try. "No, Perry. I'm not telling you a goddamn thing. We're playing this my way." *Because if you got your claws into this, the next thing I knew I'd be yanked into going to the Monde again every month.*

*And I'm sure you have something special planned for
me. Not this time.* I lowered the gun, my arm creaking
with the urge to shoot him in the head and start killing
again.

It would be bad in the long term, but oh, the instant
gratification was tempting.

Tension ticked tighter and tighter between us, a humming line. I kept staring at the bridge of his nose, breathing softly. My pulse was a steady river.

He finally hissed, a long steam-escaping sound of dissatisfaction. But my bluff held. "Very well. I warn you,
though . . ."

Leather creaked as the gun slid back into its holster.
I flipped the whip once, the flechettes jangling. "Save
the threats, Pericles. I need to see the fortuneteller's
body—or whatever's left of it. And you need to be keeping both baby blues on that goddamn hostage. If he dies,
you're the first hellbreed I'm killing."

As threats went, it wasn't a bad one. Especially considering I meant every word.

25

The tent was hung with red velvet, cheap tin spangles, and a huge ugly stink. Black liquid was splashed on every surface, including the cracked slivers of a crystal ball on a small circular table draped with purple sateen. Fine gritty dust puffed every time the breeze plucked at the tent's edges, and the slice of hot daylight from the pulled-aside front flap didn't do much to dispel the gloom.

I had an unsettling notion that this hellbreed had snarled at me, on my first visit to the Cirque. But not enough of her was left to be sure.

I was still cold. Perry crowded behind me until I stepped away, not liking the faint touch of his breath on my hair. The ruby at my throat spat a single bloody spark, and silver in my hair shifted and buzzed, warning him off. "Why aren't you watching the hostage?"

"Oh, I like it much better here with you." His usual tone, bland and interested, with just the faintest sarcastic weight to the words.

"Go, Perry. Have them bring me a bottle of Barban-court rum and some cornmeal."

"You came unprepared?" Mock-surprise, now. He skipped nimbly aside as I turned, avoiding both the sword of daylight through the flap and a bubbling streak of decaying hellbreed tissue. Fine white dust curled up, cringed away from the shine of his shoes.

"I didn't have time to stop at a *botanica*. You gonna stand here running your fucking mouth, or are you going to do what I tell you?"

"Where's your little kitty, my dear? Home lapping a bowl of cream?" His eyes glowed bright blue, the threading of indigo in his whites pulsing in time to some heartbeat too slow to be human.

"Saul isn't your concern, Perry." I was too tired to put much *fuck-you* into it. "Your concern right now is keeping that hostage breathing long enough for me to put an end to this."

"And afterward?"

Afterward you can go fuck yourself again, if it will reach. I folded my arms. "We'll deal with *after,* after. Hurry up."

"I think we should come to an agreement."

"You're about ten seconds away from me blowing another hole in your head. What you think doesn't matter."

His eyes glowed. A small flicker between his parted lips was his wet cherry-red tongue, gleaming in the dimness. "Not even if I'm the one keeping you alive? The performers here are restive, and the Ringmaster is recovering from a nasty bout of green smoke and cockroaches. Even Traders are so fragile."

Even you, he probably meant.

I am not a Trader. I'm a hunter. Don't forget that difference, Perry. "Five seconds." I stared at the air over his head. "And counting."

He sighed, spread his hands . . . and ducked out into the sunlight again, the shiver rippling through his linen suit as well as his skin as the sun, that great enemy of all darkness, touched him.

I hoped it hurt. I hoped every fucking second he spent out in the daylight hurt him.

A straight-backed wooden chair lay flung on the floor, soaked in rotting hellbreed ichor. There was something odd—a long hank of dead-black hair, tangled up in the muck. A few moments more of examination proved it to be a wig, with a kerchief tangled in it. The kerchief had once been red, and was now rotting as the acid ate at it. The wig's fake hair was stronger stuff, bubbling slightly as it was . . . digested.

"Ugh." I glanced up. *She was probably at the table when it started.*

Greasy antique playing cards scattered across the table. Five of spades, ace of spades, queen of spades, all spackled with steaming liquid rot and covered in teensy roach tracks. The crystal-ball shards vibrated slightly, and something lay tangled under the knife-sharp splinters. Even the base of twisted dull metal the crystal ball must have rested on was torn up, sharp jagged edges still quivering with distress.

The violence of this attack was far and away the worst. It looked like the hellbreed had literally exploded in chunks. Even with all the sacrifice Zamba

had performed at her house—the killing of her closest
followers—this was superlative.

Which meant Mama Zamba must've had some link
to Moragh the fortuneteller. Something physical, the last
piece of the puzzle.

Come on. Something has to be here. I was about to
start tearing the tent apart when a round silvery glimmer
caught my eye.

I crouched, the balls of my feet slipping slightly
in greasy, bubbling gunk. Each piece of silver I wore
quivered with blue light, blessing reacting with contamination.

"Bingo," I whispered. I shook a piece of fabric out of
my pocket—a red bandanna, 51 colors like Gilberto's,
left over from the last big case. I unknotted it, folded it
over, and grabbed.

The pocket watch dangled, gunk dripping off it.
Steam curled away from its steel curve. Not silver, and
not gold, but still antique. "Blessed Maria." The words
were numb on my lips, but the hellbreed ichor cringed,
turning inert and dripping free. "Watch over us sinners,
now and at the hour of our death."

Belief behind words neutralizes evil, one of the oldest
tricks in the book.

I popped the case free. The watch had stopped at
11:59, and there was no way of knowing, but I would
bet it was P.M. A plain face, with the Greek letter Omega
right under the 12. The crystal wasn't cracked, and en-
graved on the outer edge of the front casing were three
worn-down letters.

SRG. Samuel Gregory. I wondered what the "R"
stood for.

There wasn't much about this case that I could feel good about. But I felt good about this, even with my coat hanging in hellbreed muck and my heart breaking inside my ribs.

"Gotcha," I said softly. "Gotcha, you bitch."

I closed the watch up and stowed it in my pocket. Stood, my knees creaking, and surveyed the rest of the tent. A shadow fell across the flap and I whirled, hand to a gun.

It was the stuttering barker, Troy. His face twisted up, hard red flush high on his cheekbones. His mouth was a thin line, and his hair was mussed.

He held a bottle of Barbancourt rum. "H-h-h-here." The single syllable strangled itself on the way out of his mouth. "I-it w-was H-H-Helene's."

"Well, it's going to help catch her killer." I took the bottle, and he dug in his pocket. Came up with a much-wrinkled paper bag. I pointed. It seemed easier than making him talk. "Cornmeal?"

He contented himself with a nod and handed it over. "A-are y-you r-really g-g-g-going to—"

"I'm really going to fuck up Helene's killer, Troy." *Jesus. I'm reassuring a Trader.* "How's Ikaros?"

His thin shoulders came up, dropped. His eyes glittered with the flat shine of the dusted, and he seemed not to notice the stink filling the tent. The red suspenders were even more hopelessly frayed, and his white shirt looked wilted. "Th-th-they s-s-say you're n-not g-g-g-going to d-do an-ny-nything. Th-that—"

God, it was like pulling nails out of stubborn wood, listening to him talk. "I don't care what they say. I'm just interested in getting this over with. Get out of here."

His lip curled for a bare moment before turning into a thin bloodless line again, and he retreated out into the glare. I was left holding the rumpled bag of cornmeal and a half-full bottle of Barbancourt, standing in the middle of a rotting smear of hellbreed and staring at the shards of a crystal ball, clutching a pocket watch that ran with blue light under the surface of its steel casing.

I set the rum and the bag of cornmeal on one of the few unsullied spots on the table, yanked the cup out of my pocket. The watch fit inside, and when I drew the straight razor out and slid it into the cup the blue light didn't just lurk below the surface. It fizzed over, falling in a cascade of sparks. A shiver walked down my spine again.

"Oh yes." I tilted the cup, watching the blue light paint the fraying velvet of the walls, and the bottle of rum trembled against the tabletop. "I've got you now, Zamba."

So much of sorcery is pure will. You don't really have to do a damn thing except declare, *This is the way the world is.* People do it every day. The record plays just under the surface of their conscious minds, all those assumptions they make.

That's just the way it goes. Some things won't ever change.

It's also the principle that lets hellbreed, Sorrows, Middle Way adepts, and so many others slip through the cracks. People fear muggers or tax audits. They don't fear the things that crouch in the crevices, staring up with glowing eyes that don't obey human geometry.

Oh, sure, people subconsciously cringe away from a full-fledged 'breed or shiver when an *arkeus* passes close enough to touch. But they won't really *look*. They don't want to see.

And they will hurry away, if they can. Lock their car doors and forget.

Whatever weird confluence of genetics and opportunity makes a hunter, one thing is paramount: the ability to look steadily at the weirdness and the filth. The refusal to look away.

And add to that the stubbornness to refuse to accept that what you see has to stay the way you see it. I can't explain it any more clearly. It's the original sin, I suppose—the pride to stand toe to toe with God and say, *No, you did something wrong. You fucked up here, and it's my job to make it better. To fix it, as much as I can. Maybe you're too busy, maybe you have a great cosmic plan that accounts for all this suffering and hideousness—but I don't, I'm not you, and I'm going to fucking* do *something.*

It's just centimeters away from the pride that hellbreed think gives them the right to murder, rape, pillage, distort, and batten on the helpless.

But those centimeters count.

The straight razor rattled in the blue enamel cup. The pocket watch did too, blue sparks popping and fizzing as I held it in front of me, arms extended, knuckles and tendons standing up with the effort of keeping the wildly agitated metal still.

The rum burned in my mouth. I held it, my gag reflex quivering on the edge of kicking in, the alcohol fuming until my eyes watered and spilled over. The cornmeal, a

fine thin line of it in a circle around me, shifted. Little
grains of it rose, touched down again with slight whispering sounds.

They didn't scatter. They just lifted and plopped down
again.

When physical material has already been sensitized
to a load of etheric energy, it's easier to pump more force
through it. My arms burned. My throat was on fire. Tears
rolled down my cheeks.

I ignored it all. Fierce, relaxed concentration filled my
skull. The cup leapt and rattled like a live thing, jerking
so hard it would have dislocated my shoulder if hellbreed
strength wasn't pouring through my right fist, scorching sliding down my wrist and pooling in my palm. My
bones creaked. I dug my heels in, concentrating.

The pool of filth that used to be the fortuneteller bubbled. Her wig sent up curls of smoke. My blue eye narrowed, eyelid twitching madly as if I had some sort of
tic. The strings under the surface of the visible snarled,
ran together in a complex patterned knot.

Sometimes the best way to go about it is to unpick the
knot, strand by strand. Then there's other times, when
you just slice the goddamn thing in half and let the resulting reaction smack someone in the head.

Guess which one's my favorite.

In this space, half-sideways from myself, I could *see*
the fine dusting over every surface, an etheric imprint
like the scales on a butterfly's wings. Zamba had spent
energy recklessly to reach this victim.

She must be getting close to the end, or desperate.
The cup rattled, lunged forward.

The great hunter magics are largely sympathetic, as

opposed to the controlling sorcery of, say, the Sorrows. Sympathetic magic is intensely personal; you have to know yourself before you can use it. One of the greatest dictums in hunter training: *know thyself.*

And of course, there are times when brute force instead of subtle knowledge is the best way to get things done.

I sucked in air through my rapidly filling nose, my lungs inflating. The rum was getting hotter and hotter in my mouth. The cornmeal shifted wildly, with a sound like static cling on a pair of really big metallic socks.

I gathered myself. The mental image solidified inside my head, seen with the unsight of my blue eye. Long blond dreadlocks, blue eyes, a narrow waist, a bony face with smallpox scars across the cheeks, a long blue and silver caftan kilted up to her knees. Mama Zamba was crouched, looking wildly around her, fat snakes of hair writhing. She could probably tell something was gathering, but not *what.*

I spat, a long trailing mist of rum that ignited in a puff of blue flame. The cup leapt again, dragging me a few inches, my heels stapling into the dusty ground. Cornmeal popped into flame too, sizzling. The smell was baking bread for just a moment, then shaded into burning starch.

Potential shifted, *might* became *is,* and the force left me in a huge painless gout. The tent flapped wildly, straining against its moorings, and the calliope music rose to a shriek.

Rum-fire and burning cornmeal winked out. The force yanking on the blue enamel cup snapped like a rubber band, and I sat down hard, skidding on my leather-clad ass as my teeth jolted together.

Jesus. Major sorcery always ends up with a pratfall. Reaction hit, like thunder after lightning. The strength went out of all my bones and I sagged, the scar singing one wet little satisfied note against my arm.

I heard my own breathing, harsh stentorian gasps. Blinked several times. Gray smoke billowed, wreathed the entire tent. The bubbling hellbreed ichor gave one or two last pops and settled, spent.

I swallowed, the reek of rum and burning baked goods sliming the back of my throat. "Checkmate," I said, softly, and wished I could lie down and sleep.

But there is no rest for the wicked, or for a hunter who has just bought a little breathing room. Zamba wouldn't be fucking with anyone at all until dark fell and the tide of magic turned. I pushed myself up on trembling hands and knees, wished Saul was there.

It was the wrong thought. A sob escaped halfway, I set my teeth and bit, choking it off. Pushed myself upright the rest of the way, every muscle screaming in protest.

Just a little longer, Jill. You've got a plan, stick to it.

It was good advice. But I was oh, so tired.

The iron voice of duty had no truck with my complaining. *Get moving. Finish the job.* I bent wearily, scooping the watch and the straight razor back into the cup.

Time for the next part of the plan.

26

I found the Ringmaster by the simple expedient of collaring a passing Trader and putting a gun to the skinny, rhinestone-laden asshole's greasy head. I needn't have bothered—he just led me to the same broken-down Airstream trailer the hostage had been in before. There was a huge hole busted in the side of it, and a large black spot in the dirt where the Ringmaster had bled.

I went up the wrecked steps carefully as the Trader hissed behind me, set my foot over the threshold, and half-glanced over my shoulder. "Open your mouth again," I said softly, "and I will break every last one of your hell-trading teeth."

The hissing cut short as if someone had taken a kettle off the stove, and I edged into the darkness inside the ruined trailer.

Perry sat in a folding chair, leaning back, elbows on the arms and fingers steepled in front of his nose. The frowsty bed held a stick-thin blond figure, collapsed against pillows and breathing softly, with a gleam of silver at its throat.

The Ringmaster crouched easily at the end of the bed, his thin shoulders up and his top hat askew. Frayed red velvet strained at his shoulders and hung down, his jodhpurs stretched over his bony knees. He glanced back at me, his eyes burning orange in the dimness, and his lip lifted silently. I saw the flash of the boneridge that passed for his teeth, but he immediately turned back to the hostage and I let it go.

"Hello, darling." Perry's words slid against each other, Helletöng rumbling underneath them. "It has been an *interesting* morning."

"How's he doing?" My throat still burned from the rum. I wondered if he could smell it on me. A colorless fume of sorcery still hung on me too, and no doubt he could smell that.

"Oh, I didn't know you *cared*." Perry snorted slightly. "He suddenly quieted, not ten minutes ago. The magic pulling on him slackened, and he is sleeping."

"Pulling on him, huh?" *Now that's odd.* "What was the collar doing?"

"Sparking like all your curséd metal." The indigo threading through Perry's whites was black in the dimness, and the scar chuckled to itself like wet lips rubbing together. "It seemed to help, though."

I had to turn my back to him to check the hostage, and I was so tired I only felt the slightest ripple of unease up the muscles along my spine. My boots whispered through a drift of candy wrappers and paper trash. Something stuck under my heel, and Perry chuckled softly.

The sweat on me turned to ice. But I just lifted one

of the hostage's eyelids and checked the pupil reaction: none. The dust-shine on the surface of the eyeball had turned thick and mucousy, dry and veined on the surface. His breath was regular and shallow, his ribs rising and dropping. There was no spare flesh on him, and he wore only a pair of stained jockey shorts. His skin was mottled like a night-growing fungus. Lines of spidery writing sank into the stretched, sunken skin, twitching sluggishly with his slow pulse.

The writing flinched away from my touch. My apprentice-ring sparked, and the collar took on a dim foxfire glow. The biggest pocket of my trench coat flapped slightly, as if a small animal nestled inside it.

Huh. Curiouser and curiouser.

I passed my palm down Ikaros's torso, the hellish scribbles fleeing my touch. The mottling also fled a little, but it still took two or three passes before Perry made a small spitting sound of annoyance.

"Do you *mind?*"

"Actually, I really don't. Sounds like you do, though." I kept looking. I wasn't quite sure what I was looking *for,* but the way the cup, razor, and watch trio was shaking in my pocket was an odd sign.

I glanced at the foot of the bed. The Ringmaster hissed softly, the bone ridge's crevices grimed with something dark and dripping. Faint shadows crawled across his face, the traces of poisoning from blessed silver.

I stepped toward him. The hostage's breathing evened out, became deeper. The scar tingled, expectant.

"Jill." Perry's tone was a warning.

I'm in a trailer with two hellbreed I'm not killing and a Trader I'm trying to save. Jeez. "Just a second, Pericles." I eased forward another step, leather-clad shins whispering along the side of the foam mattress.

The rattling in my pocket decreased.

That isn't right. She's after the Ringmaster, isn't she? It's the only thing that makes sense. I looked back at the hostage, who stirred restlessly and curled up on his side, unconsciously making a lizardlike movement with his head to make the collar's spikes fold down on one side.

I wondered how long he'd been doing this, to be so easy with the thing.

The thought of what Ikaros might have paid for that might have made me shudder, if I hadn't been so tired.

"What did he Trade for?" The words fell into a sudden dangerous silence, filling the dark, trash-strewn interior. The jagged edge of sunlight falling over the door wasn't a beacon of hope—it was a sterile blanket. In the distance, the calliope rollicked on, and I suddenly wanted to find out where the music was coming from and fucking shoot the goddamn thing so I didn't have to listen to it.

"None of your business," the Ringmaster finally said, each sibilant laden with menace.

I turned my head, met his pumpkin-hellfire gaze. "You brought trouble to my town. There's people dead in the streets, and I've been attacked." *Besides, this is an old unfinished case, and I'm going to see it carried through.* "Any question I care to ask about, any dirty laundry I take an interest in, *is* my business. What did he Trade for?"

The Ringmaster did his best to stare me down. But Perry shifted slightly, the folding chair creaking, and the thin, crow-haired 'breed actually cowered, perched on the end of the bed like a vulture.

If this keeps up, Perry, I might just even get to like you. Or at least, hate you a very little bit less.

"Henri, this is excessively wearying." Perry sounded bored, but the Ringmaster flinched again. I took another half-step toward him, and the buzzing rattle in my pocket diminished again.

Another little piece of the puzzle fell into place. Not a big one, but one that stopped me and made me examine the hostage's face again in the dimness.

"For the same thing every hostage Trades for," the Ringmaster finally said. "For peace. Forgetting. An end to pain."

Why do I not believe that for a minute? "He had something he didn't want to remember?"

"Doesn't everyone? Even our kind has regrets." He shifted, and I saw his feet were bare, horny calloused toes gripping like fingers. The muscle under the skin flickered in ways no human meat would move. "Not many, true. But still."

Regrets from a hellbreed? Jesus. "Yeah, like you regret you didn't kill someone painfully enough? Whatever." For the hundredth time, I took a firmer hold on my temper. "What did he trade for?"

"I told you. He traded to forget. And he was valued here among us."

Valued, yeah. As a way to keep the hunters off your backs, or a way to allay suspicion? As a mascot? Don't break my heart. I let out a sigh, my cheeks puffing up and the sensation of Perry's eyes on my leather-clad back like ice against fevered skin. "I've got other business to transact. The attacks won't start again until dark, and I'll be back before sunset. Perry, you keep watch. And *you*." It was an effort not to jab a finger at the Ringmaster. "Clear out the bigtop. Before it's dark we're going to need the hostage in there and people watching the entrances and exits. The rest of your people need to be outside the city limits by the time dusk hits."

That got a reaction. The hellbreed stiffened, and the scar burned with sudden hurtful awareness. "You're throwing us out?" He showed his boneridge again, and a sudden certainty boiled up in me. If he mouthed off just one more goddamn time . . .

Calm down, Jill. Get some perspective. The exhaustion both helped and hindered. I was too tired to go on a homicidal rampage, but the chain on my temper was fraying.

Hard.

"No. I'm catching your killer and finishing this up. You give me any more flak and you're going to be auditioning a new Ringmaster instead of a new hostage. Get me?"

Hey, they're not the only ones who can threaten.

"I do not think—"

"Of course you don't." Perry's tone was smooth as silk. "It is not your strength. Our little hunter doesn't wish to lose whatever advantage she has. She will keep the identity of our killer secret until the last possible moment, to ensure we do not make alliance with him *and* to ensure this ends the way she wishes. With the Cirque firmly under control and myself, I suspect, neutralized."

It didn't sound bad when he said it, but I was kind of

irritated that he twigged to it. More irritating was how surprised he sounded, as if he didn't think me capable of realizing my best chance of wrapping this up and making it so the 'breed didn't get any funny ideas was controlling the dispersal of information.

"The thing is," he continued meditatively, "she cannot be sure what I know. And here she is, with her back to me and her throat within reach of your claws. She must be very sure, this canny little wench, of at least one thing—that I want her alive for my own purposes."

The only thing I'm sure of right at this moment is that I'm not going to murder you just yet. And that I can't trust you as far as I could throw you with two broken arms. I said nothing, but the sudden drop in my pulse-rate was warning enough. If either of them moved on me now Zamba might just be a loose end to tie up at my leisure, instead of part of a ticking time bomb of an equation. "Don't flatter yourself, Perry. You're occasionally useful, but in the end you're just one thing."

His laugh was as cold and slow as the sudden chilling of the scar, a chunk of dry ice pressed against my skin, eating its way down. "And what is that?"

"Just another hellspawn." I swung toward the hole in the side of the trailer. "I'll be back by dusk. Nothing should pull on the hostage before then."

They rumbled at each other in töng, metal rubbing painfully against itself in some deserted trainyard. The Ringmaster's tone went up at the end, an inquisitive ear-flaying squeal, and Perry's deeper answering rumble swallowed it whole.

I stepped out into the curtain of golden light. The cold around me cracked reluctantly, threads of heat touching my leather-clad shoulders. The cup rattled a few times and was still, a weight in my largest pocket.

Calliope music surged and drifted. The shadows were alive, lean dogshapes twisting and leaping through them. The sun was higher, working through the shell of ice over me. It was going to be another scorcher of a day, and I wasn't going to get any more rest.

Come on, Jill. You can rest later. Right now, you've got to break few traffic laws.

I lengthened my stride. Dust lifted on the morning breeze, and I caught a breath of cotton candy and sickness. The Cirque shimmered, even more frayed and tawdry in daylight, thick electrical cables strung between the tents. The avenues and alleys were deserted, but I could feel eyes on me.

I tried not to feel like I was retreating, and had to remind myself to keep my chin up as I headed for the entrance.

Galina met me at the door, in jeans and a gray T-shirt. "Jill, thank God. I remembered. I can't understand why I forgot—"

"Voodoo," I said shortly. *Memory is as easy as electronics to subvert. It's honest paper they have trouble with sometimes.* "Where's Gilberto?"

"Upstairs sleeping. I gave him a tranquilizer and set a healing on that arm of his. He seems okay enough." Her eyes were dark and troubled, and her marcel waves were slightly disarranged, pulled back under another red kerchief. "I was in the kitchen stirring up a batch of bone-ease and all of a sudden it hit me, like I'd known it all along. Listen—"

So Zamba's slipping and her loa *are no longer paying attention to certain things. Or it doesn't matter now that she's close to getting what she wants.* I made a restless movement. I was two steps ahead but I might not stay that way for long. "I need ammo, I need a place to work, and I need your help."

"Jill, *listen*. I think Mama Zamba is—"

"Is Arthur Gregory. He made a deal with the Twins, got a sex change or just dressed like a girl to throw everyone off the scent, and part of the deal was clouding his origins so nobody would guess or find him. It didn't work completely on you because you're a Sanctuary, and it didn't work on Sloane's files because of the defenses on Hutch's store and the standard defenses on every piece of hunter paper. I just spanked Zamba a good one this morning, and I'm working on no time and even less sleep. Can you get me some ammo and talk while I'm reloading? I'll need some other things, too."

The shop resounded around her, clear air thrumming like a bell for a moment, and I swayed on my feet. I could still smell cotton candy, and the reek of a hellbreed body boiling as it ate through cloth and false hair alike.

Galina folded her arms and examined me from top to toe. "Heavens. Where's Saul? You look terrible."

"Thanks. I think Saul left me." Said that way, it only managed to hurt like hell instead of cripple me.

"Left you?" A vertical crease showed up between her pretty eyebrows. "But—"

"Galina." I closed the door, the bell jangling discordantly. My arms ached, a low deep fierce pain. I'd probably pulled something trying to keep the cup still, and sorcery tells on the physical body even when you have the power to burn. Come to think of it, my ass hurt too. I would probably be bruised by midnight. "My love life can wait. If Zamba kills who she's aiming for, there's going to be heavy-duty problems and I'm too tired to deal with them. I've got a plan but I need your help. You can talk and help me at the same time."

"What do you need?" She was suddenly all practical attention, turning on her bare heel and setting off across the store toward the back counter.

"Rum. Hand mirrors. Florida water. Cigars. A little bit of luck, and everything you now remember about Samuel and Arthur Gregory." I took a step after her, and paused. "And . . . you wouldn't happen to have any live chickens around, would you?"

"I don't deal in livestock; I send people to Zamba for that. Or used to, anyway."

Damn. But all of a sudden, a bright idea popped into my head. "Never mind, I can get 'em somewhere else. I'm going to need to use your phone, too. Oh, and cornmeal." I paused. "And I think I might need some heavy-duty firepower."

She didn't even blink. "Like?"

"Grenades. If this all goes south I'm going to need to kill a lot of 'breed *really* quickly."

27

The sun was still a decent distance above the horizon when I goosed my Pontiac through the rows of parked cars under hoods and blankets of sparkling dust, bumped over a temporary speed bump, and got right up near the front gate. The same female Trader working the admissions booth didn't even glance up. There wasn't a single, shuffling soul in sight in the wide dusty strip in front of the booth, and a pall of white biscuit-flour dust hung over everything.

The heat was like oil, and I was glad. I'd washed my face at Galina's, but I was still grimed with dust as soon as I stepped out into the haze. The Trader in the booth stared as I opened the trunk and shrugged into the first bandolier. On went the belt, heavy with more ammo, and the second bandolier. The weight at shoulders and hips was enough to drive home just how fucking tired I was, and my eyes burned. I blinked away fine grit and picked up the black canvas bag, settled the strap diagonally across my body.

Jesus. I'm loaded up like a burro. I also got the flat-tish cage out of the backseat, thanking God I'd gotten a sedan and not the two-door coupe. If someone wanted to firebomb *this* car they had their work cut out for them, GM hadn't believed in fucking around with fiberglass in the '60s and this was one of the heaviest, widest mothers they ever built. Plus, the price had been right—it was a heap when I picked it up, but a month or two of heavy work and it was a solid, if not cherry, piece of American metal.

The chickens were okay, three balls of white feathers in a wire cage. Piper hadn't even asked me why I wanted them. "They're pecking and clucking, and I can't get rid of them until Monday," was what she said out loud. *God-dammit, take these fucking things away,* was the unspoken message.

And then she'd looked at me when I appeared in the door of her office, and said, "Jesus, Jill. You look awful."

It's about to get worse, I thought, and slammed the door. Stuffed my keys in their safe pocket, blew a kiss to my baby, and turned on one slick steelshod heel, stamped for the entrance.

"You can't leave that there!" the Trader called, her fingernails digging into the pasteboard counter. "Hey!"

My left hand had the cage, and my right actually cramped when I snatched it back from a gun butt. *Don't waste ammo on this bitch,* the cold clear voice of rationality said. *You're going to need it later.*

I didn't realize I was staring as her until she blundered backward, the spangles on her shirt sending up hard clear darts of light as she spilled right through the

back of the little hutch where she crouched, deciding
who could go in and get trapped by the Cirque. Must've
been a helluva cushy job.

But not right now.

She vanished, and sunlight bounced through the
empty booth. A flutter of small paper tickets puffed into
the air, settled. I uncramped my fingers, shook them out,
and took a deep breath.

Cool and calm, Jillybean. That's the way to do this.

I waited until I felt the little click inside my head, the
one that meant I was rising away, disconnected, into the
clear cold place where I could do what I had to without
counting the cost. The space where murder was just se-
mantics and the only thing that mattered was the task
at hand. Anything else—pity, mercy, compassion—just
fucked it up, just tangled the clarity of justice and made
everything difficult.

It was a good thing Saul wasn't here. I couldn't do this
with him around. Not with his quiet dark eyes watching
me. And that was part of the problem, wasn't it? It wasn't
him.

It was me.

But right now I hopped the stile, weighted down and
maneuvering the wire cages with one hand. The ram's
heads sparked, gathering the late hot sunlight and throwing it back viciously. I could swear I saw one of the blind
snouts move, and the stile clicked once as I landed, a dry
ominous sound.

Thou who, I thought. *Thou who has given me to fight
evil, protect me, keep me from harm.*

Usually the Hunter's Prayer calms me. This time, it
was no anodyne. It was a complement to the unsteady

ball of rage under my ribs. *Because I want to be the one dishing out the harm tonight. Some divine help wouldn't hurt, if this plan's going to pull itself off.*

It was warm and still inside the Cirque. Balmy, even. The whole place was deserted. Maybe the girl in the booth had been an early-warning system, or maybe she didn't get the memo that everyone was supposed to be gone. Nothing moved except unsecured tent flaps, and the calliope was muted and limping along through a rendition of the "Cuckoo Waltz," wheezing and popping, straining like a locomotive going uphill.

Dusk was beginning to gather. The shadows had lengthened. I've seen a lot, and believe me when I say there is *nothing* creepier than a carnival at dusk. The midway games were all lit up, but nobody was in the booths. The dust tamped itself down where people's feet had shuffled. The ghost of cotton candy turned cloying and rotten, haunted the heavy stillness. The breeze mouthed the fringe over the goldfish bowl, whistled through the pegs of the Wheel of Fortune, made the Ring the Bell, Strongman!'s bell make a low hollow sound. I caught a glimpse of a carousel down one long avenue of tents, the horses rising and falling with a clatter. The mirrors ran with soft dead light even through the red glow of approaching sunset, and where the horses shifted into shadow a ripple ran as if their muscles moved. Carved manes tossed, and some of them trickled greasy, black-looking blood from sharptooth mouths.

A mouthful of fried-food scent, old grease gone rancid and clotted, brushed by, and the chickens made soft broody sounds. A single white feather drifted down from the cage. THROW A RING, a hand-lettered sign barked at me, the white-painted words surrounded by leering faces, WIN A PRIZE. The rings chattered softly against the angled spikes, and I could almost see the pegs used to make the spikes impossible to hit.

I penetrated the tangled maze, heading for the big-top's bulk. Its pennants flapped as the wind came up the river on its evening exhale, and I heard a distant mutter of thunder behind the calliope's mournful wrangling. The flat mineral tang of the water swept the fried food, animals, and spoiled candy away from me for a moment, and I was suddenly possessed of the intense urge to set the cages down, shuck all my weaponry, go back to the car, and drive. Somewhere, anywhere. Away from here and the job that had to be done. Away from the job that would kill me one of these days.

The carnival-breath closed around me again, walling away the clean scent of the river. All of a sudden I smelled popcorn and white vinegar, corn dogs and healthy human sweat. The calliope lunged forward into "Take Me Out to the Ballgame," and I remembered one of the few good times in my childhood, when my mother was between boyfriends. She had taken me to a Santa Luz Wheelwrights game, and we'd eaten hot dogs and cheered until we were hoarse.

Two weeks after that her new guy put her in the hospital and beat me to a pulp too. I was six.

Memory exploded, calliope music wrapping around me and tapping the inside of my skull, and I had another, deeper urge. To throw down the cage and the weapons, to retrace my steps and find that carousel, and to pick a horse. Any horse, it wouldn't matter. Though I would like one with tawny sides and dark eyes, and I was sure there would be one there waiting just for me. I could climb up on its back and ride, and one by one every memory I *didn't* want to keep would fall away like autumn leaves.

And if the horse shuddered and lurched then, if it grew fangs and the other horses clustered around with hellfire in their eyes and their teeth dripping, I would not care. I would willingly lie down, and it wouldn't be rough wooden planks that I felt. It would be the killing cold of a snowbank, and I would be back in the snow before Mikhail pulled me out.

Not tonight, little one, he'd said. But even then I'd known it was only a matter of time.

I shivered. The chickens made more soft noises. The tremor passed through me, and the calliope missed a single note.

If I went and got on that carousel, though, I would forget Saul. I would forget the low inquiring purr he used when he was sleepy and I moved against him in the warm nest of our bed. I would forget the way his hair curled, and the depth of his dark eyes. I would forget his hands warm on me, and the soothing when I sobbed and he would hold me, murmuring into my hair.

Even our volcanic fights, when we screamed at each other and the ghosts of my past would rise behind each edged word. Or the silence in Hutch's bookshop when I realized he was gone, most probably for good, because I didn't deserve him.

Remembering him would be a double-edged pleasure. But it was one I would hold to me in the dead watches of the night, when I was patrolling and my city was a collection of black and gray. Filth in its corners and the cries of innocents falling on deaf ears.

If I dropped what I was holding and went to the carousel, who would even try to fight for them? And who would remember Saul the way I did?

Trembling had me in its grip like a dog shaking a favorite chew toy. Sweat slicked my skin, ran down the channel of my spine. The chickens were squawking more loudly now, because their cage was jerking back and forth. I came back to myself with a rush, and found the shadows had lengthened. One lay over my boot-toes, and I looked up, confused.

The sun was sinking. How long had I been standing here?

Silver chimed as I shook my head, the charms clattering against each other. My apprentice-ring popped a spark, and the chickens took exception to that. I let out a harsh breath, my pulse hammering like I'd just run a hard mile. Feathers drifted to the ground, and I noticed the dust had swirled around me, streaks against my leather pants up to my thighs.

As if something had been rubbing against my legs.

The calliope surged again, but I couldn't identify the tune and it didn't pluck at me. It sounded dissatisfied. I took an experimental step forward, and the chickens calmed down. More thunder sounded, closer now. I checked the deepening bruise of the sky, found no clouds.

I understood more about the Cirque now. Much, much more than I ever wanted to.

My legs stopped trembling after another couple of steps. I swallowed a horrible bitter taste and almost choked on the regret and unsteady anger.

The bigtop wasn't far. I somehow made my weary legs go faster, and I walked toward it with my head held high.

28

There was no guard at the door—just a red velvet rope I felt okay stepping over, since its arc almost dragged the strip of faded Astroturf leading into the maw. The plague-carrier's straight wooden chair was set to one side, flies buzzing around its encrusted surface. My coat whispered, and thunder growled again in the distance.

First impression: soaring space. The place was *huge*. At the far end was a collection of gleams and puffs of green vapor, and the back of my neck chilled when I realized it was the calliope, two stories high and belching lime-green steam. It wasn't any louder, certainly not loud enough to be heard all through the Cirque.

Next impression: empty seats, their wooden surfaces polished by God knew how many rear ends and backs, their arms carved. Some had straps lying open, others hungry metal hoops that clicked open and shut in time with the music, right where they could close over wrists and ankles. Some of the seats flipped up and down in tentative jerks.

Three knee-high wooden rings held vast circles of stained sawdust. The two smaller, flanking circles held all sorts of weird metal cages and implements, some crusted with nameless fluids, others gleaming dully. The light came from nowhere, and rippled on the underside of the canvas like reflections from a pond's unquiet, scum-laced surface.

The biggest, central ring was mostly bare. Dark spatters and drips spoke in their own tongueless language—*that's high-impact splatter, and right there is arterial spray, and that's where someone was bludgeoned.* I forced myself to look away.

Set in the exact middle of the middle ring was a plain metal bedstead with a thin dun mattress that looked older than I felt. The hostage lay, curled into a fetal position, his narrow shadowed back to me. He was still wearing the same ratty boxers, and the collar glinted under his lank hair.

I stepped over the border of the ring, candystriped plywood faded and chipped this close up. As soon as I did, light glared, and I almost threw myself into a fighting crouch before I realized it was a spot from high up, and it highlighted the Ringmaster, standing at the other end of the circle. His face was a cadaver's leer, and he capered a little like a tired old horse, his red velvet coat glaring and the top hat sending back jets of dispirited aqueous light. His cane whirled once like a propeller, the green crystal globe humming as it clove thick air.

He danced again, his jodhpurs flapping and the boots landing hard on springy sawdust. Then he halted, jabbed the cane at me, and hissed.

I set the chickens down. They had gone deathly quiet,

and the cage shook slightly. I didn't blame them a bit. The shadows in here leapt and swirled, but I didn't see any colorless crystal eyes or lean leaping forms. Even my blue eye was having trouble with the shifting shadows, the ether thick as pea soup.

But just because I didn't see them didn't mean they weren't there. And Perry had to be around here somewhere too.

The calliope quieted slightly, faint cheery music with an undertone of ripping flesh and splintered bone. I did my best to tune it out.

"Come on in and step right up, ladies and gentlemen! See the hunter come into the ring! Yessir it's a sight for the ages, and tonight's show will be the one to end all shows! Hurry, hurry, find your seats—"

"Shut *up*." My yell sliced right through his, and the scar woke to painful, agonized life, sending a hot bolt up my right arm. "And get out of the fucking ring."

"This is the seat of our power." All the bluster was gone. His eyes were sheets of orange fire, fat drops sizzling down his thin cheeks. He even wore stained white gloves, and the calliope agreed with him, singing along. It followed his breathing, a deep hitch whenever he sucked at the air to fuel that voice. "You heard the siren song, didn't you?"

Goddamn hellbreed. Tell me again why I'm helping you. "Henri." I sounded like a teacher addressing a recalcitrant third-grader, but it was just the exhaustion. "If you don't fucking get out of this ring I'm going to blow your head off."

The cane whirled again, once. His lips peeled back, and the faint lines running through the sharp boneridges that served him as teeth were no longer approximations of a human mouth.

No, they were all shark, and all pointed at me.

But I stood my ground, next to the chickens in their wire cage, fine white feathers now drifting upward on a random draft of air. Killing him and burning this entire horrorshow to the ground had a certain appeal.

But that would ruin the plan, Jill.

A wall of warm air flapped through the entrance, the canvas straining and ropes suddenly creaking. The shadows turned darker, and I knew instinctively that the sun had touched the horizon. *Not long now.*

"As you like." The Ringmaster capered back. "For now."

I picked up the cage and matched him step for step, forward as he retreated. By the time I reached the bed in the center, Henri de Zamba was a good twenty feet away toward another pair of flaps, a stage entrance. More spotlights buzzed into life, glaring circles of leprous white stabbing the seats. A shifting crowd murmur filled the tent. I half expected to see people shuffling in, their faces blank with the expectation of entertainment. This light would bleach them out, turn them into ghosts, and the calliope would murmur like it was murmuring now.

Another rattle of thunder sounded. I could barely hear it over the music.

I set the cage down. Dug in the black canvas bag. The white novenas in their glass sheaths went at the cardinal points, unlit. I circled around the bed and its deathly-still occupant, leaving a trickle of cornmeal. I made the circle as perfect as I could, etheric force bleeding out from the fingers of my right hand to guide it and keep it solid. The particles were unearthly yellow, like the sunlight even now bleeding away over the edge of the world.

The circle had to be big enough to contain the bed *and* another smaller circle traced at the foot. This one I tried not to hurry over, but the shadows in here were getting stronger. How long had I stood listening to the calliope and thinking about the carousel?

Just do it, Jill. Worry later.

The *veve* took shape, the spout of the plastic bottle of meal jittering a little as force ran smoothly through my hand. Alien curves unreeled, and the second smaller circle to one side grew almost without me noticing it. Cornmeal shifted and hissed over the sound of the calliope, and the lines twitched and tweaked until they were satisfied. The meal ran out, but the symbol completed itself out of nowhere.

A shiver walked down my spine again, salt crust from the cold sweat drying itched. *Great.*

The shadows were wine-dark now, well on their way to achieving solidity. Ikaros stirred and the Ringmaster hissed again.

Move it along, woman! The cigars almost fell out of my shaking hands, rolling in their sheaths. I tipped Florida water out, a sweet orange breath overriding the reek of animals and sawdust. When I looked next, the cigars had arranged themselves near each *veve,* short bristling hairs atop the circles.

The Ringmaster hissed again. I set the bottle of Barbancourt rum down, pulled the bag strap over my head, and reached down into its depths, bringing up a plastic bag of copper chloride.

"I do not recognize this sorcery." The Ringmaster paced closer to the edge of the containing circle. "I do not trust you."

"That makes us about even." I tipped all the copper chloride I could hold into my left hand. "You're the first one I'm going to kill if this doesn't work out. Just remember that."

The world held its breath. I pitched the bag and scooped up the rum, just in time. The long dusk exhale ended, and I felt the end of sunset all the way down to my bones.

I can always feel it. Sunset always wakes me up like five shots of espresso and a bullet whizzing past. I swear I can feel the deep breath Santa Luz takes at the moment of dawn or dusk, when the tide shifts and another day or night rises from the ashes of whatever preceded it.

The Ringmaster threw back his head and let out an eerie cry, the calliope pausing and thundering out every note it was capable of. The green vapor billowed, and faces appeared in it, long screaming gaunt ghostly faces. Their eyes burned orange, just like the Ringmaster's—

—and Ikaros, almost naked on his stained mattress, howled and went into seizure. His thin body bowed up into a hoop, and the collar bloomed with blue sparks as a point of violent green appeared up over the circle. It dilated, became a disc, and there was a pattering sound as roaches fell out of its glare and somehow avoided the circle I'd drawn. They landed in the sawdust and exploded in tiny gobbets of slime. The chickens made high-pitched, frantic sounds suddenly cut off in mid-squawk. Their heads had been lopped cleanly off, blood briefly spraying in high-tension arcs.

Which was a good sign, if I was looking for one.

Time's up.

The cap on the rum spun off, I took a gulp, and threw the copper chloride over Ikaros. It flashed into sparks of blue flame, the cornmeal spat points of a deeper-blue static, and I sprayed the rum—

—just as the Ringmaster launched himself over the circle's barrier and hit me full-on, bones snapping as I flew into the seats and the hostage screamed a curlew cry.

What the fuck? But I knew. The Ringmaster must've thought *I* was the one fucking with the hostage. Goddamn hellbreed, they don't even trust themselves.

Let alone a hunter.

My hand slapped a gun butt, slipped away, and closed around a knifehilt. We hit, a crunch of thunderous pain, and something warm and wet flung itself out between my lips. One of my large knives stabbed forward, blue flame catching hold on the corruption in the air, and sank into his midsection with a *tchuk*. That took a little pep out of him, especially when I wrenched the blade back and forth, hellbreed strength pumping through my arm and stink exploding around me. Wooden splinters rammed into my back, skritching against leather.

I punched him twice in the face, the scar a white-hot coal burrowing into my arm. His hard crust broke, splitting where I'd poisoned him with silver before, and I lunged up out of the wreckage, getting solid footing and *pushing* with every ounce of strength I could dredge up.

My fist hit again, the scar squealing in satisfaction

as I *pulled* on etheric energy, and the Ringmaster flew
back. His top hat flew the other direction, out of sight. I
scrambled up, my side afire with pain and the scar burning as it burrowed in toward the bone. Sick heat spilled
through me, bones melding in an instant, and I retched,
clear fluid and blood spattering through my mouth and
nose before I whooped in a breath and flung myself forward. My abused lungs burned and warm claret trickled
down my side, but I had no time to worry about that.

Because on the other side of the central ring, leaning
forward as if pushing into a heavy wind, stood Mama
Zamba. Her blond dreadlocks writhed behind her, her
hands stretched out into claws, and she pushed against
the shell of energy holding the cornmeal circle, her blue
eyes gone wide and black above her pitted cheeks.

I've got you now, you bastard. My feet touched down
and I vaulted, both guns coming out of the holsters. Her
face tipped up and filled with sick green light, cockroaches spattering behind her and flooding forward,
seeking a weakness in the circle, and her haunted eyes
met mine.

29

$\mathcal{A}$ tinkling childlike laugh. Sudden cold wetness and smell of salt and candy. And pain so immense it swallowed the world.

I'd hit something, and it had thrown me. *Hard*. A convulsion ran through me, muscles locking and nerves firing wildly in protest, a mutiny of the body.

I rolled onto my side, every inch of me protesting violently. Heaved and would have thrown up if my jaw hadn't locked. Silver crackled, the charms in my hair rustling, and my eyes were full of heat and something too sticky and red to be tears.

Thunder, again, not faraway but close and overwhelming. Ozone in the air. The calliope wheezing, limping brokenly through a descant. I pushed myself up and saw the Ringmaster's broken body trampled into sawdust. Black goop runneled his vanishing flesh. Arms and legs corkscrewed, twisting as death claimed the tissues.

I slid down the broken remains of several chairs. Gained my feet. Vomited a long string of blood. There were probably internal injuries. *Where the hell is Perry? I don't like it when I can't see him.*

It was enough that he was staying out of the way. I didn't want to deal with him *and* all this at the same time.

A barrier at ringside was just a three-bar fence, it took me two tries to hop it. And there, beyond the Ringmaster, Mama Zamba lay in the sawdust, writhing. Her dreadlocks were full of grit, and a spume of it jetted up as she convulsed, harsh ratcheting breaths blowing snot out through her nose. Bones crackled, and my smart eye saw the triple-lobed shimmering in the air over her.

The Twins were occupied with their follower. I gathered myself and bolted for the cornmeal circle. Another rattle of thunder shook the air inside the bigtop, a brief flash of acid white light made every detail stand out. Ikaros wasn't seizing anymore. He lay sprawled on the bed, chest rising and falling, the angular spiked hellwriting climbing over his flesh in fits and starts. His eyes were open, staring at the roof.

"Nooooooooooooooooo!" Mama Zamba screamed, and her voice deepened, taking on a male timbre at the end. The bone-crackles took on a deeper, wetter sound, and my feet slipped in ichor-slimed sawdust. I was almost there, *almost there*—

Another bright-white flash, smell of ozone turned thick and cloying, and a huge warm hand cupped my back and flung me. I landed in a heap inside the cornmeal circle, looked up as I reached my knees.

Mama Zamba hung in the air, but she no longer looked even faintly female. Her face had *shifted,* cheekbones broadening and the smallpox scars deepening. Her eyes were now Arthur Gregory's eyes, glowing feverish gas-flame-blue and horribly sane. The caftan flapped around her thickening legs, and he hit the edge of the cornmeal circle going full-speed.

Ka-POW! Lightning flashed. The resulting explosion knocked me back into the steel-framed bed, its footboard barking me a good one in the side, where my ribs were already tender from being broken once tonight. I collapsed, trying to get enough air in, my hands came up despite me and clutched at the bedframe. I had enough time to see the tendons standing out under my fishbelly-pale skin, blood sliming the back of my left hand and dulling the shine of my apprentice-ring, before the imperative to *get fucking moving!* boiled through me again and I hauled myself up.

Noise returned. I realized I'd been temporarily deafened as I landed hard on Ikaros, irrationally afraid the several pounds of ammo I was carrying would crush him. Squirmed, fell to the side, wrapped one hand around a bar in the headboard and braced myself, my right hand jabbing up.

The collar's spikes sank into my skin again. The pain was tiny compared to the rest of me. I found the release catch.

"Noooooooooooo!" Arthur Gregory yelled again, and I snapped a glance up to see him flying toward the cornmeal circle again. I couldn't count on a lightning strike this time. Chango and the Twins had probably both interfered as much as they were able to.

The release catch was slimed with blood. I let out a hopeless sound, fingers scrabbling, caught in the spikes coming up from the collar. My apprentice-ring sparked under its mask of blood.

The catch miraculously parted. The collar opened like a flower, and I rolled off the bed, landing hard on my ass, my head hitting the frame. Silver chimed, a small noise lost in the sudden lunging scream of the calliope. Green vapor filled the air, full of the candy-sick corruption of Hell and a darker effluvia.

Ikaros screamed. So did Arthur Gregory.

I scrabbled away on hands and bootheels, muscle pulling loose of bone with hard popping sounds, flaring with pain like nails tearing my flesh. The cornmeal scattered as I plowed through the edge of the circle, and Arthur Gregory landed on the bed. Ikaros was already gone, though, rolling away on the opposite side.

The scar boiled, burrowing in toward bone. It never got any deeper, but I sometimes wondered what would happen if it did. Right now there wasn't time. I fumbled for a gun, for a knife to fling, anything. The calliope shrieked again, belching more green smoke, its brass pipes blooming with sick *ignus fatus* light, spinning off fat globes of bobbing will o' the wisps.

The hostage gained his feet in a spooky-quick lunge. He had a lot of pep for someone who had been writhing and twisting with seizures for a day or two. His eyes lit with the dusted glitter of a very pissed-off Trader. His jockey shorts flapped, scrawny-strong muscle popping out under his skin, where the mad angry runnels of hell-script fizzed, glyphs winking out of existence with tiny puffs of steam.

He drew himself up, and Arthur Gregory hopped off

the bed. The caftan fluttered around his ankles, torn and stained all over now. The blond dreadlocks swayed.

Sudden silence filled the bigtop. My breathing was very loud, but so was theirs, twin gasps through constricted windpipes.

They faced each other, and my hand closed around a gun butt. I was moving through syrup.

Then Ikaros spoke. His face had squinched itself up, and he sounded very young.

"Arthur?" Tentatively. His broad farmboy paws knotted together. "Art?"

Arthur Gregory twitched.

Oh, holy shit. The last piece of the puzzle clicked into place. *That's why the attacks didn't kill him—they were attacks on the Ringmaster, not on the hostage! And—*

"Goddamn you," Arthur hissed. "God damn you to Hell."

Samuel Gregory spread his arms. "Already done. I've seen things you can't imagine." His face was no longer young. Instead, it was ancient and graven.

"You were here. The whole time." Arthur's hands dropped to his sides. He took two steps forward. The calliope simmered in its corner, a tremor rising up through the floor as if we were having an earthquake. "You were *here!*"

"I came here to forget it. Forget it *all.*" Samuel's hands twisted together, fingers knotting. "Him. And her. *Mother.*" The single word was loaded with hatred, and I shivered.

"Even me?" Arthur drew himself up. His dreadlocks rasped against each other.

Samuel shrugged. "Even you. I'm . . . sorry."

He didn't sound sorry.

"I did everything for you," Arthur whispered. "Everything. All this. I sold my soul."

Samuel sounded unimpressed. "So did I. And you have to come here and *remind* me."

A hand closed over my shoulder. I flinched, but the fingers dug in. "Hush." Perry's hot breath touched my bloody cheek. "Be quiet, now. This is meant to be finished."

I pitched forward, but I was so tired. And his fingers bit down again, steel pins grinding my flesh. "I said *be still*." His whisper floated to my ear, a trickle of moisture that might have been blood or condensation from his breath sliding down toward my jawline. Frantic disgust roiled through me.

They stood staring at each other. The calliope regained its voice and whispered.

"God damn you." Arthur's throat had closed down on him. All that came out was a rasp. And too late I saw the knife in his broad, long-fingered hand. It glittered, starlike in the green pondlight. I let out a warning blurt, but Perry's other hand had clapped over my mouth. Dry skin against the slick of blood on me, and he drew me back.

Arthur Gregory lunged forward. Samuel collided with him, and the knife rammed itself home in his narrow chest. Samuel's arms were spread, strangler's hands limp and loose.

He had thrown himself on the blade. He folded down like a clockwork toy run out, and the corruption racing through his tissues distorted his face into an old man's before finally draining away, his body twitching and jerking as it turned into a bubbling smear.

My eyes rolled like a panicked horse's. I threw myself forward, but Perry dragged me back down again and I couldn't get leverage. His other arm was a bar of iron across my midriff. He crouched behind me, and the heat of him was like a boiler. The smell of charring leather rose.

"Quiet!" The rumble of Helletöng scoured my ear, already half-deaf and ringing from the vast and varied noises of the night.

Arthur Gregory went to his knees. The tripartite spinning of the Twins appeared briefly, a pale oval of light. They laughed, a cruel tinkling sound, and he stretched out his arms. Their faces blurred into each other before the slim androgynous figure silhouetted in the light turned its back and danced away.

Abandoning him.

The *loa* are fickle. Just as much as hellbreed are. And Arthur Gregory had used up all his credit with them.

His wail shattered the stillness. The calliope answered it, shaking the bigtop. Canvas rippled and fluttered, the ropes singing in distress.

Perry dragged me even further back, duckwalking. One of his knees dug briefly into my ribs and I made a small sound in the back of my throat, a red-hot bolt going up my cramping side and exploding in my neck. The scar blazed, agony unstringing my nerves. The collar still tangled in my fist, its spikes buried in my wrist. Hot blood smeared my right hand, and pretty much every other inch of me. My back was hot, and Perry hissed happily to himself as he rose, dragging me upright.

They flowed past us, bright eyes and twisted limbs, a tide of hellbreed. The plague-carrier I'd seen before

was first among them, capering and jigging; he had
found another red velvet coat somewhere. It was he who
picked up the Ringmaster's cane, stealing it neatly from
under another 'breed's questing fingers, and he twirled it
neatly, cracking the other 'breed on the head and snarling. They pulled back a little, and he found the top hat
too. It went onto his lank-haired noggin, and I was suddenly aware of hellbreed and Traders packing the entire
bigtop, dancing in through the stage entrances, climbing
through the stands, cheering and rumbling in töng.

Arthur Gregory was on his knees, sobbing. He bent
over, his mouth distorted in a wet "o" of suffering. His
eyes had turned dead-dark, and cold. Snot smeared on
his upper lip. One of his dreadlocks came loose and
fluttered to the churned, wet sawdust. Others followed,
plopping free of his skull with odd little sounds.

The plague-carrier capered to Gregory's side, spinning the cane. The green crystal shivered and crackled,
and when the carrier spread his stick-thin arms, the
calliope tweeted. He jabbed the cane at it, green vapor
cringing away from him, and the first few notes of "Be a
Clown" rippled through the air.

The crowd cheered and hissed, arms raised, cheap
glass and paste finery twinkling. Their eyes were bright
and avid. None of the animals put in an appearance, but
I swear I heard an elephant trumpet and the yowls of
big cats. Yipping dogs. Perry's arm loosened. My boots
touched the ground, finally. The shadows crawled and
leapt with the Cirque's dogs, their eyes glowing and
crackling.

"Ladies and gentlemen!" It was a ringmaster's voice,
an impossible deep baritone coming from the plague-

carrier's narrow little chest. *"Welcome to the Cirque Diabolique! We're all-new and renewed! We're pedal to the metal and shoulder to the wheel! And welcome our new hostage! What's your name, sonny?"*

The cane whirled again, and the crystal jabbed toward Arthur Gregory. Who screamed, his body buckling. He lifted his face to the bigtop's fabric roof swimming with sick green light and *howled*.

Their cries rose with his. Every single one of them, Trader and hellbreed, yowled like cats at the moon. The plague-carrier danced back, whirled, and blinked through space with the eerie speed of hellbreed. Perry's arm tightened again, but the thing just halted a bare four feet from us and gestured to the collar.

"Clip him and chain him." Strings of gummy yellow ick crawled over sharp teeth, and the 'breed exhaled foulness. "You have our thanks, hunter."

I opened my mouth, closed it again. Arthur howled again, the cords on his neck standing out. The plague-carrier danced backward, spinning the cane, and Perry shook me, recently broken bones twinging hard even though my body was doing its best to patch everything up.

"Do as he says, Jill." Perry's arms slithered away, I swayed on my feet. "He is theirs now."

It doesn't look like he knows it, I almost said. But the new Ringmaster halted next to Arthur, and put down one narrow hand. He smoothed the matted blond head, caressing, and made an odd clicking noise.

The dreadlocks finished falling, and new hair was growing in. Sickly yellow, and oddly feathery.

The collar jangled in my fist. I took an experimental step forward. My knee buckled, but I stayed upright. Perry made a low spitting sound, as if to chide me for swaying.

Arthur's blind eyes passed across me for a moment, and I opened my mouth again to protest. To say something, anything.

But the Ringmaster bent down and exhaled across Arthur's wide, now definitely male face. Which turned slack and grinning, vacant.

"It is ever so," Perry intoned behind me. "A life for a life."

"Life for a life," the assembled Cirque chorused. Even the calliope, weaving notes that sounded like words between the frantic strains of a song I didn't want to identify.

The new Ringmaster twitched, and pulled Arthur Gregory to his feet. "There," he said brightly. "Isn't that nice?" Foulness dripped down his chin. "Tell the nice lady your new name, my dear."

Arthur Gregory smiled under a mask of tears, snot, and blackened sawdust. He mumbled something, his lips moving loosely.

"She didn't hear you." The plague-carrier glanced at me. His shoulders were tense, and I had a sudden insane vision of shooting *his* ass, too.

But I was so tired.

"Samuel," he said, louder, his mouth working oddly over the word. "I am Samuel. Now. I'm Sam." By the third time he repeated it, he sounded like he believed it.

The flat shine of the dusted lay over his irises, and I knew what he had bargained away. Who wouldn't want to get rid of the memories he must have been carrying? The guilt, and the shame, and the murder?

The new Ringmaster watched me avidly. I'm sure something of what I was feeling showed on my face. The biggest thing, though, was weary disgust. And relief that this was finally over.

"You have one more day," I croaked. "By dusk tomorrow I want you out of my city."

He swept a simulacrum of a bow, grinned his death's-head grin under the old top hat. The cane whirled, cleaving the air with a low sweet sound. "Of course."

I clipped the collar on Arthur Gregory and left him to his new demons.

30

It was a relief to take the heavy weight of ammo off. I stowed the grenades carefully, tossed the black canvas bag into the trunk, and slammed it to find Perry leaning against my car, his pale hair and linen suit immaculate. The night was young, and as I stood there watching him, the first few shufflers arrived. A quick flicker of movement was a new Trader in the admissions booth—a round little dumpling of a male in a bowler hat and pencil moustache. His eyes glittered as a tall heavyset man in jeans and a stained *Friends Don't Let Friends Vote Democrat* T-shirt eased up to the booth and handed over a snub-nosed .38. The man's mouth worked wetly, his hair was uncombed, and he looked like a dreamer caught in a nightmare.

The Trader stamped his hand and motioned him past. The man stumbled through the turnstile, his hands plucking at the hem of his shirt. The big stain on the front, right over his belly, was very dark against his white fingers.

"Nothing ever really changes, you know." Perry's grin was wide and stainless, his bland blond mask firmly in place.

"You knew." I meant to sound accusing. I only managed "tired." I pulled the key out of the trunk's keyhole and clenched it in one nerveless fist. The scar had gone quiescent, humming slightly as etheric force pooled in it and spooled through my body, encouraging and compressing the natural processes of healing.

I was going to be hungry, to fuel the healing. In a little while.

Perry shrugged. "Not the specifics. But this is how the Cirque gains its new hostage." His face lengthened into mock-concern, and his eyes burned blue. "You didn't know?"

God, just go away. I'm tired. I lifted my chin slightly, drying blood crusting on my face. Thunder rumbled in the distance again, a sweet cool wind touching my hair. Silver jangled, and my scalp crawled. "I'm done here, Perry. Get off my car."

He didn't move. "Where is your cat? Have you lost your taste for bestiality at last? Though that was a lovely touch, with the chickens."

That wasn't me, Perry. That was a loa, *and it was payment.* "Leave Saul out of this." God, I was so heavy. It was an effort to focus on him, to force my weary body past another iron barrier of exhaustion. My eyes were crusty and hot, and adrenaline was fast losing its usefulness as a spur.

Too bad, Jill. Deal.

"He's been looking weary lately, my dear. And you

look weary too." A pause, and then the silken trap. "I saved your life. You owe me."

So that's your game. I made a small beeping noise. "Nope, no deal. You helped out because you didn't want the Cirque loosening your grip on the city. I don't owe you a goddamn thing."

His grin widened, became sharklike. The essential inhumanity under his shell gaped and yawned. "You belong to me, hunter. It's only a matter of time."

It was a relief to find out he was lying. No matter how many times I feel that relief, it's always profound. "I'll tell you again: hold your breath until I call. Fuck off, Perry. I'm going home."

"You owe me," he insisted.

"I don't owe you jackshit." My fingers rested on a gun butt. If he attacked me now, I would probably lose—and lose badly. I was just too fucking tired.

But I would still inflict a lot of damage before I went down. And here outside the barriers of the Cirque he couldn't count on their help—*or* on them not running riot once I was out of the picture. It was the same basic situation, me playing them off against each other again.

It was necessary. But it still made me feel dirty, in the worst way. Like I might never get clean again.

The indigo threading through the whites of his blue-glowing eyes retreated a little. "Such a righteous soul you have, Kiss. I only ask an inch of it."

That's more than enough room to damn someone. "Not this time, Perry. Go home and suck eggs."

He bared his teeth, a swift snarl. I cleared leather and had both guns on him, back leg braced, arms straight. The scar woke, a blinding jolt of pain pouring salt on every recent injury. We faced each other, and the only sound was the shuffling of the doomed circling before they slid through the ramheaded turnstile into the Cirque's poisonous glow. With a *click, click, click.*

That and the calliope, singing softly. A well-satisfied, cheery little song threading just under the subliminal noise of my pulse. My coat flapped slightly, and the thunder drew closer. It smelled like rain.

Even the rain isn't enough to wash this off. I didn't blink. I barely even breathed. The world narrowed to Perry and me, facing each other over a chasm the width of a hair.

He bared his teeth again, another snarl. This one poured through the subaudible register, I could barely hear it even with the scar amping my senses into the superhuman. My pulse slowed, skin chilling under its mask of drying blood, sweat, spatters of rum and other fluids I didn't remember getting splashed with.

"Someday," he said, finally. "Some fine day, Kiss."

Maybe. But not tonight. "Not tonight, Perry. Get out of my sight."

He moved. I threw myself back and down, but he just went *over* me with the spooky stuttering speed of the damned. Hit the ground, and heard the fast light patter of his footsteps retreating toward the meatpacking district and the Monde Nuit. A chilling little laugh, fraying in the distance, and the calliope sighed.

I pushed myself wearily to my feet. Didn't look at the shuffling victims in front of the Cirque. *Not one more fucking thing tonight, please. Not one. Okay, God?*

There was no answer. There never is.

I got into my car, and got the hell out of there.

Epilogue

I sat in the car for a while. My garage is narrow, but well-equipped. I considered putting the seat back and sleeping right there. I itched all over and would feel crusty in the morning, as well as dirty inside and out. And I'm accustomed to the weight of my weaponry, but sleeping in my guns was a bad idea.

Still, the thought had merit. Especially when I thought of the empty house, and—

The door to the house opened. I blinked as a slice of warm electric light fell across the car. The figure in the door was tall, broad-shouldered, and his shorn hair was starred with silver. He stepped down into the garage and came to the driver's side, opened the door.

I shut my eyes. Tears rose.

Finally, he crouched down. His fingers touched my hair, brushed my cheek. He rubbed a little, dried blood crackling under sensitive fingertips.

"Jesus," Saul said quietly.

"I'm sorry." The words came out in a rush. "I shouldn't have said that. I shouldn't have—"

"Jill." Kindly, quietly, calmly. "Shut up."

I did.

His fingers circled my wrist, pulled gently. It was work getting out of the car, but he helped pull me upright. The door slammed, and he folded me in his arms. The sound of his pulse was a balm and blessing.

Are you staying? I couldn't make myself say it. *Don't leave me. Dear God, please, don't leave me.*

"I just want you to do one thing," he said into my filthy hair. I almost cringed.

Anything. Just stay with me. I stilled, waited.

"Just nod or shake your head. That's all. Now listen, Jill. Do you still need me? Do you want me around?"

"I—" How could he even ask me that? Didn't he *know?* Or was he saying that he felt *obligated?*

"Just nod or shake your head. I just want to know if you need me."

It took all I had to let my chin dip, come back up in the approximation of a nod.

"Do you still want me?" God help me, did Saul sound *tentative?*

It was too much. "Jesus Christ." The words exploded out of me. "Yes, Saul. *Yes.* Do you want me to beg? I will, if you—"

"Jill." He interrupted me, something he barely ever did. "I want you to shut up."

I shut up. For a few moments he just simply held me, and the clean male smell of him was enough to break down every last barrier. I tried to keep the sobs quiet, but they shook me too hard. The breeze off the desert rattled my garage door, and the last fading roll of thunder retreated.

He stroked my hair, held me, traced little patterns on my back. Cupped my nape, and purred his rumbling purr. When the sobs retreated a little, he tugged on me, and we made it to the door to the hall, moving in a weird double-stepping dance. He was so graceful, and I was too clumsy.

He lifted me up the step, got me into the hall, heeled the door closed. My coat flapped. My boots were heavy, the heels clicking against concrete. I probably needed to be hosed off.

I had to know. I dug in, brought him to a halt, but couldn't raise my eyes from his chest. "A-are you s-s-still—" I couldn't get the words out. I was shaking too hard.

"You're a fucking idiot," he informed me. "I'm staying, Jill. As long as you'll have me. I can't believe you think I'd leave you."

That did it. I broke down completely then, and as he half-carried me down the hall I cried. I couldn't tell if I was crying for myself or for Arthur Gregory, or for the whole goddamn world.

Tomorrow night I would have to get up and do this all over again. Make sure the Cirque left town and find out what new mischief was brewing under the night skies. It never ended, this job.

It never would. And now I owed a *loa* a bullet, I had an apprentice to train, and Perry was looking to be trouble again. How long could I keep up mortgaging bits of myself?

As long as you can, Jill. As long as God lets you.

But for right now, Saul held me. My legs failed me and I went down in a heap. He went down with me, and

he held me just inside the door to the living room. The
first spatters of rain rang hard on the warehouse roof. I
cried without restraint, and he held me.

We all Trade for something.

And God help me, it was enough. He was enough.

I just hoped I would always be enough for him.

Glossary

Arkeus: A roaming corruptor escaped from Hell.

Banefire: A cleansing sorcerous flame.

Black Mist: A roaming psychic contagion; a symbiotic parasite inhabiting the host's nervous system and bloodstream.

Chutsharak: Chaldean obscenity, loosely translated as "oh, *fuck*."

Demon: Term loosely used to designate any nonhuman predator with sorcerous ability or a connection to Hell.

Exorcism: Tearing loose a psychic parasite from its host.

Hellbreed: Blanket term for a wide array of demons, half-demons, or other species escaped or sent from Hell.

Hellfire: The spectrum of sorcerous flame employed by hellbreed for a variety of uses.

Hunter: A trained human who keeps the balance between the nightside and regular humans; extrahuman law enforcement.

Imdarák: Shadowy former race who drove the Elder

Gods from the physical plane, also called the Lords of the Trees.

Martindale Squad: The FBI division responsible for tracking nightside crime across state lines and at the federal level, mostly staffed with hunters and Weres.

Middle Way: Worshippers of Chaos, Middle Way adepts are usually sociopathic and sorcerous loners. Occasionally covens of Middle Way adepts will come together to control a territory or for a specific purpose.

OtherSight: Second sight, the ability to see sorcerous energy. Can also mean precognition.

Possessor: An insubstantial, low-class demon specializing in occupying and controlling humans; the prime reason for exorcists.

Scurf: Also called *nosferatim,* a semi-psychic viral infection responsible for legends of blood-hungry corpses, vampires, or nosferatu. Also, someone infected by the scurf virus.

Sorrow: A worshipper of the Chaldean Elder Gods.

Sorrows House: A House inhabited by Sorrows, with a vault for invocation or evocation of Elder Gods.

Sorrows Mother: A high-ranking female of a Sorrows House.

Talyn: A hellbreed, higher in rank than an *arkeus* or Possessor, usually insubstantial due to the nature of the physical world.

Trader: A human who makes a "deal" with a hellbreed, usually for worldly gain or power.

Utt'huruk: A bird-headed demon.

Were: Blanket term for several species who shapeshift into animal (for example, cougar, wolf, or spider) or half-animal (wererat or *khentauri*) form.

extras

orbit

meet the author

LILITH SAINTCROW was born in New Mexico, bounced around the world as an Air Force brat, and fell in love with writing when she was ten years old. She currently lives in Vancouver, Washington. Find her on the Web at www.lilithsaintcrow.com.

introducing

If you enjoyed **FLESH CIRCUS**,
look out for

HEAVEN'S SPITE

Book 5 of the Jill Kismet series
by Lilith Saintcrow

*H*ow fast does a man run, when Death is after him?

The Trader clambered up the rickety fire escape at a dead run and I was right behind him. If I'd had my whip I could have yanked his feet out from under him. No use lamenting it—had to work with what I had. He was going too fast for me to just shoot him at the moment.

Didn't matter. I knew where he was headed. And though I hoped Saul would be quick enough to get her out of the way, it would be better if I killed him now.

Or got there first. And *then* killed him.

He went over the edge of the wall in one quick spiderlike scuttle and I flung myself up, silver charms tied in my hair buzzing like a rattler's tail. The scar on my right wrist burned, a live coal pressed against my skin, as I *pulled* etheric force through it. A sick tide of delight poured up my arm, and I reached the top and was up and over so fast I collided with the Trader, my hellbreed-strong right fist jabbing forward to get him a good shot in the kidneys.

We rolled across the rooftop in a tangle of arms and legs, the leather trench coat snapping once and fluttering raggedly. It was singed and peppered with holes from the car bomb where I'd lost my whip. I was covered in drying blood and very, very pissed off.

Just another night on the job.

No you don't, you fuckwad. One hand in his hair, the other one full of knifehilt, the silver-loaded blade ran with crackling blue light as the blessing on it reacted to the breath of contamination around the Trader's writhing form. I caught an elbow in the face, my eye smarting and watering immediately, and slid the knife in up to the guard.

The Trader bucked. He was thin but strong, and my fingers slipped, greasy with blood. I got a knee in, wrestled him down as he twisted—

—and he shot me four times.

They were lead, not silverjacket slugs. Still, the violent shock of agony as four of them slammed through my torso was enough to throw me down for a few moments, stunned and gasping, the scar chuckling to itself as it flooded me with power. My body convulsed, stupid meat freaking out over a little thing like bullets. A curtain of red closed over my vision, and I heard retreating footsteps.

Get up, Jill. Get up now.

Another convulsion running through me from crown

to soles. I rolled on my side, muscles locking down as a gush of lungfluid and blood jetted from my mouth and nose. The contraction was so intense even my eyes watered, and I whooped in a deep breath. My hands scrabbled uselessly against dirty rooftop.

Get UP, you bitch!

My feet found the floor, the rest of me hauled itself upright, and I heard my voice from a dim long faraway place. I was cursing like a sailor who just found out shore leave was canceled.

Now go get him. Get him before he gets there.

I stumbled, almost fell flat on my face. Getting peppered with lead won't kill me, but if it hits a lot of vitals it's pretty damn uncomfortable. My flesh twitched, expelling bits and chunks of lead, and I coughed again, rackingly, got my passages clear. More stumbling steps, my right bootsole squeaking because it was wet. The knife spun, blade reversed against my forearm, and I blinked. Took off again, because the Trader's matted black hair puffed up as he dropped over the side of the building.

Now I was mad.

Go get him, Jill. Get him quick and get him hard.

A half-moon hung overhead. Santa Luz shuddered underneath its glow, and I hurled myself forward again, going over the edge of the building with arms and legs pulled in just in case. The drop wasn't bad—just another roof, a little lower—and I had some luck—the stupid bastard decided to stand and fight rather than run off toward the civilian he'd marked for death.

He hit me hard, ramming us both into the brick wall of the building we'd just been tangling on the top of.

This rooftop was a chaos of girders and support structure for the watertank looming above us. I got my left arm free, flipped my wrist so the knifeblade angled in, and stabbed.

Another piece of luck—his arm was up, and my aim was good. The knife sank in at a weird angle, the axillary region exposed and vulnerable and now full of silver-loaded steel. My knee came up so hard something in his groin popped like bubblegum, and I clocked him a good one with my hellbreed-strong right fist.

Stupid fuck. While he was running, or at least just trying to get away, he had a chance. But fighting a pitched battle with an angry helltainted hunter? Not a good idea.

He folded, keening, and I coughed up more blood. A hot sheen of it slicked my chin, splashed on my chest. I pitched forward, following him down. My knee hit hard, a jolt of silvery pain up my femur; I braced myself and yanked his head back.

Another knifehilt slapped my palm and I jerked it free of the sheath. My right hand cramped, kept working. He made a whining noise as I bore down, bodyweight pinning him. I'm tall for a female but still small when compared to most hellbreed, Traders, or what-have-you. The scar helps, gives me denser muscle and bone, but when it comes right down to it my only hope is leverage. I had some, but not enough.

Which meant I had to kill him quick.

The silver-loaded blade dragged across easily, parting helltainted flesh. A gush of hot black-tinged blood sprayed out. Human blood looks black at night, but the

darkness of hellbreed ichor tainting a Trader's fluid is in
a class all its own.

Arterial spray goes amazingly far, especially when
you have the rest of the body under tension and the
head wrenched back. The body slumped in my hands,
a gurgle echoing against rooftop and girders, twitches
racing through as corruption claimed the flesh. I used
to think that if Traders could see one of them biting it
and the St. Vitus' dance of contagion that eats up their
tissues, they might think twice about making a bargain
with hellbreed.

I don't think that anymore. Because when you get
right down to it, what Trader thinks about death as real?
That's why they Trade—they think the rules don't apply
to them.

My legs didn't work too well. I scrabbled back from
the body, a knifehilt in either fist. Fetched up against the
brick wall, right next to the indent from earlier. Sobbing
breaths as my own body struggled for oxygen, my eyes
locked to the Trader's form as it disappeared into a slick
of bubbling black grease starred with scorched bones.

Watch, milaya. My teacher's voice said quietly, inside
my head. *You watch the death you make. Is only way.*

I watched until there was nothing recognizably human
left. Even the bones would dissolve, and by daybreak
there would only be a lingering foulness to the air up
here. I checked the angle of the building—any sunlight
that came through the network of girders would take
care of the rest. If the bones had remained I would've
had to call up some banefire, to deny whatever hellbreed
he'd Traded with the use of a nice fresh zombie corpse.

But no. He'd Traded hard, and he'd used his bargain

recklessly, burning up whatever remained of his humanity. I coughed again, shuddered as the adrenaline dump poured through me with a taste like bitter copper.

Just another night on the job. And we were three scant blocks from Molly Watling, his next planned victim. Who was probably scared out of her mind right now, even if Saul had shown up to get her out of the way.

It's not every day your ex-husband Trades with a hellbreed and shows up with a thirst for human flesh, hot blood, and terror. He'd worked his way through his current wife, three strippers, and two ex-girlfriends, not to mention a mistress and another woman grabbed at a bus stop. His sole victim of opportunity, his practice run for the others.

I blew out between my teeth. The reek was amazing, and I was covered in goop, guck, and blood. The night was young, and I had a line on the hellbreed Trevor Watling had Traded with. A hellbreed I was going to talk to, up close and personal with some silverjacket lead, because that was my job.

Time to get back to work.

But I just stood there for a few more moments, staring blankly at the smear on the rooftop. I've given up wondering why some men think they own women enough to beat and kill them. It used to be like a natural disaster— just get out of the way and hope it doesn't get you. Then I thought about it until it threatened to drive me batshit, chewing over the incomprehensible over and over again.

Now it was enough just to stop what I could. But Jesus, I was tired of it.

A vibrating buzz almost startled me. It was the pager

in its padded pocket. I dug it out and glanced at it, and my entire body went cold.

What the fuck is he doing calling me?

I tested my legs. They were willing. My shirt was ruined, and my leather pants weren't far behind. Still, all my bits were covered, and my trench coat was ripped and tattered but still usable.

I got going.

My pager went off again, and when I dug it out Connie, the ER nurse, looked at me funny. But they're used to me at Mercy General, and Saul made soothing noises at the sobbing, red-haired almost-victim. "Montaigne at the precinct will have details," I told the ER nurse, who nodded, making a notation on her clipboard. "She'll probably need sedation, and I don't blame her."

The stolid motherly woman in neatly pressed scrubs nodded. "Rape kit?"

I shook my head. "No." *Thank God. I got there in time.*

Of course, if I hadn't, Molly Watling would have been carted to the morgue instead of driven to the ER. Small mercy, but I'd take it. Connie's expression said she'd take it too; the relief was palpable.

"It's all right," Saul said soothingly. The silver tied in his hair with red thread gleamed under the fluorescents, and he didn't look washed-out in the slightest. But then, Weres usually look good in any lighting. "You're safe now. Everything's okay."

She nodded, fat tears trickling down her damp cheeks. She flinched whenever I looked at her.

"Bueno." Connie patted the woman's arm. "Any injuries?"

I shook my head again. "Nope. Shock, though. Ex-husband."

Comprehension spread over Connie's face. No more needed to be said.

"So, sedation. Call Montaigne, get a trauma counselor over here, and Monty'll take care of the paperwork." County health has counselors on standby, and so does the police department. *Especially* in cases like this. "I've got to get going."

Connie nodded, and deftly subtracted Molly from Saul. She didn't want to let go of his arm, and I completely understood. A big guy who looks like Native American romance-novel beefcake? I'd be clinging too.

"Th-thank you." The almost-victim didn't even look at me. "F-for everything. I didn't th-think anyone would b-believe me."

Considering that her ex-husband had terrorized every woman before he'd killed them, and he'd been a real winner even *before* Trading, it made sense. "He's not going to hurt you anymore." I sounded harsher than I needed to, and she actually jumped. "He's not going to hurt *anyone* anymore."

I expected her to flinch and cower again. But she surprised me—lifting her chin, pushing her shoulders back. "I sh-should thank you t-too." She swallowed hard, forced herself to meet my eyes. It was probably uncomfortable—a lot of people have trouble with my mismatched gaze. One eye brown, one blue—it just seems to offend people on a deep nonverbal level when I stare them down.

I nodded. "It's my job, Ms. Watling. I'm glad we got there in time." *It was too late for those other women. But take what you can get, Jill.* I shifted my attention to Connie. "I need a phone."

"Si, señora. Use the one at the desk." And just like that, I was dismissed. Connie bustled the woman away out of the curtained enclosure, and the regular sounds of a Tuesday night on the front lines swallowed the sharper refrain of a terrified, relieved woman dissolving into fresh sobs. The smell of Lysol and human pain stung my nose almost as much as the dissolving reek of a Trader's death.

Saul let out a sigh. He reached out, his hand cupping my shoulder. "Hello, kitten."

I leaned into the touch. The smile spreading over my face felt unnatural, until my heart made the funny jigging movement it usually did when he looked at me and the usual wave of relief caught up with me. "Hey, catkin. Good work."

"I knew he wouldn't get there before you." His own smile was a balm against my jagged nerves. He'd put on some weight, and the shadows under his eyes weren't so dark anymore. "What's the next emergency?"

I shrugged, held up the pager. "Gilberto paged from home."

He absorbed this. "Not like him," he finally said. Which was as close as he would get to grudgingly admitting my apprentice was doing well.

"That's what I thought." I reached up with my left hand, squeezed his fingers where they rested against my shoulder. His skin was warm, but mine left a smudge of filth and blood on him.

He never seemed to mind, but I took my hand away and swallowed hard.

"Well, let's see what he wants. And then, breakfast?" Meaning the night was still young, and he'd like a slice of time alone with me.

It's kind of hard to roll around with your favorite Were when you've got a kid living with you, after all. I was about ready to start suggesting the car's backseat, but— how's this for irony—I hadn't had time yet. One thing after another, that's a hunter's life. "I don't see why not. I've got a line on the hellbreed Watkins Traded with, too."

He nodded. The fringe on his jacket trembled, and he turned on one heel. "Sounds like a busy night."

"Aren't they all." I followed him out, past other curtained enclosures. Some were open, the machinery of saving lives standing by for the next high-adrenaline emergency. Some were closed, the curtains drawn to grant a sliver of privacy. Someone groaned from one, and a murmur of doctor's voices came from another. Mercy General's ER was always hopping.

The nurse at the desk just gave me a nod and pushed the phone over, then went back to questioning a blank-eyed man in Spanish through the sheet of bulletproof glass as she filled out a sheet of paperwork with neat, precise scratches. The patient swayed and cradled his swollen hand, pale under his coloring, and smelled of burnt metal and cocaine. I kept half an eye on him while I punched "9" and my own number.

He picked up on the first ring. Slightly nasal boy's voice. *"Bruja?"*

"Gilberto. This better be good." I regretted it as soon as I said it. He wasn't the type to call me for nothing.

As usual, he didn't take it personally. A slight, wheezing laugh. "Package for you, *mi profesora*. Wrapped up with a pretty bow."

"A package?" My mouth went dry. "Gilberto—"

"And the man who delivered it still here. *Uno rubio*, in a suit. Says he'll wait for you."

A blond? The dryness poured down, invaded my throat. "Gilberto, listen to me very carefully—"

A slight sound as the phone was taken from my apprentice. I knew, from the very first breath, who was waiting for me at home.

"My darling Kiss." Perry's voice was smooth as silk, and full of nasty amusement. "He's quite a winning elf, your new houseboy. And so polite."

Think fast, Jill. My heart leapt, and the scar on my wrist turned hot and hard, swollen with corruption. As if he had just pressed his lips against my flesh again. "Pericles."

Saul went stiff next to me, his dark eyes flashing orange for a moment.

The hellbreed on the other end of the line laughed. "I have a gift for you, my darling. Come home and see it. I will be content with the boy until then."

He dropped the phone down into the cradle, and I slammed the receiver down, pulling it at the last moment so I wouldn't break the rest of the phone. The man on the other side of the glass jumped, and the nurse twisted in her chair to look at me. I didn't bother to give a glance of apology, just looked at my Were.

Saul's eyes met mine, and I didn't have to explain a single thing. He turned so fast the fringe on his jacket flared, and headed with long strides for the door that would take us out toward the exit. I was right behind him. The scar on my wrist twitched under the flayed cuff of my trench coat, and Saul's stride lengthened into a run.

So did mine.